CATCH A WAVE

A SECOND CHANCE, BROTHER'S BEST FRIEND,
SWEET ROMCOM

SAVANNAH SCOTT

❀ Created with Vellum

Connect with Savannah Scott

You can connect with Savannah at her website
www.SavannahScottBooks.com

You can also follow Savannah on Amazon.

For free books and first notice of new releases, sign up for
Savannah's Romcom Readers email at https://www.
subscribepage.com/savannahscottromcom/

For Jon
My surfer boy.
Watching you ride is poetry in motion.
I'll always be the one
holding the towel when you hit the sand.
And when you've taken your last ride,
we'll hold hands and walk the shore.

~

For everyone who ever messed up royally.
And for those whose hearts were horribly broken.
Hope is a relentless force.
And forgiveness is yours for the taking and giving.
Embrace your second chances.
🤍
Never give up on what could be.

*Second chances don't always come
in the form we wish they would.
They are always made of one common ingredient:
Sheer grace.*

MAVS & BODHi

1

BODHI

If you love something so much, let it go.
If it comes back it was meant to be;
if it doesn't it never was.
~ Albert Schweitzer

Not one of us seems to be breathing, our eyes riveted to the big screen as we watch Kalaine being towed into the thirty-foot waves at Mavericks.

I'm torn between acting nonchalant and chill and showing the depth of my concern. Kalaine—or Mavs, as I nicknamed her a lifetime ago—has everything it takes to dominate this wave. She's been surfing since she could walk, literally. Her dad took her out on Oahu's North Shore on his shoulders. Once she was a toddler, he propped her up on his board and held on to her hands as they surfed the smaller sets near shore. By the time she was five, she was paddling out into the surf on her own board.

Of course, when her older brother, Kai, started competing,

she fought tooth and nail to join him. Even though her parents raised her to surf, they didn't like the idea of her entering contests. Female athletes have to work doubly hard to prove themselves in this male-dominated sport.

But women like Mavs earn all our respect.

She earned more than my respect at one time.

And now her brother, Kai, is my boss and housemate—and, my best friend. And his baby sister is about to ride one of nature's most challenging waves. The sheer power and force of this northern California break makes riding Mavericks life-threatening. Only the best of the best surf here. The contest had been shut down for years due to the potential danger to surfers if conditions aren't just right.

I should know. I used to ride those beasts, preparing all year for the amount of time I'd potentially spend shoved underwater, building the strength I'd need to paddle and pop up, and honing the skills it takes to navigate once I was riding. I claimed my spot in the top two or three men to compete—even taking first place at Mavs the year before my career as a pro ended.

A vein in Kai's neck bulges. His elbows rest on his knees, and his eyes don't even blink as he watches his baby sister get towed out into the line up. She's one of four women out there in this forty-five minute heat. The goal is to grab as many good waves as she can, taking her turn with the other surfers out in the designated zone. After their performance is ranked, two of them will advance to the next round.

The jet ski takes off, manned by Dan Hale, Kalaine's long-time partner and coach. They look like a beetle being dragged up a glassy blue mountain. Kalaine rides behind, standing on her board, ready to be let loose when the wave crests.

The moment comes. Kalaine releases the tow rope and Dan disappears behind the wave, riding ahead of the peak, while our girl shoots down the front of the massive wave, leaving a trail of white foam slicing the blue water behind her. And then the wave breaks and it's like she's being chased by a liquid avalanche. I feel it in my blood—the sympathetic adrenaline rush, the way everything goes still and you feel like you're flying or floating, but you've never been so focused in your life. She's in the perfect spot to get tubed for a moment, riding in the curl of the wave. Surfing what we call the greenroom is the closest thing to heaven I've experienced on earth.

The closest thing except one—holding Kalaine in my arms.

I shake that thought from my head. She's not mine. She belongs to the ocean, like I do now. The sea's been a better companion to her than it was to me. But we're getting back on good terms, me and the water, these days. Me and Mavs, not so much.

The room erupts in a gasp when Kalaine goes under, her board shooting about ten feet away from her. My heart feels like it's trying to beat its way out of my throat. But Dan's right there, speeding in a circle on his jet ski, finding her and hauling her out of danger within moments.

A raucous cheer fills the room. Kai jumps up. "That's my girl! That's how you do it!"

I smile broadly at him. It's a smile that says I'm glad his sister made it, not one that says she's everything I ever wanted, and if I could turn back clocks and calendars, she'd be the one thing I'd get right—the one I'd never leave behind.

Ben and Cam are jumping around high-fiving too. Ben's a surfer, even though he grew up in the midwest. Cam plays around on a board occasionally, but he's not nearly as devoted as Ben. Their girlfriends, Summer and Riley, are chattering and cheering too.

"She's amazing, Kai!" Riley shouts.

"Girl power!" Summer echoes.

"She's the best of the best," I say to myself more than anyone else. On or off the water, she's the best of the best.

We simmer down, settling back into our seats to watch the

rest of the competition. We'll hear her score in a minute. A portion of her rank depends on the ocean. But what she does with what the ocean deals her makes all the difference. She caught a killer wave. It appeared to be bigger than some of the others. That helps. And she owned that thing—made it hers. My chest swirls with a mix of emotions—pride, longing, and a huge dose of regret. It's a sour cocktail.

"Don't you and Kalaine have a history?" Summer asks, knowing full well I dated Kai's sister.

I catch Kai's glance in my direction and hold his gaze. I'm talking to Summer, but I'm looking at my best friend. "A while ago. She and I rode the circuit together."

"Water under the bridge," Kai says with a nod toward me.

His face is neutral, but he sends me a message. He warned me then. *Don't mess with my sister, man. There are plenty of other girls you could hang with. Not her.*

I told him we were only friends. And along with everything else I felt for her, we were friends. Mavs and I had an ease between us. She's the type of person who gets along with everyone. But we had a certain chemistry from the moment I met her. That sparkle in her honey-gold eyes. The way she'd look over at me sideways, tilting her head and sending me a coy smile. She made me want to impress her. And yet I always felt like I was fully accepted by her despite my flaws. I didn't mean to fall for her. It just happened. And when I found out she felt the same, Kai was the last person on earth I considered.

He says everything that went down between us is in the past, but moments like this tell me he's never quite forgiven me for pursuing his sister. And even if he did forgive me for overstepping his clearly drawn lines, he'll never forgive me for the fallout when things ended between us.

I'm half watching the three other women in the heat, half up in my head, until it comes time for Kalaine's next wave. The room isn't nearly as tense as it was when she went out the first time. We're fueled by confidence from watching her master that last one. The other surfers have all ridden well, though Kalaine's wave was superior. And she got tubed, which gave her the competitive edge she needs to advance. Still, the anticipation is thick. Everyone gathered in our living room wants to see her move on to the next round. And we all know the risk she's taking each time she approaches another colossal wave.

Dan tows Kalaine in, and just like clockwork, he takes off as soon as she releases the line, racing ahead along the backside ahead of the peak. Mavs shoots over the top of the wave, and it looks good until the wave breaks prematurely.

Everything happens in slow motion. Kalaine's body looks like a doll being spit off the lip of the wave, flying headfirst toward the water twenty or thirty feet below. Her board flies away from her in another direction.

My eyes are glued to the screen. I feel my jaw tighten so rigidly I could break my molars. I sense Kai shoot up off his seat next to me. I don't look over. I can't. My whole body and mind are focused on the woman I still love being thrown into the water. We don't see her after she goes down. The wave tumbles over her with a force and magnitude I won't ever forget.

It feels like an eternity.

I'm a restless ball inside my perfectly still frame.

Zodiacs swarm the ocean immediately.

The announcer's voice tells us what we can plainly see.

"Kalaine Kapule has been underwater for more than thirty seconds, going on a minute now. The turbulent foam makes it difficult to even tell where she got thrown to. Her surf partner and coach, Dan Hale, turned the jet ski around and is searching the water near where she dropped."

Another announcer's voice chimes in. "That was quite a drop, Steve."

"It was. I'm not going to speculate, but I've seen other

surfers fall from big waves, and they've rarely come out of a fall like that without some sort of injury."

"Wait!" the first announcer interrupts. "I think I see some action out there."

I see it too. We all do.

"That's her!" Kai shouts from next to me. "Get her out of there, Dan!"

I squeeze my eyes shut, sending up the closest thing to a prayer as I know how to utter. When I open my eyes, Dan's jet ski is the main object the camera has zoomed in on. He's off the Zodiac and in the water, tugging Kalaine with him. He manages to pull her out, drape her across the jet ski, and then he zooms toward the shore where he's rushed at by a team of medics and lifeguards. When Dan carries Kalaine's limp body onto the sand, it's hard to see what's going on through the throng of bodies instantly surrounding him and Mavs.

On our side of the screen, no one dares utter a word.

A phone rings. I swivel my head to look at Kai. He pulls his cell out of his pocket and answers.

"Yeah. ... we're watching." Kai's eyes don't leave the screen where Kalaine is being placed on a stretcher.

She's not responding yet, according to the announcer.

I'm numb. Seeing her fall was like witnessing my surfing accident from outside my own body. But this time, it was her. I sat here, completely powerless to do anything, my hands itching to grab a Zodiac and speed through the water to her rescue—to be the one carrying her out of the water. I should be standing next to her now, holding her hand in mine and not letting go until she wakes from this nightmare.

But I waived those privileges a few years ago. I'm an afterthought in the middle of this family's crisis. An interloper.

2

BODHI

Aren't we all tormented by past relationships?
~Alex Rosa

"She's doing better," Kai tells the customer as he rings her up for a beach towel and some sunscreen.

The customer smiles and tells Kai to pass along her positive thoughts and prayers for Kalaine. She even pronounces Mavs' name right: Kah-lah-ee-nay. Everyone gets it right now that Mavs has been immortalized for surviving her accident. Even people who aren't into our sport have heard something about the young woman who defied death at Mavericks. The news spread—because she's a woman doing something as dangerous and life-threatening as big-wave surfing.

Kai thanks the customer and starts working on inventorying our full wetsuits.

It's mid-February, not exactly the height of our busy season, but we attract a whole other set of tourists this time of year. People from truly cold climates come to Marbella, despite the foggier mornings and cooler temps of winter on the island. They consider our highs of sixty degrees balmy since the weather where they're coming from usually requires a snow-blower and an ice scraper.

It's been four weeks since Kalaine's accident. She stayed in the hospital for a week.

I ran the watersports shack here at Alicante Resort and Spa while Kai took his first vacation since I've worked here to go sit by his sister's side until she woke. And then he stayed on until she was released with a concussion, sprained ACL and broken ankle. According to what I overheard Kai telling Ben, Kalaine insisted on staying in California despite her parents begging her to come back to Oahu with them. From the little I know, she had been living somewhere in South America with a group of female surfers before the accident.

I know Mavs. She's easy going—a total free spirit—but also driven. Anyone who rides big waves has to be. And when she makes up her mind about something, not even her dad will convince her otherwise. According to Kai, she's staying with a friend up in Scotts Valley outside of Santa Cruz.

Couch surfing: It's the worst kind of surfing. Been there, done that, got the water sports job to prove it.

I don't ask about Mavs, but my ears perk up anytime someone else does.

Kai and I have been like ships in the night since he's been back. He's hiding himself away and avoiding his emotions by throwing himself into work. He's always done some handyman jobs around the island to make a little extra cash here and there. But since Kalaine's accident, he's been working the water-sports shack most days and then leaving work to go fix or build something for someone nearly every night. He's burning the candle at both ends.

I get it. What we witnessed took a toll on each of us in its own way.

I'm giving him space—for now.

We all process traumatic experiences in our own ways. I'm pretty sure he'll burn off his grief within a few more weeks and things will go back to some semblance of normal.

"We've got to talk," Kai says, looking up from the wetsuit he's holding.

His finger pokes through a hole in the neoprene near the neck.

"I've gotta try and patch this," he says, as if he didn't just say we need to talk.

Another customer walks in, asking about surf lessons. I field all his questions since I'm usually the one doing surf instruction these days. Ben gives some lessons too, but we leave him to run the tours during the winter months.

Between the steady stream of customers, and Ben coming in to work the afternoon shift, Kai and I don't get any time alone all day. His words—we need to talk—hang like an ominous cloud between us. By the time we close, I'm racing home ahead of Kai. I had planned to have a group of friends over for burgers and hanging out. Kai and I are sort-of known for our regular barbecues. A bunch of resort employees will come over and fill our space until everyone gets too tired and starts to peel away to their own places for the night.

Kai disappears after work and doesn't come home until after everyone's left. I'm already in bed when I hear the door open and shut behind him.

I shoot him a text.

Bodhi: What did you need to talk to me about?
Kai: It's late. We can talk tomorrow. I don't want to talk by text.
Bodhi: I can come out of my room if you want.
Kai: It can wait.
Bodhi: K. Night, bro.

Kai: Night.

I don't fall asleep right away. It's been this way for four weeks now. Whenever I shut my eyes, I see Mavs being thrown off that wave. I try to shake that image, only to have it replaced with the sight of all the jet skis swarming to find her when she was held under by the whitewash, or the sight of her limp body being placed on the stretcher.

I've started to text her hundreds of times, just to tell her I'm thinking of her, or to say I'm glad she survived. But I'm the last person she needs to hear from right now, so I delete every message before I send it. I know what it's like to come out of a wave like that. Everything you believed and thought gets questioned—by you and everyone around you. She doesn't need her ex-boyfriend stepping into the mix and complicating things right now.

I wake later than usual the next morning. Saturday's my day off this season. I didn't set an alarm since I knew I didn't have to be anywhere. I'm working on shaping a board in the garage, so I have the door wide open, even though the view is only of the alley that runs behind our house. I've got my Airpods in, an old Sublime album setting the tone for my work. I hear a banging noise, so I turn off my power planer and pause my music.

The banging starts up again. Someone's knocking at our front door.

I walk through from the garage into the house, brushing dust off my hands onto my board shorts as I go. I'm a mess. Shaping boards leaves me coated in grime and dust, but it's work that gives me a purpose and something to focus on besides Mavs.

I open the door and blink.

Mavs is standing on our porch, a crutch under one arm, her ukulele case in her other hand and a paisley duffle bag sitting at her feet. Her long, wavy, dark brown hair is pulled up into a ponytail. She's got several strands of wooden beaded necklaces around her neck, and she's wearing a long flowing cotton skirt and a loose blouse that makes her look like the Hawaiian reincarnation of Janis Joplin.

Her golden brown eyes pierce right through me.

Mavs moves a little and her crutch pivots, sending her toppling toward me.

I reach out on instinct, cupping her elbow in my hand, my other hand grasping her waist.

The first words to come to mind fly out before I give myself a chance to think of what to say. I've dreamt of this moment for years. Then I trained myself to release that dream.

Here we finally are, and all I can think to say is, "What are you doing here?"

3

KALAINE

It is so strange, to encounter an ex.
It's as if you're in a foreign film, and what you're saying face-to-face
has nothing to do with the subtitles flowing beneath you.
~ Jodi Picoult

"What are you doing here?" We both blurt the words at one another simultaneously.

Bodhi.

The man broke my heart and wrecked me in more ways than that wave at Mavericks did a month ago. Ironic: the nickname Bodhi gave me became the place to nearly take me to my death.

What is Bodhi doing *here*?

And why didn't Kai tell me Bodhi was on Marbella Island?

His hand is still on my elbow, steadying me. I pull back, wobbling again. For a woman who makes her living balancing on a board on water, I can't seem to find my equilibrium these days. Some of my unsteadiness is the aftermath of the concussion. My one-legged status doesn't help. Most of what's throwing me is the man standing in front of me, his shoulder-length, brown wavy hair bleached with surfer-blond streaks that tell me he's been living in the sunshine again. He smiles that smile—the one that won my heart. The one that haunted my dreams. The one I worked so hard to forget.

Some pieces of the past become so deeply embedded in the heart and mind, woven in like an original thread. Everything about Bodhi feels familiar, from the cleft in his chin, hiding just beneath a little scruff that tells me he didn't bother to shave this morning, to his nearly shoulder-length brown hair held back by a bandana, to the piercing gray-blue eyes pinned on me right now. His hands fit my waist and elbow like an old pair of slippers, the ones you ought to throw out, but you keep hanging on to because you've broken them in just right.

I thought I had moved on. I believed I was over him. I foolishly assumed we would never see one another again. But here he is, looking tan, rugged, windblown, and giving me that look that always undoes me. I used to love the way he made me feel lightheaded and disarmed. Right now, I just want him out of my brother's house so I can settle in.

We both start to answer simultaneously.

"I live here," Bodhi says.

I blurt, "I'm moving in," my words tumbling over Bodhi's.

"You ... what? You live on Marbella Island?" I ask, certain I heard him wrong.

"You're moving in? Here?" Bodhi answers me with a look of confusion mirroring my own, only he's smiling and I'm so, so not.

"Where do you live?" The crutch bears into my armpit, a tangible reminder of everything I've lost, including the gorgeous man standing across the threshold of my brother's house from me.

"Here."

"You said that, but here where?"

"Are you asking to see my bedroom, Mavs? That's moving a

little fast, don't you think?" He teases me, but his eyes are soft. And, wait. *Whaaaat*? His bedroom is ... here? As in, *this house*?

I tilt back to double check the address number.

Thirty-two. That's what Kai said.

"This is it." Bodhi smiles softly. "My place. Well, Kai's and mine."

"What ...? How ...? When ...?"

Apparently, I've decided to recite all the question words in our language.

But seriously, my brother has been living with my ex. And I'm just now finding out about it the day I come to *move in*? In what universe are Bodhi and I going to live under the same roof?

Bodhi looks suddenly nervous, moving to shove his hands into his pockets, only he doesn't have pockets because he's wearing board shorts and the flimsiest T-shirt, his pecs begging to pop free of the fabric. He catches me staring and I blush.

"I uh ... I started to text you a bunch of times." His voice quavers in an uncharacteristic show of nerves. "It's good to see you ... up and about."

Bodhi is the quintessential surfer boy, raised in Ventura on the coast of California. He's got enough of the slang, and the swagger, and the sun-bleached looks to give him a free lifetime pass to any woman he sets his sights on. At one point in time, that woman was me.

"I'm supposed to ..." I attempt to ignore the way my body is firing to life at the sight of my ex-boyfriend. Bodies are like mischievous adolescents, sneaking out to do whatever they please. My urges are officially grounded. I'm taking away all their privileges. Someone has to play the adult here.

I wave my extended hand toward the room behind Bodhi, indicating I'm supposed to move in there—into the house where he apparently lives. What is my life?

"Yeah. Right. What did you mean when you said you were

moving in?" Bodhi bends to pick up my bag and the scent of him rushes over me. He's waves and salt, coconut and sand, ocean and a cozy beach bonfire—everything that draws me in even while it screams *danger*.

Bodhi backs up, making room for me and my crutch to awkwardly amble past him. I don't dare look in his direction. I hobble into the living room. Yes. I had another crutch. I ditched it, insisting I only needed one. I'm not usually this headstrong, but losing everything that mattered most to me—nearly losing my life—apparently brought out my ornery streak.

I look around the cottage-style home. A familiar photo of me and Kai sits on the mantle. We're at Pipeline. He had just won first place. I didn't win anything that day, but I didn't care. I was so proud of my big brother. My lying big brother who couldn't bother to tell me he's shacking up with my ex. I wonder how much damage I can do to him in my current condition.

I finally turn to Bodhi.

"Have a seat," he says. "Do you want something to drink?"

"I'm good."

I'm not. Not at all.

Better just unload everything and get this over with. Not that anything I say will do me any good. Bodhi lives here. It's not like he's about to move out.

I sit on the couch. It's cream with beachy throw pillows in varying shades of blue. Prints of beach scenes line the wall along with a few photos of my brother on waves. None of Bodhi. Interesting.

I lean back, wishing I had asked for water. I'm thirsty from traveling, and I'd like something to do with my hands.

"Dad wants me home. He and Mom would coddle me. The accident scared them, and their reaction is to grip tighter, to hold me near. Of course they feel that way." I pause, swallowing hard. I don't mind crying, but I don't want to lose it in front of

Bodhi. "Dad said he never should have let me compete—like ever."

"As if he could have stopped you? You were born for this. Kai might be named after the ocean, but you were born to ride the waves. Born to dominate your sport. You're never more alive than when you're on the water. It's like it's your natural habitat. Maybe you were a mermaid in your past life." He chuckles at his own joke.

His quiet confidence in me draws out a reluctant smile while his words remind me how all-too-familiar he is with me. What kind of warped fate is it that I would wind up here, talking to him, and he'd be the first person since my accident to tell me I belong in the ocean?

Even Dan is second guessing everything, and Dan has always believed in me. He had always gone beyond merely acknowledging how natural of a surfer I was, and pushed me as every good coach should. Until now. Now Dan is hesitant, reworking everything in his head over and over as if he caused me to go over the falls. This isn't about Dan. But I know my accident threw him into nearly as bad of a spiral as it has thrown me.

I don't know where I stand with the ocean now. I'm wary. For the first time in my life I feel afraid of the place that was my second home. I don't know if I can get back out there and do what I've always done. And if I don't surf, what will I do with my life? I've never wanted anything else. I can't share these thoughts with anyone. My competitors are my friends. They have the same hunger I did. I'm a reminder of how quickly the ocean can turn on a person, a living talisman of the fact that they are risking their lives for a sport we all love fiercely. My family wants to keep me landlocked. My coach is caught up in his head.

Everyone around me wants to put me on tenterhooks. Not Bodhi. He never questioned my love for the ocean or my need to keep testing my limits. He believes in me. He always did. I shake away the consolation of his words. He's not mine. He left me. He broke me in ways I never knew I could be broken. The jagged edges of our breakup threaten to sever my tenuous grasp on my dignity and self-control right now. It would be so easy to collapse into Bodhi's arms, to feel the familiar warmth of his comforting embrace, to let him kiss my forehead, to allow his lips to travel lower ...

The look in his eyes makes me feel like he's reading my mind.

"Yeah. Anyway, I didn't want to go back to Oahu. I need space. Time. Just somewhere that isn't under my parents' watchful eyes. I've got a lot to figure out. And my friends are all traveling to the other contests. It's peak season. You know?"

Of course he knows. This was his life too.

Bodhi's quiet, studying me. Giving me the space I just said I needed.

Oh, he's good at giving space alright. Too good.

"I don't want to go back to Santa Teresa quite yet," I add.

Bodhi's face scrunches slightly.

"Costa Rica," I clarify. "That's where I've been living. It's like a surfer commune down there. It used to be more sleepy. Now it's growing. There are some mid-level consistent breaks and some more gnarly points. Have you been?"

I forget my walls too easily around Bodhi. It's been that way since the first day I laid eyes on him. He's got me opening up, relaxing back into the sofa, sharing my thoughts. And all he did was answer the door, grab my bag, and offer me a drink.

KALAINE
(THE FIRST DAY I SAW HIM …)

I knew the second I met you
that there was something about you I needed.
Turns out it wasn't something about you at all.
It was just you.
~ Jamie McGuire

"Who is *that*?" I ask my best friend, Leilani.

My eyes catch on a boy I've never seen before. He's standing at the tailgate of a pickup truck on the other side of the parking lot. The energy in the air is electric. It's January, overcast, and the conditions are just right for a big break here. Surfers line the lot at the backs and sides of vehicles, all in various stages of dress and undress, towels wrapped around their waists to provide a modicum of privacy while they don wetsuits and prep to go into the water at its peak. When Mavericks breaks, you get a twenty-four-hour notice, thirty-six if you're lucky. People charter planes, grab bargain flights, take six-hour road trips—whatever it takes to get here and be a part of this moment.

The guy at the back of the truck looks familiar, but so do so many of the dudes out here on the cliffs of this northern California surf break. Half of them have been on the pro circuit for a while. Many of them have sponsorships. I would remember that face, though. No way I'd forget a guy who looked like *that*. His messy waves fall just above his shoulders in such a stereotypical surfer style it should look contrived. Instead, he looks like he invented surfing—and invented sexiness while he was at it.

Leilani follows my gaze and a slow smile spreads across her face. "Oh that guy? He's Bodhi Merrick. I think Kai knows him pretty well. He's officially competing as a pro now. All the surf blogs have been following him as he's been training for big waves. I think he got a Red Bull sponsorship too."

"Hmmm." I hum, trying to feign disinterest.

I cradle my tumbler of coffee in both hands, taking a sip to stave off the chill of the mist in the air.

Leilani laughs. "You're so transparent. Don't even pretend you don't want to just run over there and write your digits on his palm in Sharpie."

I laugh back. "I've got more class than that. I was going to use a tattoo gun."

She bursts into giggles. "That's what I'm saying. A guy like him would need it tattooed too. Otherwise, he'd be on to next week's girl and forget you as soon as you walked away."

"You think?"

"Look at him. He's hot and he knows it. He's young, in top shape, getting attention from companies and judges. He's at the top of his game. No guy like that is looking to put a ring on it."

"*I'm* not looking to put a ring on it. Sheesh. Settle down. I just noticed him."

"Who didn't?" Leilani looks around and I follow her gaze. More than a few other girls are staring at Bodhi.

Some of them are wahine—female surfers. Most of them are just honeys—girls dating one of the surfers, or hoping to. Nothing wrong with that. When and if I ever date a man, he'd better love the ocean. I can't imagine dating a kook. I live to surf.

My eyes drift back across the cliffs to the spot where Bodhi is tugging the zipper pull up the back of his wetsuit. He bends down to wax his board and on the way, he catches me staring. I look around like I'm busy doing who knows what, and then my gaze drifts back to him. I glance at him through my lashes. At this angle, half of my hair covers my face. At least my Hawaiian heritage is good for something. My crazy-thick hair feels like a curtain right now. But he sees through it. I can tell by the smile that curls his lips into a lopsided grin. He's smiling right at me, and I can't help but feel like I'm lit up from the inside.

My brother walks over to where I'm standing at just this moment. Of course he does.

"Look but don't touch, Keiki." He calls me *child*. The nickname used to be sweet, but now it's more annoying than anything. I'm nearly twenty. But to Kai, my older brother by four years, I'm always a baby, even if I surf waves that are double overhead. I've never surfed this place, though.

Mavericks.

In my bones, I know I will. I can feel the call of these waters —the magnetic invitation to come take a ride. Even without seeing them in person, I sense them. Maybe it's the challenge of taking on something so few men have, and even fewer women. I want to be one of those women—the ones who surf the giants.

I'm already training with BWRAG for safety awareness. My ohana insisted on it. If I'm shooting to ride double and triple overhead waves, I have to prepare to be safe. I agree with them, even if they make demands like the brood of wild, squawking chickens roaming around our neighborhood on Oahu.

I shrug at Kai as if I have no clue that he was warning me off Bodhi. Kai has no business telling me which guys to stare at ... or tattoo with my phone number. I'm a young woman. I'm going pro. I've got a life of adventure and freedom ahead of me.

I'm going to surf the world. And, maybe I'll find a man to share my adventures with. Maybe not. The ocean is, and always will be, my first love. Men are merely pretty—and fun. The most fun is flirting with them, especially when they know we're flirting. Like that one does.

Bodhi's watching Kai speak to me. He nearly rolls his eyes. I stifle a giggle, while holding his gaze. My brother keeps his serious look locked and loaded for my benefit. He should know by now his bossy big-brother stance has no impact on me— well, very little impact. I'd do anything for Kai, but at the end of the day, I'm my own person.

Leilani approaches my brother. Her crush on Kai is so obvious it's nearly embarrassing. I don't know why she's so into the serious, older-guy type. The idea of her and him ... just ew. She could do better. I love my brother. He's been my best friend ever since childhood. He's even the one who talked Mom and Dad into letting me pursue surfing as more than a hobby. And, Kai's the reason Mom ended up letting me finish my course-work for high school online so I could travel with him while he competed. But I don't love thinking of him kissing anyone.

"I thought Bodhi was a good friend of yours." Leilani practically bats her lashes off, looking up at Kai like he's beyond special.

"He's a good friend." Kai says. "We're getting closer the more we travel together. Why?"

"You'd think you'd want your sister to flirt with him instead of someone you barely know."

"I don't want my sister to flirt with anyone." He says it like it's so obvious.

"Good luck with that." Leilani giggles, and Kai smiles a little back at her. Huh.

Kai eventually wanders off, leaving me and Lei to boy-watch and chat here on the side of the road facing the path that leads to the cliffs of Mavericks. We're a safe distance from shore. Any closer and we'd be forced to turn around by the law enforcement they require to stand guard out here on days like these. The surfers will be allowed through, looky-loos aren't allowed on the cliffs since some spectators have been seriously injured by rogue waves in recent years. So, we'll wait for the guys to go out, and then we'll pack it up and swarm some restaurant where everyone who braved the waves will eat and drink their weight in healthy food and coffee while we all talk over one another about the rides they took.

Bodhi stands and stretches, preparing his body and mind for what he's about to endure. I watch him bend and extend his arms down to the ground. Then he reaches overhead in a stretch I know all too well. I'm shameless in my perusal. He looks over and I can make out his wink at me from a distance.

"Surfers are so beautiful," Leilani says softly from beside me.

She's not wrong. Surfers are beautiful—especially *that* one.

4

BODHI

If I had a flower for every time I thought of you ...
I could walk through my garden forever.
~ Alfred Tennyson

C *osta Rica*, Kalaine says.

She's been living in Costa Rica.

"Nah. I've never been," I tell her. I shift a little on my feet. I still haven't gotten to the bottom of her showing up with a duffle and one crutch, but Mavs is relaxing on our couch, and the story will come. It's beyond surreal to see her here, in my space.

"I always wanted to check out Costa Rica. Pura vida, right?"

Mavs smiles and nods when I quote the unofficial motto of that country. Saying *pura vida* is nearly the same as saying *aloha* in Hawaii. It's a greeting, a farewell, and a way of life.

"I surfed Brazil. Some breaks in Peru. A bunch of guys and I took a trip before I went pro. We traveled down the coast of

Peru, hitting Máncora, Cabo Blanco ... Lobitos, Chicama, and Huanchaco."

"I've never surfed Peru," she says.

Her voice is wistful like she never did, and she never will.

"Hashtag goals, right?"

"Did you seriously just say 'hashtag'?"

I chuckle. "I was trying to make you laugh."

She shakes her head lightly, her smile is dim. There's a weariness to her—one I recognize. She had the wind knocked out of her in more than one way.

"You look like you were in the middle of something," she says, eyeing me from head to toe.

I always liked when she looked at me like that, taking in every inch of me, never hiding the fact that she was checking me out. The heat is gone now, though. This is different.

Kalaine lived life filled with helium. Buoyant, light, rising above, reaching upward. Now she's a deflated version of the girl I loved—the girl I still love, definitely still love.

"Yeah. I was shaping a board."

"For yourself? You're surfing?"

The incredulity in her voice is warranted.

"I don't do anything too rad anymore. Mostly just teaching at the resort."

"You teach surfing?"

"I do."

"With Kai?"

"Yep. He's my boss."

Mavs laughs at that—a full belly laugh. And once she starts laughing, it's like a dam broke. She's laughing hard, her eyes squinched up, her mouth wide open. She places a hand on her stomach and bends slightly while she cackles, looking like she could double over at any minute.

I can't help but smile, watching her come undone. She's gorgeous. I'd say exotic, and she'd correct me, saying she's a dime-a-dozen in Oahu. She's not. There's no one like her. And I thought I had rid myself of the way she affected me. I moved on, started a life without her, married myself to the ocean and grew content to go out with girls from work here and there. I knew I'd never settle down. Kalaine was my one. And when I blew it, I knew I'd never try to make my forever with anyone else. But, here she is, losing it on my couch, laughing like she used to. And my heart has officially entered a time warp.

"I'm getting you water." I walk toward the kitchen.

I need to put space between us—to breathe through the urge to sit next to her. She's hurting. In the past, I'd have held her. I may never hold her again. It's not even fair to her for me to be thinking of anything but what she needs right now after taking the fall of her life.

"I take it you came over on the ferry?" I say from the kitchen.

She's still giggling. "Yeah." Her softening laughs trail into the kitchen and I indulge myself in a full smile. Mavs is sitting in *my* living room, laughing. If you'd have asked me if this would ever be my life, I would have sworn you were out of your mind to even consider it. Sure. Kai's her brother. But she never visited him. They'd meet up at their family's home in Hawaii. I honestly never thought I'd see her in person again, let alone have her here, in my own house.

I walk back into the living room and hand Kalaine the glass of water. Our fingers brush and our eyes lock, and for the briefest moment it's like we're catapulted back in time to over two years ago.

I step back and she regains composure, or maybe she never lost hers.

"Kai. Your boss. Man. That's ... that's just crazy."

"It's really not as crazy as you'd think. He's chill. I came here after the accident."

"You did?"

"Yeah. Not right away. But ... yeah."

"You've been here for ..."

"Almost two years."

The truth hangs between us. I feel like a jerk. Obviously, Kai hasn't told her I live with him. He's never mentioned me to his sister. I get why. I'm not sure she does.

"So, you mentioned moving here?" I circle back around to her original declaration.

"Yeah. That's ... well, after I kill my brother, I'm not sure how things will end up."

"Unless I'm in the will for his half of the house ..."

She chuckles, but it's not the laugh she had a few moments ago.

"He told me he had a spare bedroom. I basically begged him to let me come here."

Kalaine looks up at me, the clear evidence of her trauma written all over her face. "I told him I didn't want to be alone in my place in Costa Rica. Besides, I didn't really want to have to face everyone there—not yet. The whole town's heard about what happened—seen the recording on YouTube. I don't want a million questions every time I leave the house. Kai tried to talk me into staying with our parents. When I refused, he admitted he had a room where I could stay. He said something about a detail he needed to iron out ..."

Her voice trails off and I raise my hand. "Me. I'm the detail."

"I kinda figured that out. Kai didn't say anything to you?"

"No. But he did say there was something he needed to talk to me about. He's kind of been ... busy. And we haven't had any time alone. I had people over last night. We've had customers constantly coming into the watersports shack where we work. Did Kai know you were coming today?"

"I didn't give him an exact date." Mavs' lips draw thin and her eyes crinkle with amusement. "I guess telling him when to expect me would have helped. But he really could have mentioned you living here at some point over the past two years."

I don't say anything. If I defend Kai, I'm asking for all Mavs' irritation to be turned on me for something I wasn't party to. If I don't defend him, I'm throwing him under the bus when he's done nothing but help me rebuild a life. I deserve Kalaine's anger—just not for this.

"Well. I don't know what I'm going to do." Mavs' voice is small again, her shoulders slumped.

"You'll just stay here."

"What? No! No way. No offense, Bodhi, but you and I ..." she waves her pointer finger between the two of us. "We're not at the point where I can live under the same roof as you."

Sobering reality. Her words feel like a slap.

She's right. We're not what we were. I did that. And some harms may never be undone no matter what I'd give to turn things around and give us both a second shot.

This short respite today has been sweet, but in another way it's the worst kind of cruelty because I got a taste of her. And I want more. I always wanted more with her. She's the only woman who ever made me want more.

My craving for her may never diminish. But I forfeited my right to pursue her. And now, she's at her most vulnerable point. It would be the height of selfishness to pursue her when she needs time to sort out her thoughts and her life. I know what she needs more than anyone. I've been right where she is. Only, when I turned to Kai, I didn't have to run into an ex while I was seeking a safe place to stay.

"I spend a lot of time at work," I find myself convincing her before I've even considered the ramifications of what I'm offering. All I know is I can't stand to see her so unsettled. She's the freest spirit I've ever known. I won't be the reason she sinks and can't get back up again. "I can stay out of your way. I mean, if you stay here, I'd make it easy on you."

"It wouldn't be—easy on me. It wouldn't be easy on you either, I imagine. You're being naive if you think it would. But I don't really have another option. Kai was my last stop."

"Well then, it's settled. Let me show you to the guest ... I mean *your* room."

5

KALAINE

Sometimes the hardest part isn't letting go,
but rather learning to start over.
~ Nicole Sobon

I hobble behind Bodhi, down a hall that feeds off the living room. Doors line the hallway. He points to each one as we pass.

"That's the coat closet. There's the guest bath. We'll turn it into yours."

Just like that. I've got to hand it to him, he's as unrattled as ever. The only time I saw Bodhi come unglued was after his accident. Then, he was unrecognizable to me. It was like someone had stolen in overnight and switched out his personality. Where the easy-going, carefree, winsome flirt of a man had taken up residence, a shell remained. And that shell was filled with a sullen, lost soul.

Bodhi said something about the rooms just now but my mind was off in the past somewhere.

"What?"

"I said, that room's mine and that one's Kai's. You want to put something like itching powder in his sheets? Or we could short-sheet him. Maybe switch out his toothpaste for some sort of senior citizen muscle rub?"

"I use that muscle rub now."

"I'm sure you do." He winks at me, and it's meant to be friendly.

I appreciate his attempt to lighten the situation and distract me from the reasons forcing me to be here bumming a room from my older brother.

"Anyway," he clears his throat. "This is your room. We leave it pretty untouched. I had been keeping my guitar in there. I'll just ..." He goes to move past me and we brush against one another.

"Sorry," we both say at the same time.

And then we're standing here in the doorway, stuck in this awkward position. He's mere inches from me, looking down into my eyes. I'm staring right back up at him.

"I can't ... maybe this isn't such a good idea, Bodhi."

"No. No. Just let me get my guitar. I'll get out of your hair. I promise we'll make this work, Mavs."

Mavs.

The nickname just rolls off his tongue. I can hear him murmuring it into my hair after kissing me, or affectionately tacking it onto something sweet he'd say when we'd cuddle up on yet another beach, watching the stars. He always said it with a certain kind of reverence. Only he and I know why he gave me that particular nickname. It's a name only he used.

He doesn't seem to be the least bit aware of even having said it just now. *Mavs.*

I'll never be able to forget—what we were and what we lost. Everything that name stood for is gone now.

"Okay." Bodhi lifts his guitar case higher than needed. "Got it. I'm out. I'll be in the garage if you need me. Saturdays are my day off. I'm usually out there. Or I can be scarce. Or ... whatever you need."

"Don't." I look at him with a plea in my eyes.

"Don't what?" He's already walking toward my doorway.

"Nothing. I ... just probably need to lie down for a bit."

That's not a lie. My ankle hurts and I feel light-headed. I'd love to ignore all those telltale reminders of my new reality if I could.

Bodhi nods and walks the rest of the way into the hall. "I'll leave you to it. If you wake, and I'm not here, it means I figured out what to say to your brother and I've gone to pay him a visit at the shack."

I smile faintly.

And then Bodhi's gone. And my foolish heart has this unwelcome yearning for him to turn around and come back.

I hobble over and shut the door. Then I look around my new room. The term *my* being a stretch. This room belongs to my ex-boyfriend and my soon-to-be ex-brother, God rest his soul.

The double bed sits in the middle of the main wall, flanked by two bedside tables. There's a window looking out toward the front yard, though the curtains are drawn shut right now. Behind me, next to the door leading to the hallway are two sliding doors to the closet. No desk. No other furniture. Just a bed and two side tables. My paisley duffle taunts me from the floor where Bodhi dropped it.

Will you unpack me and settle in, or will I remain untouched and ready for an easy getaway?

I mutter to my travel bag, "I'll get back to you on that."

Bending down, I pull my cell out of the front pocket.

Then I prop my crutch on the wall and make my way to the bed. The doctors said to put weight on my foot in the boot during this stage of healing. I'm not sure if a full day of travel using one crutch was what they had in mind. I collapse backward onto the bed and turn so my leg is up and then I unfasten the boot, setting it on the side table. I wiggle my toes and twin sensations of pain and relief travel up my leg.

Then I pull up the contact for my oldest and best friend in the world and hit the button to dial her. Leilani's in Oahu right now—where I would have been—where we grew up. She's surfing a big wave contest called the Eddie, named after the champion surfer and North Shore lifeguard, Eddie Aikau.

"Hey, Lei," I say when she answers.

"Girl. I've been waiting to hear from you. Did you make it to your brother's house?"

"You could say that."

"What do you mean?"

Voices chatter in the background behind her, probably other surfers. A pang of longing throbs through my chest. I'm a few blocks from the ocean, but I may as well be landlocked.

"I mean ... he shares a place with another guy." I look toward the door where Bodhi walked out of my room only moments ago.

"Oooh. So, is this guy cute?"

I giggle. Leilani is shameless in her appreciation of men. She's more of a Type-A than I am when it comes to setting goals and pursuing them. And she doesn't take crap from anyone. I'm more of a live and let live person. She's more of an, *Oh, no you didn't*, type. We mesh somehow. Perfectly.

"I used to think he was beyond cute."

"What? Do you know him?"

"Yeah. I did."

"Stop being so mysterious. Who is this man?"

"Bodhi."

"WHAAAAAT?" Leilani shrieks. I hear people around her go quiet. "Sorry. What did you say? I know you didn't say Bodhi, as in the man who shattered your heart into so many fragments it took me at least a year to put Humpty Dumpty back together again."

"It wasn't as bad as you make it sound."

"Um. Beg to differ."

"It was a rough year. Can you blame me?"

"You, I never blamed. Him ..."

"I know. And, there's more."

"Shut the front door. More? What more? Don't you think you've been through your quota of bad juju with him?"

"Yeah. Well. Apparently Bodhi has been living here for almost two years. He came to Kai's after the accident."

"Um. Am I missing something? Why didn't Kai say anything about this minor detail? Like, oh, I don't know, *Hey Kalaine, your ex is now my housemate*?"

"Right? Trust me. That's going to be the very first question I ask my brother."

"You haven't seen him yet?"

"No. I got off the ferry and a resort employee drove me to Kai's ... well, Kai and Bodhi's ... in a golf cart. Then I knocked on the door and Bodhi answered. Kai's at work."

"Awkward." She pauses. Then her voice brightens. "Or ... maybe it's fate. No. It's not fate. Unless fate has a vendetta against you."

"Nope. It's not fate. It's just awkward."

"Hmmm. I don't know. Let's run the statistical probability here ..." Leilani pauses her train of thought to answer someone. "Yeah. I'll be right there. Go ahead without me." Then she says, "How likely is it that you and Bodhi would end up crossing paths again? And then, on top of that, what's the likelihood that you would end up in Bodhi's actual house? I think this could definitely be fate."

"If fate is out to get me, then yes. I'll agree."

"Despite the way you moved on with life, you have to admit you never got over him. It pains me to admit that." Her voice is calm and gentle, like she's trying to coax a toddler to give back an open bottle of nail polish while standing over a white carpet.

"My old feelings for him are completely irrelevant, and also highly inconvenient. I need to have gotten over him. And I'm angry enough to override any reaction to his hotness."

"His hotness. I know. Girl, if he's as hot as he was when he was surfing ..."

"He is. And it's a troublesome aggravation I'll have to live with temporarily. I'm obviously not staying here." I don't know where I'll go, but I can't stay here with Bodhi and my lying brother.

I sigh. "I'm a pro surfer. I can overcome my physical urges in order to attain a higher goal." I pause. "Well, I was a pro surfer. I don't know what I am now."

"I'll tell you what you are. You're still the top surfer in female heats, and in big wave surfing you're one of the best of the best. You kick booty and take names. You even out-ride most of the men. Mark my words. You will be proving all that and more in the years to come. Don't give up on yourself over this one experience, Kah."

"I know. I won't."

I can't bring myself to tell her I won't ever surf again. I know it in my bones and my bones don't lie. Sometimes you have to leave a bad relationship. The ocean showed me something at Mavericks. I'm not the surfer I thought I was. That's a lesson I won't have to learn twice. If I can't surf the kinds of waves I used to, there's no use doing less. That would only depress me more.

"Good. That's my girl. You'll dominate again, sweet wahine. If can ... can, right?"

"Yeah. Right. Did you need to go?"

"Yeah. They're all getting açaí bowls at Sunshine Shack. I'm meeting them there. No rush."

I picture all of the surfers gathered around the little yellow hand-painted hut, the low mountains in the background and

the ocean across the road with the *Grommies Crossing* sign
hanging there. I would have been laughing and coming off the
adrenaline high of my rides right along with them. We'd all be
comparing notes about who caught the best wave, tricks that
were landed, fails and misses. That's my community—or it was.

"I'll let you go. I'm tired after traveling. Ride a wave for me,
m'kay?"

"They're all for you until you can get back and ride your
own. I love you, sis."

"I love you too, ke kika." I use our slang Hawaiian word for
sister, it's what I've called her since high school, or maybe even
junior high.

We hang up and I text my mom just so she doesn't worry.

Kalaine: *I made it to Kai's.*

Mom: *Good. Do you want me to call?*

Kalaine: *No. I'm going to lie down and rest. I'm good, don't
worry.*

Mom: *Good. You rest. You need rest. The doctors said so. Call me
later with Kai.*

Kalaine: *I will.*

I won't. I don't even know what I'm going to say to Kai, let
alone how I would manage a phone call to our parents without
turning him in for living with Bodhi. My family is no longer a
fan of my ex after watching me go through the kind of heart-
break I never thought a person could experience. My ohana is
loyal to a fault—always taking my side.

I fluff my pillow and lie down on the bed in the room that
does not feel even remotely like it will ever be mine—probably
because it won't be.

6

BODHI

We are all trying to get over the person
who broke our hearts.
~ Alex Rosa

I try to get back to shaping the board. My mind keeps traveling the short distance through the house and down the hall to the second door on the left. Mavs is right here, in my home. And Kai didn't prepare either of us for the life-quake of seeing one another for the first time in years—the first time since I blew everything with her.

I set down my tool and run a hand through my hair. I should shower, but I'm too keyed up to wait. I have no plan, no words prepared, just a raging need to confront my best friend and the co-owner of my house. The second year I lived here, Kai said it didn't feel right to have me pay rent, so we renegotiated the mortgage and I gave him a wad of cash for the down payment. We own this place fifty-fifty. If one of us ever needs to move, we'll sell and split the profit, or one of us will buy the other out. Thankfully, all my sponsorships and championship earnings gave me a good nest egg. I make barely anything working at the shack, but it's enough to cover my monthly expenses, including my half of the mortgage.

That's all the more reason Kai should have stepped it up and told me about Mavs coming here. This isn't just his place. And she's not simply another down-and-out girl he wants to help. The woman in my spare bedroom never wanted to see me again—that much is obvious. And, yet, she had to beg for a place to stay. I'd move out if I didn't own half this house, just to give her some air.

I hop on my mountain bike and ride the few blocks to the sand. Then I park my bicycle in the racks at the beach's edge and walk down the boardwalk leading to the watersports shack. The little white wooden building sits on a wider section of a dock. We stash kayaks next to a supply shed behind the main building. A few benches flank the spots in front of the windows. Customers use those for gearing up before a lesson or going out on rentals.

The door is almost always open, even with our cooler temps during these winter months.

I walk in, knowing full well no one is expecting me on my day off. We love this place, but we all need our time away from it too.

"Bodhi? What's got you coming in on your day off?" Ben asks.

The three of us, Ben, Kai, and me, are the main full-time employees for watersports. We're all certified in water safety, diving, lifesaving and boater education. We've got a few part-timers, and we hire some mainland college kids over the summers to help offset the flood of tourists who come here May through September. But today, it's just Ben and Kai working.

"I've got something to discuss with Kai." My eyes scan the shop.

Ben lets out a low whistle. "This oughta be good."

"What makes you think it's not?"

"Your face, for one. And the fact that you left your pet project on a Saturday—looking like you've been wrestling with a powder puff—to come down here."

"Yep."

I don't say anything else because Kai appears through the back door. When he sees my face, it's like he knows.

"You wanted to tell me something?" I ask.

"Let's step out back."

"Nooo." Ben nearly whines out the word. "I never get to have any excitement in my life anymore. If your bromance is hitting the rocks, I want to watch."

I can't help but chuckle, even though I'm livid, and confused, and probably other things I can't even figure out yet. This is all fresh. Mostly, I keep picturing the way Mavs looked at me and how the last thing she needed was to come seeking refuge and end up bumping into her ex after all she's already endured.

"Fine," I say to Ben.

I turn to Kai who's still a store-length away from me. "Mavs?"

Kai runs his hand down his face from his forehead to his chin.

Stevens, our resident marine biologist, comes in the back doorway behind Kai.

"What's up, Bodhi?" His tone is casual until he reads the room. "Uh. Everything okay?"

Ben smirks. "No. Totally not. Kai did something. And Bodhi's upset, and he just said, *Mavs,* whatever that means. Get a bowl of popcorn. It's just getting good."

I give Ben a look. He just smiles that lopsided, golden-boy

grin of his. You can't get mad at that guy. He's like a mischievous puppy who's always cuter than he is annoying.

"Mavs, as in Mavericks? The big wave spot?" Stevens asks.

"No." Kai's eyes are steely.

He knows he messed up, but he does not like me using the nickname I gave his sister. I guess I said it on purpose. But also, it slipped out—like it did in the guest room when I was alone with her. The air nearly whooshed out of the room when I said it. I averted my eyes and played it cool, but I felt the way everything shifted for a moment, the memories rushing us like a rogue wave full of enough power to take us both under.

"He's talking about my sister."

"Your sister who is currently in our guest room."

"She's here?"

"Yeah. She showed up about an hour ago, hobbling on one crutch, only a duffle to her name, and a look of bewilderment when I answered the door. Imagine her shock, finding out you've been living with me for two years."

"Oh, man."

"Wait, what?" Ben asks. "No way! Dude. You never told your sister you were living with her ex-boyfriend?"

Stevens looks at each of the three of us. "You dated his sister?"

"Yeah. I did."

"Big mistake," Kai adds.

"You're not really in the position to call out my mistakes from where I stand."

"Yeah. True." Kai's shoulders slump the slightest. "I meant to tell you. I didn't know she was coming today, though. I thought it would be next week. I was going to tell you. And her."

Ben can't help himself. "What were you thinking, Kai?" He shakes his head. "Man, you are in such deep, deep yogurt. Stinks to be you, bro."

Kai looks properly remorseful. "I know already. I messed up. It seemed like a good idea at the time. The last thing my sister needed was a reminder of Bodhi. She would have felt like I was betraying her." He looks at Ben. "That's a long story. One I'm not going into here. Bodhi's my best friend, and when he needed me, I didn't hesitate to take him in. Over time it just got harder to mention him to Kalaine. She never visits. Our ohana —our family—meets up in Oahu, or at her competitions when I can get away for them. I figured no harm, no foul."

"Until she called to tell you she needed to stay somewhere," I add.

"Yeah. And I couldn't turn her away. I've been racking my brain for a way to break this to both of you." He pauses, his face filled with the appropriate amount of agony. "Sorry, Bodhi."

"I get it."

I actually do. I don't condone the way Kai covered facts, but having lived through my own accident and then seeing Kalaine today, I do understand why Kai hid my presence and why he'd be struggling to tell her. Without a doubt, she needs to stay here. I just need to figure out how to make living around me easy on her.

I hang out at the watersports shack for a while after Kai and I talk things through. There's really not much else he needs to say to me. I want Kalaine here. Even though it's heck-ah awkward, I want her to be able to hide out and take her time. She needs that. Kai is sincerely sorry. It's not me he needs to worry about. He's got to figure out how to smooth the waters with his baby sister. And even though she's normally as chill as they come, right now she's vulnerable, and that makes her easily riled up. I'll leave all that to him, though. His mess, his shovel.

Once I get back home, I spend the afternoon in the garage. And as far as I can tell, Mavs sleeps like the dead for the duration of the day. I'm done with my project for now. Not finished with the board, but I've done enough and I don't want my work to get sloppy by staying longer at this than I should. When I hear the front door open, I step up into the house from the garage. Kai looks around. I point to the guest bedroom.

"She went to sleep hours ago. I think she may still be out. I remember how that was for me. Sleep is the only mental break you get—as long as you don't have nightmares."

Kai nods. He's obviously still knee-deep in the reality of everything that happened to Kalaine and the fact that he still has to face her when she wakes.

"I'll go pick up tacos," I offer.

Making a food run will give Kai and Kalaine the space they need for starters. And Mavs hasn't eaten since she arrived, maybe most of the day. I'll feed her. I always loved taking her out or cooking for her. She loved cooking for me too. Those days are gone, though. I'm going to need some sort of mantra to remind myself to keep the past where it belongs. Mavs needs a safe place to land. She doesn't need me strolling down memory lane trying to revive what once was.

That's what I'll give her. A safe place to land.

Even if I have to die a little every day to do it.

7

KALAINE

You can close your eyes to
the things you don't want to see,
but you can't close your heart
to the things you don't want to feel.
~ Johnny Depp

I wake disoriented. The room I'm in is dark.

Kai's house.

Bodhi's house.

Bodhi.

A sigh leaves my lips before I'm able to control my instinctual reaction to him.

Why does he have to be so magnetic? And kind? And gorgeous. He's more than gorgeous. He's beautiful in this sun-kissed, sea salt baptized, rugged, effortless way. And he's the last thing I need to be thinking about right now.

I blink my eyes and my surroundings come into focus.

Sparse furnishings—totally a room set up by two single guys—functional with no frills.

And then my dream comes rushing back at me. I'm on that wave again. The edge approaches. Dan drives away on the backside of the lip. I scream out to him, "Dan! Dan! Dan!" My heart races and I reach a fevered panic. Then the water is like ice under my feet, sliding and pulling me before I take the near-fatal dive over the falls. Everything goes black then. Every. Single. Time. Why does my brain insist on reliving that wave over and over? I don't even know if the dream mimics reality because I can't bring myself to remember even being towed out. My neurologist said a blank spot in memories surrounding a crisis is normal after a traumatic episode, especially one that led to a concussion.

A part of me is grateful. Why would I want to remember the wave that ended my career? But another part of me won't settle until I know and see it all, pick it apart, and discern what went wrong. But I won't watch the YouTube videos or news clips. I don't want to see myself in third person. I do want my memories back—and my life.

I hear shuffling in the main room.

Kai might be home by now, considering the level of darkness filling my room. I pick my phone up off the bedside table. Six forty-five. Yeah. Kai's home and the sun set a while ago.

I pivot and reach for my boot, securing it around my foot and ankle. Then I stand and grab my crutch. Once I've used the hall bathroom, I make my way into the living room. Kai is sitting on one of the two couches. He looks up and sees me. A myriad of emotions cross his face.

"Kala," he calls me by his pet name for me.

It means princess, but it's also a kind of fish with a spike on its tail. At least he doesn't call me limu kala which is the seaweed those fish eat.

"Kai." I regard him from the hall doorway, leaning on my

crutch in a way my physical therapist told me not to—not if I don't want to hurt my armpit.

"Hey," he stands and walks to me, tugging me into his arms.

His arms slipping around me and the feel of him holding me unhinges the emotions I've kept locked up tight. My defenses fall, and regardless of my desire to stay angry, I'm leaning into my big brother, allowing tears to flow down my cheeks like a waterfall. Within seconds, I feel his soft sobs joining my own. The weight of everything rushes up and out of me into Kai's embrace.

He runs his hands down my hair without saying a word. Kai simply holds me, like he always has. My big brother. In Oahu we have a saying. Of course, it is told in connection to a story about two brothers. Nearly every piece of proverbial wisdom my parents raised us on has a story or a legend behind it. The saying is: *The older sibling cares for and protects the younger. And the younger listens to the older.* Those principles may feel commonplace, but they go deeper with us. They are a way of life—timeless truths passed through generations through oral tradition and common practice in our extended community. They have become a part of how we've built our lives—Kai and I. The culture shapes us, and even though we no longer live in Hawaii, we are always Hawaiian.

"Kala, you scared me." Kai's voice is rough with emotion.

My head is still nestled under Kai's chin. I feel his shaky breath as he tries to contain his reaction for my sake.

"I know."

"You'll be okay." The way he says that platitude feels like he's trying to convince himself along with me. "You survived. We're going to get you through this."

I pull back and look my big brother in the eyes. "And by we, you mean ..."

"Yeah. About that." Kai steps back. "I am really sorry. I

wanted to tell you before you showed up and had to run into him."

"Don't you think telling me before I decided to come here would have been a little more fair—to Bodhi and to me? I am here because I don't want to face a surfing community, having to tell everyone I'm doing fine every time I leave my house to get fruit or put gas in my moped. Instead, I came here and had to face the biggest regret of my life right in the flesh."

"The flesh?"

"You know what I mean. Not flesh, flesh. He was dressed. I was dressed. Well, he was wearing a very flimsy shirt that showed off his ... nevermind. We were dressed. No flesh. Flesh-free. Fleshless. Gah. Fleshless? That sounds like a skinned fish. But then again, fish don't have flesh, do they? They have scales. Unless you're talking about sharks. Which you aren't. We're talking about Bodhi. A very dressed, not fleshy, in-the-flesh, ex-boyfriend whom you should have warned me about, and not just this week."

I take a breath and look up at my brother who is wisely stifling a grin at my nervous word-vomit. He straightens his face, the seriousness of his omission reminding him we're not joking around.

"I should have told you a long time ago. I just didn't want to upset you."

"So you hid the truth. You harbored my ex for two years and never thought it would be a good idea to share that with me?"

"At first I didn't say anything because your breakup was so fresh. He was hurting. You know how it was."

"Actually, I don't. If you remember, I wasn't privy to any of those details."

Kai looks at me with a look of sympathy so powerful I almost forgive him on the spot. Almost. But he's not getting off that easily.

"What am I supposed to do now?"

"Stay. Bodhi wants you to be able to have what he had. He knows you need it. More than anyone, he knows. Just stay. We'll work this out. It will probably be awkward at first, but I think we'll all get used to the new normal eventually. I want you here. I've been worried sick about you."

"Great. Another lālā ʻohana worrying over me."

"I'm not going to baby you. I know you. If you wanted to be babied, you'd be in Haleiwa with Mom and Dad."

"Thanks for that, at least."

Normally, I'd give Kai more heat. And he's not off the hook. I just don't have a lot of fight left in me. And whatever I thought I was going to do to make him pay seems to have fled when he held me and comforted me like only he can.

The front door swings open and Bodhi comes in, carrying two take out bags. He holds them up like a peace offering.

"I didn't know what you'd want so I got a bit of everything."

His face looks sheepish, and he's adorable—the man who left me. I remind the little voice in my head of that glaring and overwhelming fact. Maybe this is just what I need—time around Bodhi to work out my residual attraction. Over time my longing for him is bound to fade out and diminish into nothingness. I'll just give it time.

"Thanks, bruh," Kai says. Then he turns to me. "You hungry, Kala?"

"I could eat." A house. I'm starving. But I don't want to tell Kai I haven't eaten since I gobbled a protein bar this morning. My metabolism hasn't gotten the memo that I'm no longer an elite athlete.

"Let's dig in." Bodhi walks past me, the smell of amazing tacos wafting behind him—as if I needed one more reason to trail behind him like he's the Pied Piper and I'm some lost waif of a child.

Kai lingers behind us silently, entering the kitchen and grabbing down three plates, then placing them around the wooden table. Bodhi opens the bags and sets them in the middle. And the three of us sit, facing one another.

"Well, this isn't awkward at all," Bodhi says with a carefree smile.

"Not at all," I agree.

I stare at the bags, unable to meet Bodhi's eyes.

Kai doesn't say a word.

Instead, he fishes through the bags, obviously familiar with which colored paper wrap holds which taco. He pulls two out. One in white and one in yellow.

"You've got to try their carne asada." He plops one of the tacos on my plate.

I don't fight him. I mean, it's carne asada. Choose your hills to die on. Tacos aren't that hill.

We eat in silence except the occasional hum or moan of appreciation, most of them coming from me. Not only was I beyond hungry, but these tacos are amazing.

"Mexican tacos are so good. I had forgotten how good." I mumble around a bite. "In Costa Rica they roll them and fry them."

I'm totally talking with my mouth full, so I raise the back of my hand to cover my lips while I lick a stray bit of sauce from my lip.

Bodhi smiles over at me. I concede, and smile a flash of a smile at him. The expression doesn't say, *green light*, but I hope it says, *thanks for dinner,* and also *leave me alone.*

There's a knock at the door while we're all digging into our second tacos. Bodhi and Kai look at one another.

"I'm not expecting anyone."

"Me neither."

Bodhi wipes his hands and stands. We can see straight through the kitchen and living room to the front door. When Bodhi opens it, two young women who look slightly younger than me stand side by side on the porch.

"Hey, Bodhi!" one of them says with a whole lot of enthusiasm.

She's got brown hair and is wearing the kind of makeup that says she put in some effort.

"Hey, Emily." Bodhi's tone is friendly, but guarded. I can't tell if that's because of her or me. Probably me, since he's usually one of the most outgoing and confident people in any crowd.

"Thanks for having us over last night," the other girl, a beautiful blond, says to him.

"No problem. What can I do for you two?"

"Sheena left her jacket in your room last night," the one named Emily says.

"Oh, yeah. Come on in." Bodhi glances briefly at me as the two girls enter the room.

"Hi, Kai!" the one named Sheena says. She notices me like an afterthought. "Who's this?"

"Hey, Sheena. This is Kalaine, my sister. She just arrived today."

The girls both say hi, but Sheena turns and walks down the hallway, following Bodhi like she's made the trip to his bedroom before—probably more than once.

My taco feels like it's turning into a ball of lead in my stomach.

Here's something I should have thought of before now.

Bodhi. And women.

He's always been this magnetic force. Between his looks, his easy-going personality, his sense of humor and his prowess as a surfer, he's the perfect man. Most women are drawn to Bodhi. I'm used to it. But I'm also used to being the one he focused on no matter who was around us. He never flirted with other women. We had female friends. But I never had to worry about Bodhi being unfaithful.

But we're not together anymore. He doesn't owe me

anything. We haven't been a couple for two years. And he's still a magnet, and a man who enjoys attention from women. Before I think better of it, I'm closing my eyes and placing my head in my hands, my elbows resting on the table.

"Are you okay?" Emily asks me.

"Me? Yeah. I'm great." I lift my head and meet her eyes, pasting a smile onto my face.

"Long travel day," Kai supplies.

Not long enough.

"How long are you visiting?" Emily asks.

Her smile is warm, and normally I'd be talkative. *Never met a stranger*, my mom used to say about me.

"It's ..." I start to answer.

Kai cuts in. "She's here for a while. She's got some time off work."

"That's so great. Sheena and I work at the resort. Bodhi and Kai always throw the best barbecues. A bunch of us come anytime they put the word out—some townies and a whole group of resort staff usually swarm this place. I'm sure you'll be here for the next one."

"Sounds fun." I smile again.

I wonder if I look like I just ate a bug, or if I'm pulling off the smile. I'm betting I've got bug face.

Kai sends me a sympathetic smile.

Sheena and Bodhi come out from his room. She's carrying a jacket and smiling up at him with that same look I've always seen women give him. He's not paying special attention to her. I can't get a read on what she is to him. But her jacket was in his room. That tells me pretty much everything I need to know. Doesn't it?

"Do you two want some tacos?" Bodhi offers.

"Oh, no thanks. You're so sweet," Emily coos to him. "We already ate. We just wanted to grab Sheena's jacket since it's so cold out lately. We didn't mean to barge in on your dinner."

"It's fine," my brother says, even though he can clearly tell it isn't.

"Well, we'll see you around, Bodhi," Sheena says.

"Yeah." Bodhi stands between the dining table and the living room, looking at me with a conflicted expression on his face.

"Nice meeting you two," I say, standing to take my plate to the sink.

Only, I'm wearing my boot, and I admittedly pushed myself too hard today, so I pivot and then I nearly drop the plate when I grab for the table to keep myself from landing on the floor.

Awesome.

Bodhi is next to me before I have time to fully catch myself. His hand is under my forearm, steadying me, and his other arm lands around my waist for the second time today. Our faces are less than a foot apart and our eyes lock.

"You okay?" he asks, as if we're the only two people in the room—or on the planet.

"Yeah. I'm fine. Good. Great."

I pull my arm away and stand on my own two feet. Or one foot and a boot, but at least I'm holding myself up now.

Bodhi has the nerve to wink. Or maybe it's just a reflex. He probably winks all the time now at every woman on the island. He just goes around winking like he's campaigning for office. He's the Oprah of winks. You get a wink! You get a wink! You get a wink!

I look away from Bodhi, severing the stare down we had been locked into ever since my almost-fall. And when I glance over to gauge my brother's reaction, he's near the front door, walking Sheena and Emily out.

"She's not ..." We're no longer touching, but Bodhi's still up in my personal space.

"Don't, Bodhi."

"I just want you to know ..."

"No. I don't have any claim on you. We don't belong to one another. It's okay."

"Mavs." There's a plea in his voice.

"If I'm staying here, you can't go around calling me that. I'm not Mavs. I'm Kalaine."

Bodhi looks at me for a long moment. Then he breathes out a slow breath.

"Okay. Cool. Gotcha."

Bodhi takes a step back and I want to grab him and drop into his arms. It's not that I want to kiss him. Oh, I do. I remember what Bodhi's kisses felt like. They were other-worldly. I could lose myself in his kisses. Bodhi didn't merely kiss me with his mouth, he kissed me with his whole heart. But more than our chemistry, I miss him—the way he'd hold me and the world would feel right. No one ever believed in me like he did—not even my coach.

Kai comes back into the kitchen and shoots Bodhi a look. Whatever passes between them causes Bodhi to start clearing the table quietly without another word or look in my direction.

"I think I'll head to bed," I announce.

"After sleeping the day away?" Kai asks.

"How do you know what I did all day?"

Bodhi turns around. "That would be me and my big mouth."

"Great. Yeah. I took a nap. But I'm ready for bed. It's been a day."

"Do you need anything?" Kai asks.

"No. I'm good."

The list of what I need feels so long—too long to go into, especially with my big brother and my ex.

"Okay. I'll see you tomorrow." Kai steps in and pulls me into another hug.

I melt into his arms. Being here might be the worst decision of my life, but at least I can have the comfort of my big brother's arms wrapped around me when I'm about to come undone.

He looks down at me. "Let's go check out the island tomorrow, just you and me. I've got the day off."

"Okay. Sounds good."

I walk down the hall to my bedroom, and get ready for bed, even though I'm not the least bit sleepy.

I'm sure I'll get used to sharing the same square footage with Bodhi in time.

I have to.

BODHI

(THE SECOND TIME I EVER SAW HER …)

Ever since I met you,
no one else has been worth thinking about.
~ Kim Karr

"Who is *that*?"

I glance over to where my friend, Gull, is looking. His real name is Brad Gulliver, but we all call him Gull because he's always swooping in on everyone's leftovers.

And there she is.

Kai's sister.

I asked for her name a year ago when we were all surfing Mavericks. Kai wouldn't tell me. He turned all uncharacteristically alpha and said, *her name is stay away from me Bodhi.* I chuckled and acted like I was satisfied with his answer. Then I asked around until someone told me: Kalaine. I don't think I've ever heard a more beautiful name, or seen a more beautiful woman. And she surfs.

Not only does she surf, she rules the waves. To see her on the water is like artistry. She moves with grace and precision, maneuvering her board like she was born on it. I'll admit I checked out her socials to see videos of her ... more than once. I can't bring myself to stop watching videos of her on the water, or photo shoots she's done for her sponsors. And, conveniently enough, Kai likes to watch his sister's heats. So if a contest she's in is televised, we're tuning in.

"That's Kai's sister," I tell Gull. "He'll kill anyone who gets within ten feet of her."

"Too bad," Gull says.

"Yeah. Too bad ..." *for you.*

I'm not afraid of Kai. He may be my best friend, but that doesn't mean I'm not going to talk to his sister. I've thought about her ever since last year, always keeping the little non-verbal exchange we shared in the back of my mind. We only looked at one another across a parking lot, but it felt like we had shared a whole conversation. And as utterly crazy as it sounds, I believe we made promises to one another—promises I intend to keep. That's what's had me wondering where I'd bump into her again. And it's not a matter of if, but when in the pro surfing circuit. We run in tight circles, even though we travel the world. We're bound to see one another somewhere. Once I found out she surfed, I knew our paths would cross again. I merely had to be patient.

And, just my luck, Kalaine surfs big waves. So, here we are on Oahu's North Shore. And she's less than forty feet away from me, waxing her board, getting ready to ride in the Eddie. She wasn't on the main invite list this year. She's still making a name for herself. But she was on standby. And, as it happened, one of the invited surfers couldn't make it, so she's set to ride.

Gull wanders off to talk to someone.

I tip my chin in Kalaine's direction and she smiles at me. It's a full smile, lighting up her face. Then, she surprises me by setting her board on the sand and walking in my direction. I look over my shoulder, even though I know no one's there. Then I look back at her and point to myself with a questioning look on my face. She smiles even bigger and nods at me. And she keeps walking toward me, in her orange flowered, Hawaiian-print bikini, her brown hair wild and loose, hanging past her shoulders, being lifted by the wind. If I didn't know better, I'd think she was a dream or the best figment my imagination had ever cooked up. I'd have to treat my imagination to dinner for outdoing himself.

"Hi," she says when she walks up to me.

I'm never at a loss for words, but for some reason, I stare at her, unable to come up with anything cool or easygoing to say now that she's this close.

"Aloha?" She tries again.

"Hey," I say, looking down at where she's got her hand extended for a handshake.

I grasp her hand and shake it lightly and then I just stand there holding her hand like I'm a dork who never met a pretty girl before and just learned how to shake hands this morning. Only, it was my first lesson, and obviously I'm failing the class. Her hand is soft and warm, and I might have just brushed my thumb across her knuckles—yep. Pretty sure I did that from the look of surprise on her face.

Man, I'd give anything not to fail here, because even though I've never officially met her, I think she may be the only girl in the world who matters.

"I'm Kalaine."

"I know."

She giggles in this soft, easy way. "You do, huh, Bodhi? And how do you know that?"

I'm still holding her hand, and my eyes glance down to the place where her soft fingers rest in my grasp. I let go, and she pulls her hand back slowly.

"I asked about you—at Mavericks last year."

"You did?"

"Yeah. I did."

"Who did you ask?" She reaches up and tucks a strand of hair behind her ear. The movement does her no good. Her hair is wild and loose and thick and wavy. The curl breaks free as soon as her hand moves away.

"I asked your brother."

"And my brother told you my name?" She sounds as shocked as she should be.

"No. He told me your name was *stay away from her.*"

Her laughter this time is hearty and full. It's not feminine or soft, and I love it.

"That sounds like Kai. So how'd you end up finding out my name if Kai was being difficult?"

"Big Joe was the one who finally told me."

"Ah."

"Who told you my name?" I ask her, even though I think it was her friend.

"My best friend, Leilani. She surfs, but not the big waves. She's around here somewhere."

"I know who she is. She was the one talking to you last year at Mavs."

"Yeah. We're pretty inseparable. You know, unless something comes up where we have to separate ..." She blushes.

Her awkward moment makes me feel bolder. At least I'm not the only one struggling here. Maybe she wants to get to know me as much as I want to know her.

"What was it like?" Her eyes widen and her brows raise.

"Mavericks?"

"Yeah."

"Like nothing I've ever surfed. Unpredictable. Breaking closer to shore than a lot of the bigger wave breaks I've surfed in other places. That spot at Mavericks has an energy I can't describe. It was ... life altering. Does that sound corny?"

She shakes her head, quietly waiting for more from me. Plenty of women follow me around or show interest in me.

Kalaine's different. She's not as interested in me as she is in Mavericks. And something about that gets my blood pumping. For once, I think I've met my match.

"That day was massive. Mountains of water, like giant slopes, chaotic, and full of life. You could feel the sheer power of nature all wound tight beneath the water's surface. It was terrifying and exhilarating. When I took off behind the ski, I knew that might be my last wave ever—and I didn't care. That might sound reckless, but ..."

"You had to ride it." Her voice is soft, nearly a whisper. She gets it.

"Yeah. I had to. And there has never been another like it. I've had some killer rides since then. Big waves, long waves, tropical waves. Tubed out in the greenroom, landing perfect tricks, doing aerials off the lip, all of it has been gnarly. I'm blessed to get to travel the world and surf. But that day at Mavericks? I've never felt so alive and so fully in the moment as I did when I took off down the face of that first wave of the day and rode it all the way until I met my partner on his jet ski at the bottom."

She just nods. And then in a voice so quiet I almost don't hear her, she says, "I'm going to ride Mavericks some day."

I nod back at her. I am sure she will. There's a fire in her honey-gold eyes. Determination. I recognize her hunger. If you've got it, you can spot it.

"I bet you will," I say.

The smile she gives me might just tide me over until we cross paths again.

8

KALAINE

Other things may change us,
but we start and end with the family.
~ Anthony Brandt

"Wake up, sleepyhead!" my brother's obnoxiously happy morning-person voice booms from the hallway.

The door to the guest bedroom opens a moment later.

"What if I was getting dressed?" I ask him.

The raspy tone from my unexercised vocal cords makes me sound like I'm a pack-a-day smoker.

I pull the covers snugly against my chin, emphasizing my intention to make a permanent home in this bed. I could end up in the Guinness Book of World Records for people who stayed in bed the longest. Now there's a contest I can get behind.

"You should be getting dressed. I let you sleep in. It's already eight-thirty. Time to get coffee and get your tour on.

Come on. Get up."

He has the nerve to pull my blankets back. And of course, at that moment, Bodhi walks by. Our eyes lock. I'm wearing a pajama set of silky pink shorts and a matching tank. I could be on the beach wearing less. He's seen me in much less on my board in the water. Somehow, I feel more exposed right now.

Bodhi mumbles, "Good morning," and keeps walking.

"He's going to work. You are going to play. Let's go." Kai's bossy tone only comes out in his relationship with me. Yay, me! I won the bossy-brother lottery.

"Why does it feel like work? Play feels fun. This is not fun. I wanted to sleep in."

"You napped all day yesterday. Come on. I have to show you where to get the best coffee on Marbella. And I want to introduce you to a few friends, tour you through the resort ..."

"Can we get food?"

Kai chuckles. "Yeah. We'll get food. Come on."

Without another word, he's out the bedroom door, snicking it shut behind himself. I hear the low rumble of conversation between him and Bodhi in the living room while I stand, grabbing my boot and a change of clothes and making my way across the hall into the bathroom.

By the time I'm showered and dressed, Bodhi is long gone.

Kai's relaxing on the sofa, scrolling his phone. He looks up. "Ready?"

"I guess?"

"You are going to love Marbella, Kala. It's beautiful and chill. All the island vibes, but California style. And the resort has a lot to offer."

I can't help but smile at Kai's enthusiasm.

"I should have come sooner—under other conditions."

"I should have invited you. And I should have told you about my housing situation."

"Yeah. You should have. And I'm still mad at you. I might

look like a normal, happy girl with only one functioning leg and some serious equilibrium issues, but don't let my smile fool you. You should definitely keep one eye open when you sleep."

"Noted." He laughs and his eyes crinkle at the edges, but then he turns toward me with a softness in his eyes.

I know Kai's not making light of his choices. He's just happy to see me, and probably relieved I'm not holding a full-blown grudge. I don't know why I'm not, except I'm just so tired of hurting and struggling over the past four weeks. I don't have it in me to maintain anger.

Besides, I have to admit, I'm beyond happy to see my brother in person. Kai and I were always close. We were raised to put ohana first above everything. That means our blood family members, but also adopted family—people who come into our lives and feel like they belong to us.

"I missed you." Kai looks down at me when he opens the front door so I can hobble out past him. "I watched all your contests."

I look up at him and nod. I can feel my smile. It's not full, but I am glad he watched me. Sometimes he'd call me after a contest, or text. I knew he followed my career. But we weren't very good about connecting when we weren't together. We both live too much in the moment to be skilled at long-distance relationships. Maybe if he had been my sister we would have done better. Barely a day goes by that I don't text Leilani. But she would hunt me down if I didn't.

"So, where are we headed?" I ask Kai.

He walks toward a golf cart parked in front of his home and steps into the driver's seat.

"Is this yours?"

"No. I borrowed it from the resort. They let employees use the carts as long as we check them out and return them within the designated time. People don't drive cars on the island. We use bikes and these carts, or we hoof it everywhere. Some people use power scooters."

Kai drives us down his street and out of his neighborhood until we're making our way along a paved road that isn't even wide enough for two full car lanes. The beach is to our right, and rows of quaint shops line the left side of the street.

Then we pass an elegant array of cultivated palm trees with a pathway leading to a grand building. The marble embossed sign out front reads, *Alicante Resort and Spa*.

"That's the main resort building," Kai explains, as he continues to drive along the edge of the sand past the pier I docked on when I arrived. He points out toward another pier further to the north. Boats are moored on one side of that dock.

"That's my office."

"Your office?"

"Yeah. Can't complain. I work on a dock every day. Or in the water. It's a dream job."

"With Bodhi."

I can't help the way my brain circles back to my ex, like something swirling down the toilet.

"Yeah. With Bodhi. Sorry, Kala."

"Let's make a deal. I'll stay mad at you for a while, because you totally deserve that, and you stop apologizing. I know you're sorry. Your words won't make up for the way you betrayed me. But I do know you're sincerely sorry. So just give me time. Okay?"

"Yeah. I can do that."

Kai pulls into a spot at the side of a cafe that sits right on the sand. The sign over the door says *C-Side Coffee*.

"This is the best coffee on the island. Thank me later."

It takes me a minute to maneuver out of the cart, and Kai lets me wrestle through on my own. I'm grateful. For the past four weeks I've had nurses, friends and family hovering over my every move. It's a relief to bungle along without commentary or a safety net being flung out underneath me.

Kai holds the door open, and when I step over the threshold a brunette behind the counter shouts out, "Kai's here. Ooooh! It's Kalaine!"

I'm not used to being recognized. It's not like many people outside the surfing world follow world-class surfers.

Kai strides to the coffee bar which is situated like an island in the middle of the room full of cafe tables. Behind us, sliding glass doors open to a patio leading out onto the beach. Customers fill the outdoor umbrella tables and their chatter filters into the restaurant at a low murmur. The soundtrack overhead has beachy tunes on a low volume. I already love this place and I haven't even had their coffee.

Another woman, probably old enough to be my mom, or at least an aunt, is next to the bubbly brunette. She gives Kai a wide smile. Then the blond sitting on one of the bar stools turns and I recognize her right away. Summer Monroe.

"Riley," Kai says to the brunette barista. "This is my sister Kalaine. Kala, this is Riley. She's my friend Cam's wife. And this is Clarissa. She owns C-side." Kai points to the middle-aged woman. "And this is Summer, Ben's fiancée. Ben works with me at the watersports shack."

All three women greet me. I turn to Summer and gush. I'm not usually affected by a person's status, but I'm a little starstruck seeing Summer Monroe in person.

"I loved you in *Untethered*. You were awesome."

"Aww. Thanks so much. I loved watching you surf. I saw your ride at Mavericks. We all watched the contest at Kai's. That first wave was amazing. And ..." she trails off, but doesn't shy away from what she was about to say. "I just have to say, I'm so glad you survived that fall. It was so scary there for a minute."

"Thanks. I can't believe you saw it." I hadn't considered the fact that Kai and his friends would be watching me.

"I was glued to the screen. The whole pro-surfer lifestyle amazes me. When you have time, I'd love to hear all about how you got into surfing and how you train for big waves. You're incredible. Awe-inspiring, really."

Summer Monroe is telling me *I'm* awe inspiring.

"I've got nothing but time right now." I look down at my boot.

Summer looks down too, completely unfazed by what she sees. "Great. Because I'm between projects. I'm reading through scripts and I have a few auditions coming up, but I'm free as a bird. Let's plan to meet up. Do you have your phone?"

I pull my phone out of my pocket, and just like that Summer Monroe has punched her digits into my cell.

When I look up at her, I swear sparkling glitter is spritzing out of my eyes. I have officially lost my ability to be chill in the face of this starlet.

Of all the things, I blurt out, "I won't stalk you, I promise."

Gah! Dork-o-meter in the red! I'm sure my face is starting to blush. Thankfully, between the amount of time I spend in the sun and my natural skin tone, the pinkening hue won't show too much.

"I won't stalk you either," Summer says casually, as if I hadn't just put my foot in my mouth, boot and all.

"Deal?" She smiles a commercial-worthy smile, only it's genuine.

"Deal."

Kai and I order our drinks. My eyes wander toward the patio. If Summer and Riley weren't here, we could sit out there and watch the ocean. I may never put my feet in her waters again, but I still love her ebb and flow into the shore and away again, cresting and breaking, always tugging and calling to me. Maybe it's a lot like my relationship with Bodhi. I won't swim into those waters again either, but I feel the tug. How can I not?

It would be nice if he didn't invade my thoughts every five to ten minutes. Maybe in time my preoccupation will diminish. I can only hope.

Riley serves up our drinks and then she joins the conversation. "How long will you be staying on Marbella, Kalaine?"

"That's the million dollar question." I glance at Kai.

He smiles softly at me.

"It's complicated." I admit.

"Because you dated Bodhi?" Summer asks.

"You knew?"

"Not until this week. These guys. I tell you." Summer rolls her beautiful eyes.

She's even more stunning in person with her sun-bleached blond hair and perfect skin. She's the type of person you turn your head to look at twice when they pass by. It's no wonder she's on the big screen.

"Ben told Cam, and Cam told me," Riley says.

"Ben told me right when he got off work yesterday. He said, and I quote, 'Kai's in deep, deep yogurt.'"

I laugh. "He is. So deep."

"I'll never look at yogurt the same way again." Kai hangs his head.

"I'm still upset." I find myself confiding in these two strangers. I'm not sure why. "And, yeah. It's super awkward. Bodhi and I didn't end on the best of terms. And I didn't know …"

"You didn't know Bodhi was here on Marbella," Riley finishes for me.

"Exactly."

"And now you're living in the same house as him." Summer shoots Kai a look.

"For now. I don't know if I'll stay."

"I'd say you could move into my place, but I'm planning a wedding and I've had a temporary roommate staying in Riley's old room ever since Riley moved out eight months ago after she and Cam got married."

"And we have a spare bedroom at our place, but we're upstairs," Riley adds.

"I haven't gotten the whole stair thing mastered quite yet. I can do two or three, but a flight multiple times a day might be above my skill level—not that I'd move in. It's sweet of you to even say you'd consider it. The good news is, I should ditch the boot in a few weeks, though, if all goes well."

I pause, letting the reality that two total strangers just offered me a place to stay sink in.

"You two don't even know me. Why would you even consider letting me live with you?"

"You're Kai's sister," Summer says as if that's reason enough.

"And we girls need to stick together," Riley adds. "I didn't have an ex, but if I did, I wouldn't want to be forced to live with him."

I chuckle softly. My life. One minute I was on top of the world. The next, I'm a couch-surfing charity case.

"You can stay with me, Kala." Kai's eyes meet mine from his spot at the bar.

We regard one another and I can tell he wants me in his space, to care for me. It's like he's paying me back for not telling me about Bodhi by letting me crash with him. Also, I know he wants to practice what he knows is right. The principle is malama kekahi i kekahi—the way we care for the ones we love and all those around us.

Can I let Kai care for me?

I don't know. I might not have a choice.

9

BODHI

A true friend won't sugarcoat advice.
~ Unknown

"So, you got mail ... again." Kai says, from his position of superiority in the overstuffed chair across the room from me.

Ben and Cam are at our place to chill for the evening. We get together about once a week or so, just the four of us. Kai almost canceled with Mavs living here, but she found out he was adjusting plans because of her and told him she didn't want his life altered at all because of her. As if her being here isn't a huge alteration.

Kai is already acting way less relaxed and laid back than usual—not just at home, but at the shop. It's like Kalaine's appearance reminded him of all my past sins. It surely reminded me. All I seem to think about nowadays is how I blew it with the most amazing woman on earth, and what I'd give to turn back time. And then I always follow those thoughts with a brainstorming session as to what I can do now to make it up to her and to help her through this transition to life after a surfing accident.

She's been here five days now. That's five mornings waking to her in a robe or pajamas. Five evenings of eating at the same dinner table as her, bumping elbows as we rinse plates and grab for a dish towel. Five nights of knowing she's just down the hall from me while I try to drift off to sleep.

She has no clue. I get it. Surfers wear wetsuits in cold water, but otherwise, she always lived in a bikini. What she wears to bed might as well be a parka over a snow suit compared to that. Annnndd ... now I'm thinking of Mavs in a bikini while her brother stares at me with a look that says I am not wiggling out of his confrontation about the piece of mail that arrived today.

"Mail? Isn't that a droll topic for guys' night. Why don't we fire up the XBox and the grill instead?"

"Coals are already on the grill," Kai informs me.

He insists on using the old-fashioned Weber pit instead of a gas grill like the rest of our non-prehistoric society. I'm surprised he isn't out there with a flint and a stone, grunting while he casts sparks on a rock circle fire pit. Kai's only two years older than me, but he's so much more of an old man at heart. I'm surprised he doesn't invest in sock sandals.

"What mail is it?" Ben asks from the other end of the couch he's sharing with me.

I nearly groan. Ben is almost as gossipy as a nosy group of gray-haired women. After all, he's the one who spread my history with Mavs to Summer and Riley. He's not malicious, just curious. But still, his interest in that letter means I'm really not getting out of this conversation without going through the agony of opening a can of worms I'd hoped to ignore.

"It's an invitation." I hedge the topic with some of my typical vagueness.

Kai supplies the missing details. "An invitation to surf in a contest in San Diego."

"Whoa. That's awesome, bruh!" Ben smiles over at me. "When's the contest?"

"It's the Bro-Am in Encinitas this summer. It's an event that combines concerts with surf contests to raise money for youth organizations in San Diego."

"Dude." Cam looks over at me. "That's awesome. You'll get to compete again."

"Yep. Awesome." My eyes dart to Kai's.

"Awesome if he'd answer. And, an old friend of ours has a band that's opening for one of the headliners. They asked Bodhi to join in while he's there. *If* he's there ..."

"What do you mean, if?" Ben asks in his usual naive tone.

He's so all-in and fearless. Always goes for what he wants. Like when he pursued Summer even though she shut him down ... and down ... and down. Paid off. That's what persistence will do for a man. But I'm not made of that same cloth.

I'm more of a ... well, I *was* a risk taker. Used to drive my mom nuts how I'd leap first and think later. But either maturity, or my accident, or both had their way with me and now I just don't step outside the box. It's a sweet box. Why should I? I work on the ocean. I have a great roommate. I have a full social life with lots of friends.

Only, this week's events have awakened something in me and now I'm restless for the first time in over a year. I missed the best chance I had—a life with Mavs, traveling the world together. Eventually settling down—or not. Her in my arms every night. Us possibly starting a family. We dreamt of all that once. Lived out part of it. And then the rug was yanked and I blew it.

I thought I had dealt with my regrets. But seeing her tells me I never got near to anything but the tip of the iceberg of my grief over that season of my life and what my choices cost me.

"You're going to do it, right?" Cam's voice snaps me out of yet another mental spiral.

"Not sure."

I'm still looking at Kai, who has a very smug look on his face. He knows his work here is done. He doesn't have to nag me now that Cam and Ben are joining him in the choir of men chiming in on my life choices.

"Why not?" Ben asks. "I'd kill to get a chance like that. Well, not kill. But man. That's awesome."

Cam studies me. "What's holding you back?"

"I don't know."

Kai's face softens. He knows. He walked me through the first year after my accident.

I finally throw my friends a bone. "I haven't competed since my accident a few years back."

"Time to get on the horse and ride, then," Ben says. "You're not getting younger. It's never good to let our final experience be a fall. I get it if you don't ride double overhead again. But this isn't big wave surf, is it?"

"Nah. Maybe overhead on a freak day, but it's usually more chill there in the summer. Clean rights and lefts under the right conditions, but nothing too gnarly."

"Sounds like a good day on the water to me," Ben says breezily.

He makes it sound like a no-brainer.

"We could make a trip of it," Cam suggests.

His gaze tells me he's reading all the layers beneath my hesitation.

"Maybe," I say. "Let's check the coals before they burn down. I got steaks and have been marinating them since this morning."

"Say less!" Ben says, hopping up. "Summer's been trying to learn how to cook again. I'm starving."

We all laugh at that, and Kai gives me one more meaningful

look before following Ben and Cam out our back door to the large side yard where the grill is sitting ready for the steaks.

KALAINE
(THE THIRD TIME WE SAW ONE ANOTHER ...)

When I follow my heart, I wake up in Bali.
~ Unknown

"Welcome to Uluwatu," the hotel bellboy says as he drops my duffle on the floor by the foot of my bed.

It's not a glamorous bag, but it suits me and my lifestyle. I bought it last year at a flea market in Hilo when my family visited my mom's relatives for a weekend. It's paisley and floppy and whimsical. My duffle feels like me—but in luggage form. The porter turns and pulls Leilani's three designer suitcases off the rolling cart and carefully wheels them one by one into the closet.

"Oh my gosh!" Leilani practically squeals. "This place is perfection."

"You know that, right?" Leilani turns to our bellboy. "You live in freaking paradise."

"Yes, ma'am. If you say so, ma'am."

"I do. I do say so. What is your name?" She squints at his name badge. "Arif. Arif, this is paradise. And I'm from Hawaii. I know paradise. But, hello. Look at this."

She waves her arm toward the corner of the room where one wall of windows meets another adjacent wall of windows. Only that second wall has double glass doors leading to a wooden deck with stairs heading down to a pathway.

Arif tries to stifle his chuckle. "Yes, ma'am."

"Oh, Arif. Is that all you have to say?" Leilani teases him. "If I said I was going to blow something up, would you just say, 'yes, ma'am'?"

Arif smiles politely again. "No, ma'am."

"Good. Good for you, Arif. I hope you go a little crazy when you get off work. All this *yes ma'am* and *no ma'am* has to get old after a while. Doesn't it?"

She parrots his response with him in stereo when he answers her. "Yes, ma'am."

Then she laughs her trademark giggle and slaps an Indonesian 20,000 rupiah in his hand. He smiles widely at her. "Thank you, ma'am."

Leilani curtseys like the goofball she is, and says, "You are welcome, sir."

Arif backs out of our room with a bright smile. "Have a good day, ma'am. And you, ma'am. Just ring the main desk if you need anything."

These separated cottages are on a property with one main building. That central building holds a restaurant, a bar, some ballrooms, a few conference rooms, a spa, and a fitness center.

Leilani turns to me. "It feels so decadent giving him twenty K, but not when I think of how that's only like ... five dollars? Or is it three?"

She doesn't really want me to break down the currency exchange rates—again. I walk over to the double glass doors that take up most of one wall of our cottage room. This room is a square fishbowl. They're not much into privacy here, I guess. The ceiling fan swirls at a low continuous oscillation, stirring the warm, humid tropical air through the room but doing nothing to cool it down. My hair is at an all-time record-high frizz.

The twin beds are made in an identically organized fashion with a decorative swath of fabric across the footing and matching throw pillows along the wooden headboards. Three-foot-wide framed photos of surfers are tastefully centered over each bed.

Yep. We're in Bali.

The view out our doors and across our deck has a glimpse of the ocean. The lush grounds with grassy lawns and winding pathways give way to white sand and the ocean beyond. And this time of year, April through summer, the waves are ripe for big wave surfing. Leilani and I are here with a group of hosted surfers for two whole months. No contests. No travel. Just surfers hanging out and riding waves, coaches working with us, yoga instructors leading classes on the beach, and a lot of relaxing in the local surf towns. And, of course, obligatory photo shoots for the sponsors who are floating the bill for the bulk of this getaway.

Leilani isn't here for the surf as much as the experience. But I'm here to paddle out through the sea caves and surf the larger swells. And to sample each break along this section of the coast. And to mingle with a few great surfers I only get to see once in a while when our paths cross at competitions.

As if she can read my mind, Leilani says, "Do you think he'll be here?"

She falls back onto the bed with a relaxed flop, her arms out like she's about to make a snow angel.

"He?" I know who she's thinking about. I try to play it cool even though I am the farthest thing from it.

"He ... Bodhi. And you knew who I meant."

"I don't know. He might be."

"I hope he is."

"Why? Are you going to hit on him?"

"As if. That would break the girl code. He's a cutie, but he's not mine."

"He's not mine either."

"But you want him to be. And what better time for you two to get better acquainted than us all being here for nine glorious weeks together? Surf trip romance. Am I right?"

"Hmmm." I hum.

"Don't you play coy with me. I know you want him. I think this is your lucky trip."

"We'll see. Either way ... we're in Bali!"

10

KALAINE

Why are old lovers able to become friends?
Two reasons: They never truly loved each other, or they love each
other still.
~ Whitney Otto

"Where's Kai?" I ask Bodhi.

I stretch my arms overhead and catch him watching my movements. We're stuck in muscle memory, or whatever the equivalent of that is. Everything about Bodhi and our proximity pings off automatic responses I thought had died a slow death and been buried long ago.

It's late enough in the morning that Bodhi's up and dressed in a faded T-shirt and cargo shorts, but it's still far earlier than I've been waking since I arrived. I'm still in my pajamas, a sure sign of my lack of direction or purpose these days.

Bodhi reaches into the cabinet and pulls down a cereal bowl.

"Kai left for work already?" I look around as if my brother will just pop out of a cabinet.

Of course he's not here. If he were, he'd be playing monkey in the middle like he's been doing all week whenever Bodhi and I are in the same room. It's nearly comical how hard Kai's been working to insert himself between Bodhi and me, as if we need a barrier bigger than the reminder of how our relationship went up in smoke, leaving only ashes in its wake.

"Yep. Kai had an early lesson and he has a meeting in the main building." Bodhi pauses and flashes me one of his killer smiles. "Perils of being the manager. I skirt all that crisp shirt tucked into my trousers, indoor meeting business. Give me a wetsuit or some board shorts any day."

I smile. I've seen Bodhi in a suit. He's delectable. But the idea of him suiting up to sit around a table for something official makes me grin even wider. His natural posture in a chair is leaned back, sometimes arms propped casually behind his head, his legs stretched out long in front of him. He managed to make a living on the water for years. Most people can't. Now he's still making a living on water. I admire him for bouncing back, even if it baffles me how he managed to make himself venture out into the ocean again.

I've been on Marbella a full seven days, but Bodhi and I haven't been alone in the house since that first day I arrived. He's been kind, but formal, mostly going about his life and nearly avoiding me. You'd think him giving me a wide berth would make things easier. After all, I'm getting the space I said I needed from him.

I still can't shut down my preoccupation with him. If he's here in the house, I feel him, even if he's out in the garage shaping his next board. My mind and body are auto-tuned to his presence. If he's gone to work, I sense his absence. I try to distract myself, but I end up wondering what he's doing—if he's riding waves, helping customers, or interacting with other resort employees.

Maybe he's with Sheena and Emily. Though, neither of them have been around all week. He could be seeing Sheena somewhere else to keep things from getting awkward. It's possible he's not seeing her at all. Those thoughts keep me spun out if I indulge them. The idea of Bodhi cupping someone else's cheek, staring her in the eyes with the look that used to belong to me ... I can't go there.

"You don't have to work?" I grab down my own cereal bowl.

"Not until this afternoon. I've got a snorkeling lesson and outing with a couple. Then I've got a little break at dusk, and tonight I'm taking a group out on the glass-bottom boat with Stevens. He's our marine biologist."

"Oh."

Bodhi smirks a little at my one-word answer, but then he straightens his features and moves around me to grab the cereal.

Like a familiar onshore breeze blowing toward me off the ocean, Bodhi turns his body so he's angled in front of me. His face softens and his voice matches his expression. "How are you holding up, Ma ... Kalaine?"

I hear the whisper of my nickname float away before Bodhi says my proper name. The sound of it feels too right—too easy and intimate falling from his lips. Even the hint at it catches on something in my heart. That's why I banned him using that name. I can't take the way the word "Mavs" sends my heart floating into realms of possibility and hope, longing and recollection. My heart needs to stay here, in my chest, keeping me alive and keeping me far from the edge of the perilous cliff that is Bodhi Merrick.

I step back and grab the box of cereal he just set on the counter.

"I'm good." I lie.

I'm not good. I'm all messed up, and I'm about to come out of my skin with boredom and claustrophobia. Not to mention the residual body aches from my fall, and this wretched boot, along with the occasional bouts of dizziness if I stand up too quickly. But I can't tell Bodhi any of that, even when he's looking at me like he still cares deeply for me. I'm probably mistaking his concern for interest. Not that it would matter.

Bodhi tilts his head, obviously trying to get a read on me. Then his eyes catch mine and I know he sees everything. I can't hide my heart from Bodhi. He knows me too well.

We stand facing one another, frozen in place, a thousand unspoken words and emotions swirling between us like a tsunami of regret and longing. Memories and dashed hopes. Love and loss. It's all there.

Then Bodhi mercifully steps over to the fridge and takes out the milk.

"Ladies first."

He hands the carton to me. I fill my bowl and grab a seat.

"Big plans today?" He finishes making his cereal and pulls out the chair across from me.

Even that movement draws my attention to everything about him, the way his wavy hair falls toward his face, the stretch and bulge of his arm muscles, the fluidity of his movement. And more than all that, he's Bodhi: casual, confident, full of some sort of magnetism that God only doled out to a fraction of the population. Looking at him now, I can easily see why. He's potent, and he doesn't even know how deeply he affects me still.

"Plans? Actually, yes. Summer's coming to pick me up just before lunch. We're going to meet a friend of hers further up the island."

Bodhi smiles. "I hope it's Phyllis."

"I think the name was something like that."

"You're gonna love her. She's a kick in the pants."

"Okaaay."

He's smiling again, free and breezy, and I only see a moment of hesitation which might reveal something other than ease in the way he's treating me. Maybe he's trying hard to smooth out the waters and move on. God knows I want to. Our past tugs at me like a riptide. My accident weighs on me like a boulder in my arms dragging me deep under the waves.

Bodhi tips his head down to take a bite, and I study him. The features I know almost as well as my own have only changed in nearly imperceptible ways since I last saw him. The way he carries himself is lighter, though. His ghosts and demons seem to have vanished. He's more like the man I fell in love with, not the one I reluctantly left behind two years ago. It's obvious Bodhi's happy here on Marbella. I get the distinct feeling he truly moved on. I'm simultaneously relieved and crushed by the realization.

"What are you doing before you go to work?" Small talk. I can do this.

Maybe if I act like Bodhi's just my brother's housemate, I can curb the way my fingers itch to reach up and brush across his chin dimple. My mouth wouldn't mind a refresher as to how his stubble feels against my lips. I feel the blush rise up my neck. I duck my head and stare into my cereal.

"I'm going to do a little yoga," he looks up, swallows his bite, and winks at me.

Gah. That wink.

"Yoga?"

"Yeah. It's good for keeping me limber and centered. I've stuck with it ever since Bali ..."

His voice trails off as memories wash over both of us. *Bali.*

"That's great," I say with a bit too much brightness in my voice.

"Yeah. I stopped for a while ... after ..." He sighs. "But I picked my practice up again about a year and a half ago."

His eyes drift toward the front of the house, but it's like he's watching something that isn't there.

"Look, Mav ... Kalaine." He turns his face back to me. "This whole situation can be awkward if we let it. I know it is at times —and that's probably unavoidable. I'm trying to make it less so. But I think I'm messing up. I give you space, and I feel like I'm ignoring you, which I'm totally not. Then I talk to you, and ..." His eyes plead with me. His voice lowers to a quietness nearing a whisper. "I know how badly I hurt you. I'd do anything to take that back. All of it." He looks down and then back up at me. "But what I want more than anything, now, is to be friends and move past all of what we left behind. Maybe when you're ready ..."

Friends. I should be thrilled. He's been nothing but accommodating, or at least trying to be. This *is* awkward. He's not wrong—and it's awkward for both of us, not just me.

"Yeah. I think we can be friends," I agree.

My heart throws a fit rivaling a toddler in the cereal aisle. I push the cart onward. Nope. No. I'm not going to wish for more. And holding a grudge is way too exhausting when I'm already overwhelmed with the state of my life.

Bodhi's right. We need to aim forward.

Friends. That's what we're going to be.

"Would you be up for a little yoga?" He stands and takes both our bowls to the sink.

"I can get that." I stand and follow him, clopping more steadily in my boot than I had even a week ago when I arrived here.

"Nah. Let me." He turns on the faucet. "So, yoga? Are you down for a little sesh?"

"In this?" I point to my boot.

"Yeah. I've seen paraplegics do yoga in chairs. And I went to one class with a dude who only had one leg. You'll manage."

I'm standing next to him now, reaching for the bowls Bodhi

washed and rinsed. He bumps me playfully and I wobble just the slightest.

"Okay," I hear myself say.

"Great. I'm going to get changed. You might want to change too." His eyes take me in and I realize as an afterthought that I'm still in my pajamas. "Meet me in the side yard in ten."

He leaves me holding a dish towel. My thoughts swirl as I watch him retreat down the hallway.

Growing up, there were trails through the hills around our home—ruts and clearings forged by repeated footfalls. Being with Bodhi is like walking a well-worn path. The sights and smells, the scenery, every root and branch of our connection has been etched into my subconscious. We travel too easily down the way we've always gone. Looking at his lips doesn't make me wonder what he tastes like or what his mouth would feel like against mine. I already know. When I studied his mouth at breakfast, I remembered what it felt like to be held in his arms, to be the object of his joy and desire. I might have even craved him again.

I know just what I need.

Sanity is a mere phone call away.

Slipping into my bedroom, I lift my cell from my bedside table.

"Kalaine! What is wrong?" The scratchy, shrill tone of voice is not what I expected when I dialed Leilani.

"What? Why do you think something's wrong?"

"Do you know what time it is?"

"Sure. It's ..." I pull my phone away from my face, and then it hits me. "Oh! I'm so sorry. Were you still sleeping? Go back to sleep. It's nine here. That's ... seven in Oahu?"

"It's fine. I should get up and take a run anyway."

"A run, on a day you'll be surfing?"

"Yeah. Running gets my adrenaline pumped out so I can

focus—or something like that. Besides, this guy, Rip, is heading out for a quick run. I might join him."

"Rip Tanaka? Aka Rip Curl?"

"You know him?"

"I've seen him around. He's the one with the tattoo of a rooster on his bicep, right?"

"Yeah. That tattoo. It's so ..."

I giggle. "Have you seen him do that thing where he flexes a bunch of times? Flexing makes the rooster strut!"

We both laugh.

I grab a pair of shorts and a tank out of a drawer in the dresser and start to get dressed. "Are you, like ... seeing him?"

Leilani's never too serious about any given man. I don't picture her with Rip, but maybe I don't know him well enough.

"We're going on a run. That's it. For now. He's cute, though. But I don't know if I can date another surfer—especially one with a strutting rooster on his arm."

"Shut the front door. You can so. You know you love surfers most of all."

"I love you most of all. Now, what has you calling and waking me from my beauty sleep this early in the morning?"

I question myself. Should I really bring Bodhi up to Leilani? She already has a rap sheet on him a mile long. But who else will I talk to if not her?

"It's Bodhi."

"Is he giving you trouble?" She sounds all fierce and protective. My smile is instantaneous.

"Not at all. I wish he were. It would make things far simpler if he were being a jerk or anything besides what he's doing."

"What's he doing?"

"Basically, giving me the space I asked for, like I told you. Then, this morning, Kai was at work, and ..."

"And you kissed him? Kalaine!"

"No! I didn't kiss him! Calm down." The sound of my words

fills the small bedroom, so I muffle my voice. "No. I didn't. There was no kissing, and there won't be any kissing."

Not that the thought didn't cross my mind, but of course I didn't kiss Bodhi. I'll never kiss him again. He said, friends. And that's what we need to aim for, I think.

"He asked if we could be friends."

"Can you?"

"I think so. I'm so tired of holding this grudge. And I'm just ..."

"Reeling from the accident. Vulnerable. Looking at a huge question mark as to what lies ahead. I get it. You don't need to decide to forgive him right now, sweet Kah."

"Thanks. I know. It's just ... maybe I want to?"

"Want to what?"

"Isn't that the question." I flop onto my bed, half dressed, holding my top in my hand.

I want so much with Bodhi, or I did. Now, I don't know. He may even be seeing someone. Can we be friends? Where do I put all these inconvenient feelings for him?

"How about this?" Leilani suggests. "How about you take it day by day. If you feel like being friendly, be friendly. If you need space, take it. If you're angry tomorrow, even after you felt all clean-the-slate today, give yourself permission to be angry. What you went through wasn't fair. He's sorry, sure. But that doesn't make up for the fact that he single-handedly dismantled your future."

"True." I agree, but I don't feel the weight of it.

Bodhi's obviously different. He's gone through something. Granted, I should have been by his side while he worked through the aftermath of his accident, but maybe this time apart is what he needed most. Either way, I don't see the purpose in staying angry. When I think of trying to be his friend, anger isn't the problem. Attraction definitely is.

"I still feel ..."

"Like he's one of the hottest men on the planet?"

"Ugh. Yes!"

"You'd officially be dead if you didn't feel that way. That man is something to behold. All it takes is one glance from him through those obnoxiously long eyelashes and most women nearly faint. He's got those raging good looks and he knows how to use them. And all that was yours. I can't imagine living in the same house with him after having been his girlfriend for over two years."

"It's not the easiest."

"Stay strong. And maybe keep a safe distance from him. Six feet? That's what they say for germs, right? Maybe giving him a healthy amount of personal space will make you immune to sexiness too?"

"I don't think so."

"Stinks to be you, then." She chuckles. "But seriously, guard your precious heart. I don't want to have to fly over to California to kick his muscular booty."

I laugh. "I gotta run. We're ... uh. I'm doing a thing."

"Don't you dare hang up on that note. What thing? With him?"

"Yeah. He asked me to do yoga with him. And I said yes."

"Oh girl. Forget about it. I predict it's less than two weeks before you're in his arms again."

"What? No. It's just yoga, Lei."

"Just yoga, she says."

I hear Bodhi's voice from the door leading into the garage. "You coming, Kalaine?"

"He's calling me. I better go."

"Guard your heart, Kah."

"I will. Thanks. And enjoy your run with Rip."

"Now all I'll be thinking of is that tattoo!"

"Ask him to flex for you!" I giggle. It feels so good to laugh—like a reprieve from reality.

"I won't dare."

"I bet you will. And he'll gladly strut that thing for you."

Leilani makes a pfft sound and then she says, "I'll call you tomorrow."

We each say "I love you," and then I hang up and throw my shirt on.

Despite what might be my better judgment, I hobble out the door to meet Bodhi for yoga.

11

BODHI

How you spend your morning can often tell you
what kind of day you are going to have.
~ Lemony Snicket

Mavs steps around the corner of the house, and I feel my chest tighten. I'm like a tightrope walker: thrilled, focused, and aware of how fatal any misstep with her could be.

"Well, this should be interesting." Her tone is more snarky these days than it used to be.

I can't help but think back to my own accident and what I was like two months out.

"You're so brave." The compliment leaves my mouth before I think better of it.

"Brave to do yoga?"

"Brave to even get out of bed."

She nods. Our eyes catch, and it's nearly too much.

The urge to hold her sweeps over me. I told her the truth.

Living together is awkward. But Kalaine doesn't even know the half of what I'm battling. Every day I'm pushing down the irrational urge to rekindle our relationship. I told her I wanted to be friends. I know I can't ask for more. My attraction to her has always been nearly overwhelming. She's like no other woman. Being separated for two years—which was my own fault—has only heightened my awareness of the connection between us, the way she affects me, and the reality that she's the only woman I will ever want like I want my next breath.

"I laid out a mat for you there." I point.

She makes her way to the mat.

"I start with simple poses and then move to the more complex."

"Are you going to lead us?"

"Is that okay?"

"Someone better." She smiles a shy smile.

"Well, let's get to it."

Mavs watches me with an expectant, but hesitant look. I thought being so near to her in the kitchen would be my undoing. I was wrong. This. This moment is testing everything in me.

I start with mountain pose. We stand straight, facing the side of my neighbor's house.

"Breathe in and out, Ma ... Kalaine. Gentle breaths, count of four in, hold four, exhale four."

If I'm reading her right, she has a glint of awe in her eyes. I'm pretty sure she's thinking how far I've come since the last time we were together. I wouldn't have been doing yoga, let alone leading someone else back then. Seeing her reminded me of my mistakes, but today she's reminding me of my triumphs too. Kai was so instrumental in making sure I got past what was holding me back and gained a new lease on life. He never stopped believing in me.

Mavs and I stand together, breathing in and out. Then I

lead her into a forward fold, her body bending at the waist and her hands dropping toward her toes. She wobbles a little, but makes it.

"Can you make it into plank pose?" I ask her when we finish running through a few reps of forward fold.

"No."

"Come on, Ma ... Kalaine. You don't know if you don't try."

"It's really hard for you not to call me that, isn't it?"

I look her in the eyes, "Yeah. It's hard. But you're worth the effort."

She nods again. This more subdued version of her makes my breath hitch in my throat. She's still wrestling with the aftermath of her accident. I don't want to push her, but at the same time, I know she needs it.

"I'll help you make your way to the pose."

"Uhh ..."

I don't give her time to protest. Kai pushed me. He's not going to do the same thing for his sister. She's in a different category for him. He feels like he has to be a shelter and guardian in her life. She needs someone to push her—someone who loves her enough to believe she can move past the wreckage of the wave.

My hands are on her waist, annnnd I really didn't think this through. Touching her feels like coming home. The electricity surges between us the moment my hands land on her waist. I don't dare look her in the eyes or the thin strand of my remaining self-control will snap.

I clear my throat and pretend I'm a personal trainer—or a monk. Or a personal trainer to monks. Or a monk who does personal training on the side of whatever it is monks do to help raise funds for orphans. I picture that sidekick to Robin Hood. What was his name? Friar Tuck? Yeah. That dude definitely wasn't a personal trainer. Then I see Dwayne "The Rock"

Johnson in a brown robe with a rope belt. Yeah. That's more like it. I'm Dwayne, the monk.

Whatever it takes to deal with Kalaine for her sake and to ignore the raging fire that sprung to life as soon as I stepped into her space.

"Bend down and stretch your arms out. You can rest on your knees instead of using straight legs. I've got you."

She surprises me, by extending her arms and bending her knees more than she would if her boot weren't a factor. Between the two of us, we get her into a modified plank pose.

I let out a whoop of celebration. "That's what I'm saying!"

"I don't think I've ever been in a yoga class where they shouted before."

"I have my own brand." I smile over at her as I join her on my mat, emulating the pose she's in, only my legs are extended straight.

"You most certainly do."

She looks across the yard. "Is that your neighbor? Is she spying on us?"

"Yeah." I chuckle. "She sometimes peeps out while I'm doing my practice."

"Oh my gosh! That's hilarious."

"Hey, Margaret! Good morning!" I shout over.

The curtains drop a little, but Margaret stays there, a small slit revealing her presence.

"How old is she?" Mavs asks.

"Who knows. Too old to be an option."

Mavs laughs again. "That's either creepy or adorable."

"Let's go with adorable."

"You are blushing!" Mavs drops to her mat when her laughter overtakes her.

I hold my pose, turn into a side plank pose, holding myself up on one arm, and then I extend into a side plank split by raising my leg and holding it in the air while balancing on one arm.

"Show off," Mavs teases me.

"You want me to show off?" I wink over at Mavs.

I move into a crane pose, extending both arms onto the ground and tucking my legs up under me with my knees touching my forearms, then I slowly extend into handstand pose. I finish this show of mine by lowering myself onto my forearms and contracting into a hollow back pose, where I arch my back and point my toes toward the ground so I'm basically in a sort of backbend, but my arms are supporting my whole body.

I tuck down slowly and risk looking over at Mavs. She's smiling a smile I haven't seen in years. It's the smile she'd give me right before I kissed her. I won't kiss her now—probably not ever. But I'm tucking that smile away for safekeeping. She gave it to me. It's mine. I never thought I'd see that smile again.

"Wow."

"Really? I impressed you?"

"Yeah. You actually did."

"One day you'll be doing all those moves."

Her eyes dart away, and the pain that's always just beneath the surface returns. I regret my words right away.

"Or not. Up to you. But you could. You can do anything, Kalaine."

"Not anything. I proved that, didn't I?"

She sits up, tucking a strand of her hair behind her ear.

"You didn't prove that to me. You proved you're one of the few humans on the planet who face down waves the size of skyscrapers. You proved you're a beast and a fierce spirit. You proved the ocean is unpredictable and wild, and what we do when we ride is one of the greatest risks and thrills to be had on earth.

"Did your accident knock the wind out of you? Yes. No one

gets that like I do. But you're a fighter. I believe you'll come back from this like a phoenix. In time. When you're ready."

I don't give her a chance to answer me. "Now quit disrupting my yoga practice." I smile softly at her so it's clear I'm teasing. "Let's do the rest of the positions. Next is downward dog."

12

KALAINE

Aging is an extraordinary process where you become
the person you always should have been.
~ David Bowie

O kay. Yoga with Bodhi was either the best or worst
idea on earth.

Watching Bodhi control his body with such precision made me feel like the temps outside were spiking. And all that mastery revealed the work he'd put into recovering and moving on. He's come so far. Without me.

The combination of his soft words and the way he believes in me left me confused and shaken.

I can barely believe I did a plank, even a modified plank, and then I went into downward dog and a few seated poses. There aren't words for how good it felt to move my body, and to do it with Bodhi.

Again: confusion.

I'm grateful he's off to work, and I have plans. Hanging

around here at Kai and Bodhi's after the morning we shared would be way too much for me. Vestiges of his presence permeate every room. And I've been dying to peek into his bedroom, just to see how it's decorated and to experience the place he's come to call home. I won't. But it sure is tempting.

Summer's knock is firm and repeated.

Summer Monroe is knocking on my door.

Okay. Get a grip.

She's just another human. She eats and poops like the rest of us.

And, great. Now I'm thinking about Summer Monroe in the bathroom.

I stand and hobble to the door.

"Hey, Kalaine. Are you ready?" Summer's smile is broad and welcoming.

"Yes. I'm ready to blow this place."

"Cabin fever?"

"Something like that."

"Last year Ben got a gash on his foot surfing an area they call Dead Man's. He had to wear a boot for a while. Not the most fun time trying to get around."

"I get this off in a week. I have an appointment in Santa Barbara with a specialist."

I climb into the passenger side of the golf cart and Summer takes off down Kai's street toward the main road that runs along the beach.

"That's such good news! We'll have to host a party to celebrate. A boot's off party. Maybe everyone can come barefoot. And we can do the boot-scoot boogie ..."

"Aren't you planning a wedding?" I laugh softly at Summer's enthusiasm.

Kai warned me that she could come across as private and reserved, which would make sense considering her recent rise into stardom. So far, she's treated me like a long-lost friend. I haven't experienced anything closed-off about her.

"Yeah. I am. My wedding. It's pretty crazy. Especially planning it around auditions and potential shooting schedules."

"Kai told me your story—well a little of it. You weren't interested in Ben at first?"

"That's the actual understatement of the year. Ben did not impress me—at all. I thought he was a player. And those pick up lines. You should have heard him. Wisconsin never saw so much cheese."

"Really?"

"Yeah. Really. But that man is persistent to a fault, and he won my heart over time. He's nothing like I assumed he was. He's so much better. So much. I never knew how it could feel to fall head over heels for someone. But here we are."

Summer glows talking about her fiancé. It's a feeling I remember, the way just mentioning Bodhi's name sent a dreamy rush of near levitation floating through my body. I couldn't contain my smile when I thought of him. I wonder if I'll ever feel that way about another man again.

We're quiet. The ocean rolls in off to our right across the sand, deceptively inviting.

"So, you and Bodhi, huh?"

Summer's question should be harmless, but hearing our names smooshed together like that brings back memories of this morning—his hands on my waist as he lowered me into a yoga position. He didn't seem as affected as I was. If he was, he held it together out of respect for the lines we've had to draw just to cope with me living in his home.

"Old news. We dated for over two years. He had an accident. We stopped dating. He moved here. This is the first I've seen of him since our breakup." I'm purposely giving the Reader's Digest version of our situation.

"I can't imagine."

"What part?"

"Dating Bodhi, for one. Then seeing him after all that time. Then having to live with your ex and your brother under one roof."

"Yeah. All of that. It's ... awkward." My mind hears Bodhi saying *awkward*, and I replay his apology and the request to be *friends*.

"We're trying to be friends now."

"How's that going?" The teasing lilt in her voice and sparkle in her eyes helps me see my reality with an ounce of humor.

"It's going."

I don't say anything else. And Summer, surprisingly, doesn't push. I'm used to Leilani. She could make pushing others into a profession or a sport. Leilani's a champion, world-class pusher. And I love her for it. Mostly.

But this is nice too, just being with someone, knowing I don't have to spill the beans or make any changes. And that someone is *Summer Monroe*! My inner fangirl squeals, while outwardly I'm chill. At least I hope I am. Summer acts like she's just another young woman with ambitions and feelings and a life she's building. But I saw her face on the big screen. She's a star. It's a little intimidating, even though she's doing her best to make this all feel normal.

We drive up a hill and a different part of the coastline comes into view off to our right, the beaches are less occupied, no resort loungers or umbrellas, just sand and rocky outcroppings and the waves pulling in and pushing out. The tide is high right now, but the waves are mushy, ending in a foamy shorepound. There must be a dropoff somewhere offshore here.

"Are you sizing up the ocean?"

"It's my second-nature. Must be a reef there with a dropoff in the near distance."

"There is. It's jagged underfoot at spots, but then there's a softer spot and, like you said, a dropoff a little way out. It's impressive that you can tell that by a mere glance. I kayak the shoreline a lot. It's a way for me to forget everything and lose myself. You know?"

"Do I ever."

"So, you and Bodhi? Friends, huh?" Summer circles back to the topic I'm trying hard to avoid.

"I had such a grudge against him. And I guess I still do. I don't know."

"I can't imagine you're really in the headspace to decide where you stand with your ex-boyfriend. You're coming off a hugely traumatic experience."

"That's beyond true."

I need a change of subject. Though, talking to Summer has been calming in a way I didn't expect. She's not Leilani who has her own history with Bodhi and a healthy-sized grudge to nurse on my behalf. Summer loves Bodhi, you can tell. And, yet, she's not biased against me.

"So, tell me about Phyllis." I'm curious about this woman we're going to meet—especially after Bodhi said she's a kick in the pants.

"There's just no way to describe her. She's quirky, but not in a weird way. Full of wisdom. Kind of like the grandma you always wished you had, except one who'll drive you off a cliff if you let her behind the wheel. Do not get in a golf cart with her. Consider yourself forewarned."

"Gotcha." I smile.

Back home, extended relatives were always around. Some of them lived in our neighborhood, others on Kawaii and the Big Island. I'm used to being surrounded by elderly family members. They always pulled us kids aside to share legends and stories with us, taking every opportunity to drill the island ways into our hearts and minds. Hawaiian pride is a generational gift and my tūtū wahine made sure I received it.

We pull a left onto a street lined with beachy little shops that are so quaint I almost ask Summer to park so we can go exploring. She steers up some light hills and we're in neighborhoods with cottage homes. She parks in front of a house that's larger than most. A set of broad wooden steps lead up to a wide porch. A swing is hung on the far end and some chairs are set out around a tea table to the side of the doorway.

"This is it. Phyllis' home."

An older woman with wavy gray hair comes out the front door. She's wearing a pair of palazzo pants and a gauzy blouse with a patterned silk scarf around her neck. She looks like she could be Meryl Streep's sister.

She waves and Summer shouts out, "I brought you a treat, Phyllis! This is Kalaine. She's Bodhi's ex-girlfriend, Kai's sister. And, best of all, she's a big-wave surfer!"

That last sentence glues me to my seat. *Best of all.*

I shake the urge to pout and spiral into self-pity, and turn so I can put my weight on my good foot to get out of the cart.

"Welcome!" Phyillis says. "I'm so glad you came. Summer told me she was bringing a guest. I've got tea and lemonade, or if you want something warm or spiked, I've got that too."

I smile. "Nice to meet you."

"Goodness, you're a vision. Aren't you just beautiful?" Phyllis says as I approach her.

"Thank you."

"Isn't she stunning, Summer? Are you a Pacific Islander?"

"Phyllis! Give the woman a moment to hobble up here before you start taking the Census Bureau forms out to check her nationality."

Phyllis laughs this full, yet feminine laugh. "Right. Right. I forget myself."

Then she looks at me. "Watch yourself as you age, dear. The filters just disappear. It's refreshing and very liberating, but also can be a bit much."

"I don't mind. And, I'm Hawaiian. My family is mostly from the North Shore of Oahu."

"Oh, yes. I've been there. Years ago. Filmed there. And visited. I'll tell you a secret." Her voice is far too loud to be secretive. "I love Kawaii best."

"I don't blame you. It's beautiful."

"You know what we don't have that Hawaii has?"

"Luaus?" I guess.

"Well, that too, now that you mention it. But we don't have those wild chickens. I was enamored with them. They just roam around like any other bird, bold as you please."

"Chickens are birds," Summer says.

"Yes, but you should see the ones in Hawaii. Have you been?" Phyllis asks Summer.

"When I was young. Daddy always insisted on vacationing in certain places. Hawaii wasn't one that made his list very often."

Phyllis nods her head as if she knows some backstory.

Phyllis leads the way up the steps. "My sister is out for the day. But Mila's coming by this afternoon. It's a shame you'll miss meeting both of them. Maybe next time."

"Mila?" I ask as I make my way up to the porch. I grasp the railing and go slowly. I didn't even need a crutch today, so that's progress.

"Mila's my niece, but she's more like a daughter to me. She runs a little bed and breakfast on this side of the island. We call it the North Shore too." Phyllis smiles over at me. "Your brother helps out with little odds and ends when she needs it. You may have heard him mention it."

I have not heard him mention it. I know he does handyman work around the island during his time off from the water-sports shack.

Phyllis' home is light and airy. The white beadboard walls are filled with watercolor paintings of the shoreline and some fiber art weavings. A decorative glass cylinder sits on the coffee table, filled with shells. An artful piece of driftwood the size of my forearm is nestled against it. Everything feels welcoming and sings of the love of the beach and the ocean.

We settle in with drinks and some finger foods Phyllis sets on the coffee table. She entertains me with stories Summer prompts her to share about her years in the film industry. Before I know it, we've spent nearly two hours with Phyllis. I've laughed and smiled and settled in for probably the first time since my feet hit the sand of the Alicante beach over a week ago.

"We'd better get going," Summer says, standing from the couch and stepping toward Phyllis for a hug. "I've got to run through some scripts."

"Anything interesting?" Phyllis asks.

"Maybe. I'm not supposed to discuss it. You know that."

"And I'm not supposed to eat too much butter. Life is more fun when we skip a few of the supposed-tos." Phyllis winks.

I smile. That was definitely my philosophy before my accident. Bodhi used to accuse me of being the freest spirit he ever met. His eyes always lit up with admiration when he said it, like he cherished my carefree, spur-of-the-moment way of living—he cherished me. I wasn't necessarily a rebel, but I definitely twirled to my own inner ukulele.

"I'll tell you what," Summer smiles at Phyllis. "I'll bring the scripts by this week if you'll make lemon bars."

"Oh, that's an easy yes. You really should come up with something more challenging."

"Lemon bars. That's what I want. I'd choose them for my wedding cake if I could."

"Ah. The wedding. We have so much catching up to do. You'll definitely have to come back this week. And Kah-la ... Oh dear. How do you say it again? It's so lovely."

"Kah-lah-ee-nay." I enunciate each syllable.

"Right. Well, you need to come back too. Anytime. Don't wait for Summer to bring you, either. Just come."

"Okay. I will."

After we say our goodbyes, Summer drives us back toward the resort side of Marbella.

"What'd you think of Phyllis?"

"She's so fun. Thank you for bringing me along."

"It made her day. She'd have been so upset if she heard about you and didn't get to meet you."

I wonder why she would hear about me.

"Small town." Summer answers my unspoken question. "This island is a little spread out, and it always feels more full because of tourists, but those of us who live here year-round are like any small town—well, a small town with an ocean and a dress code of sundresses and flip flops."

She flashes me an easy smile. It's the smile of a woman whose life is on track.

"So, what you're saying is everyone knows Kai's baby sister is staying with him."

"And that you and Bodhi were a thing? Yeah. Most everyone. And also, we've seen you ride big waves. The ones before the fall. Those are the ones we think of, Kalaine. We all know you fell, but the point is, you were out there." She shakes her head. "I never actually knew someone with so much courage and athleticism. I hope my fangirling doesn't show too much."

"You? Fangirling over me?" I laugh.

"Why wouldn't I?"

I just stare at her. "I fangirl so hard over you."

"Well, that's a level playing field if I ever heard of one." Her soft southern accent peeks out.

Kai told me Summer was originally from Georgia. She completely covered her accent for her movie. When she's more relaxed, I hear that sweet drawl creep into certain words.

"Wanna pop in on the guys?" she asks as we approach the area where the boat dock leads into the ocean from the sand.

"The guys?"

"Yeah. I won't get to see Ben as much as I'd like once I'm filming. And I'm still at that stage where going a few hours away from him makes me miss him. You can mock me all you want. I mock myself."

"I think that's beautiful."

"You could say hi to your brother ... see him at work ... maybe see anyone else there?"

Her voice is light and playful, but my stomach flips at the thought of watching Bodhi at work—seeing him even more settled here in his new life without me.

I don't want to keep Summer from seeing Ben. That's what I'm telling myself when I say the next thing that comes out of my mouth. "Sure. Let's pop in on the guys."

13

BODHI

You can never just be friends
with someone you fell in love with.
~ Unknown

"Just hold the board like this, on the rails."

My student, Jenny, holds the rails like she's trying to snap the board with her bare hands. Her knuckles are white, her body stiff, her eyes wide.

"Hey," I say in the calming voice I've learned to use with novice surfers. "I'm not going to let anything happen to you."

"Okay," she says, smiling over at me. It's forced, but it's a smile. I'll take it.

"We'll just paddle out past this mushy stuff and then you can sit up on the board. You don't have to do more than that for now."

She nods.

"Ready?"

"As ready as I'll get out here. Do you know if there are sharks?"

"Sharks do live in all ocean waters. Mostly smaller species if you're close to shore. They're more afraid of you than you are of them. We haven't had a shark attack here on Marbella ever."

I never like this line of conversation once we're in the water. Wouldn't you know? Talking about sharks doesn't help a student relax—like, at all. But she asked. So, I'll do my best to help her feel confident.

"I snorkel out here all the time. And surf. You are safe."

"Okay. I'm going to do this." She nods her head imperceptibly. The shift in her mindset from panic to resolve is palpable.

"Good. You start paddling. I'm right here with you."

Jenny takes one arm off the board, loosening the death grip she has on one side, and then she starts to take a stroke, but she's still clutching the board on the other side, so her movement is unbalanced. I grab her board to steady it.

"Hold on a minute." I catch her eyes and look at her calmly and with the confidence I've worked hard to regain out here in the waves. "Can you trust that I teach people to surf all week long?"

"Yeah. Okay ... yes."

"And those surfers are mostly new to the water and the sport—otherwise they'd come out here without me, right?"

"Yeah."

"Okay. So, when I tell you to do something, you need to do what I say because I'm trying to help you succeed. Alright? I won't lead you astray. I'm going to help you do this. You will ride a wave if you keep following my directions."

"Okay."

"You have to let go of the board with both hands or this isn't going to work. Your body is going to stay on the board. Your wetsuit and the wax help keep you in place. And if you don't stay up, you've got your leash, and I'm right here. And my buddy, Wyatt, is over there on the lifeguard tower."

I turn to wave to Wyatt. He waves back, and then my eyes catch on a woman on the dock near the shack. I'd know that wild dark-brown hair anywhere. Mavs is here—and it looks like she's watching me. I nearly lose my focus on my lesson at the sight of her.

Normally, if I got this twisted up over something, I'd talk things out with Kai. Obviously, I can't tell him I'm struggling over Mavs.

"Okay," Jenny says, tearing my gaze away from the dock.

"Okay. Release the board. Then slowly drag your hands through the water. Paddle just like you're swimming. When we approach a wave, nose up like I showed you."

"Okay."

Jenny's eyes focus like it's her against the ocean. Thankfully, I know it's not. These waves are tame and easy. To her they feel intimidating, and this stuff close to shore is not fun to sit in unless you like being surrounded by sloshing foam and spray.

We paddle out next to one another where the waves are more spread out and the ocean is glassy. Jenny makes it there on her own power, and the resulting smile is one I love to see— one I can relate to. There's nothing like this.

"Okay," I tell Jenny. "You can sit up on your board. I've got you. Just hoist yourself up like you're doing a pushup, and spread your legs so you're straddling, then sit the rest of the way up."

She does as I told her, and then we're just two surfers, bobbing in the water, letting the ocean roll beneath us. We spend the next thirty to forty minutes mastering paddling into the waves and turning so we're ready to take a wave. Jenny belly boards a few, gets tossed twice, and finally lands a ride. She gets a few more before it's time for the lesson to end. We're both running on adrenaline and endorphins when we let the last wave take us in and walk our boards onto shore.

When I look up on the dock, Mavs is still there. She turns away, avoiding my gaze, but we both know she's been there—watching me teach Jenny to surf. I thought Jenny catching a wave was something. It's nothing compared to knowing Mavs cared enough to spectate. I try to talk my heart down from the thoughts I'm entertaining. It's not working. I'm nearly buoyant with hope. Maybe I'm a fool. But if I'm not ...

"You can leave your board here," I tell Jenny. "I'll come back and get these. Let's get you out of that wetsuit."

We walk side-by-side up to the shack. When we approach, Mavs ducks through the door into the shop. I walk Jenny around back and show her where she can dump the wetsuit once she's changed out of it in the outdoor dressing room.

I change out of my own wetsuit, washing under the outdoor shower and drying off with one of the towels on the bench. My clothes are inside the shop. I walk in, wearing only the swim-suit I had on under my wetsuit. The first thing to catch my eye is Mavs, staring at me like I'm indecent. You have to know her to know when she's blushing. And I know her. I wink and allow a slow smile to spread across my face. I'm not trying to toy with her. She just brings out the same side in me she always did—playful, daring, flirty, but also protective.

Mavs looks away, and then moves closer to Summer who is chatting with Ben near the cash register.

Kai approaches me. "Get dressed, dude."

"Just coming in off the water."

"How was the lesson?"

"Good! She stood up."

"That's always the best moment."

"It's almost like catching the wave of the day for yourself—watching someone else find their way out there."

I look over toward the cash register. Mavs is studying me. I can't quite decipher the expression on her face. Is she sad? Angry? Uncomfortable? Curious?

I wonder what she feels when she's watching other people surf. I remember being so angry it felt like lava had replaced the blood in my veins and my skin was too tight. Even when other people took easy waves, I had a grudge against the ocean for all it stole from me.

I turn to Kai. "Thanks, man."

His face contorts in confusion. "What for?"

"Helping me move on."

"That's what friends are for."

I look at Mavs. *That's what friends are for.* My mind scrolls through images of our yoga session this morning. I can do this for her. It's the least I can do.

Jenny comes through the shop, thanking me profusely and setting up another lesson for two days from now. She's hooked. My job here is done.

I walk down to the sand to collect our boards and then I head to the back of the shack to rinse the wetsuits and hang them to dry. After I change into my clothes, I'm behind the shop, singing a song that's going through my head while I collect towels that were left scattered back here. The familiar noise of scratching paws on the planks of the dock means only one thing. I turn and look down.

"Hey, little buddy," I say quietly.

This mutt of a dog has been hanging out around the pier for at least a week. I don't tell Kai, but I slip some food into a bowl out here every day. The dog looks a bit mangy. He obviously hasn't been living in anyone's home. Who knows how he got here, but I'm not going to let him starve.

Another noise catches my attention while I'm bending to scratch my little buddy behind the ears. He's smiling up at me. I call it a smile. His tongue lolls part way out of his mouth and his face has a wide grin on it.

If Kai would let me, I'd bring him home. But that's not going to happen. We're gone too much to have a pet, that's what Kai says. I'd be the type to have a dog and let him follow me around. This guy's chill. He'd lay on the dock and leave people alone. Probably would settle onto the beach while I surfed too. I picture him just waiting for me to come off the waves so I could take him back home. But I've got a housemate, so I can't make that call. Actually, I've got two housemates.

I look up to see Mavs leaning against the side of the shack, her arms crossed over her chest and a soft smile on her face.

"Who's this?" she asks.

"Dunno. He comes around here most days. Doesn't look like he's been inside for a while. He could use a bath among other things, but he's super chill."

"Awww." Mavs says, more to the dog than to me. Then she's bending over to scratch his head, her hand landing next to mine. Lucky dog.

The dog turns and practically leans into Mavs. He knows a good thing when he sees it. Smart little guy. She smiles wider.

"I wonder why he keeps coming here."

"Might have to do with me sneaking him leftovers." I look up at her and smile a sheepish grin.

"Oh, you are, are you? You know he's yours if you feed him."

"If only. Your brother's not too keen on pets."

"Did you ask him?"

"About this one? No. But in the past when I brought up getting a dog he said we're gone too much to care for a pet. We're always here at the shack, or out in the water. We're only home at night or sometimes on our days off."

"Seems like this little sweetie would be fine with that arrangement. Anything's better than what he's got going right now."

"You make a good point."

I can't help smiling up at her again. Her long, full hair

drapes down around her face while she leans in and pets the dog again. He looks up at her like he's in love. Yeah, man. That makes two of us. Just don't break her heart. She's had enough of that to last a lifetime.

"This can be our little secret." I wink at Mavs.

"Hmmm. Maybe." She straightens, steps back a little and then says, "Well, I'd better go. I just came here with Summer. I met Phyllis, by the way. She's great."

"Told you. She's special. I bet she loved meeting you."

"We had fun."

Mavs smiles this shy smile. It makes me itch for the days when her smiles were mine—freely given, wide-open smiles. She smiled and laughed all the time back then.

That's what friends are for.

I might never get her back, but I can at least help her smile like that again. At least I can try.

Mavs and I walk back into the shack through the back door together. My little furry friend stays out on the dock giving me a classic look full of those puppy-eyes.

"You're killing me, man," I tell him.

Mavs giggles for the briefest moment. We glance at one another and that little ball of hope inflates just the slightest bit more. It's dangerous to hope, but I'm a man who always sought out danger. You could say it's my natural habitat. Nothing ventured, nothing gained.

My phone buzzes in the pocket of my board shorts.

I pull it out and read the text. It's from my friend in San Diego.

Jammer: *Any word on the contest, bro?*

I quickly type out a response.

Bodhi: *Working on it.*

Jammer: *By working on it, do you mean, avoiding it?*

I'm so busted.

Bodhi: *Just thinking through the whole thing. Not completely avoiding.*
Jammer: *I saw Cap the other day. He said you didn't put the application in yet, so I wanted to crawl into your messages and push you, knowing how you love being pressured to take action.*
Bodhi: *It's my favorite. No need to get me a birthday gift now. You've outdone yourself.*
Jammer: *Seriously tho, bro. Send it in. This is a low-key event for a good cause. We'll hang out, ride some waves. Raise some money. Play some music. It will be like old times.*

Old times. Only all of these guys still compete and travel with sponsorships or partial sponsorships. Or they at least surf with the old group of friends regularly if they've quit competing. Jammer owns a surf school. He still does events like this one at least twice a year. Some of the guys even have their own brands now, and they're the ones sponsoring young up-and-coming surfers. Being around them puts salt in a wound. They all stayed with the surfing life and community when I dropped off the face of the earth.

Jammer: *I hear those gears grinding from here. Stop over-thinking. Come hang with your friends. We miss you. And bring that girl of yours.*
Bodhi: *We'll see.*

I look up right then to see Mavs reading the whole text exchange from over my shoulder.

"Sorry." She nearly winces. "You ... I just ... I better go."

"Mav ... Kalaine. Wait."

Kai gives me one of his overbearing brother looks. I tuck the urge to run after his sister into my pocket and turn so he can't read me like a book. *His sister.* Why did fate lure me into falling for my best friend's sister? As if our situation isn't hard enough with the massive load of baggage from our past.

I text Jammer and then shove my phone back in my pocket.

Bodhi: *She's not my girl. Not anymore.*

BODHI
(THE THIRD TIME WE SAW ONE ANOTHER ...)

If you keep looking at me like that,
I'll have no choice but to ask you on a date.
~ Unknown

She's here. *Kalaine.* I saw her at a distance, and it felt like one of those optical illusions where the whole world narrows so you're looking through a tunnel. She's here with that friend of hers, Leilani. Only, Leilani's here for the surfers. Kalaine is here for the surf. I've been watching her stats for a while now, and she's been making a name for herself.

It's only our second day here, and I'm riding the high of catching some massive waves this morning. A bunch of us will hit the evening glass-off later. But between now and then, I have a mission: finding the girl who captures my interest enough to make me think of her even when we're on opposite sides of the globe from one another.

A knock at my door disrupts my thoughts. I open it and take in my best friend, Kai. He's wearing a huge smile and board shorts.

"Let's hit the pool before lunch." He tips his chin toward the door at the back of my room leading out to the resort property.

"Because we're not getting enough time in the water here."

"Because we're in Bali, man! Bali!"

Kai is usually pretty laid-back, but he's right. This trip is amazing. Out of all the surfers in the world, we're the ones who were selected to come here. It's the trip of a lifetime.

I'm already in my trunks, so I shuck my T-shirt and grab a pool towel from my bathroom and follow my best friend out the sliders at the back of my room. We meander down a path that leads straight to the pools. They have the kind of pool that edges right up to the cliff, giving the illusion that the water is nearly a part of the ocean below.

Kai's sister is stretched out on her stomach on a chaise lounge at the other side of the pool. Her head turns, and her mouth spreads into a soft grin when she sees me. *That's what I'm saying.* I smile back and wink. She pulls her sunglasses down off the top of her head, places them over those honey-gold eyes of hers, and turns toward her bestie.

"Nope," Kai says in a less cheery voice than when I let him in my room. "Off limits, bro."

"What?" I'm so taken aback I don't even register what he's saying.

"My sister. She's not available."

"She has a boyfriend?"

I'm confused. All the signals I've gotten anytime Kalaine and I have been within a football field's distance of one another tell me we're flirting and enjoying the possibility of entertaining pursuing more with one another.

"No. Of course not. She's single and she's going to stay that way for a while."

Kai sounds so overprotective now, I almost tease him. What happened to my easy-going friend? And who is this caveman who took his place? I've never seen this side of Kai before.

"What do you mean, of course not? She's over eighteen. She's not allowed to have a boyfriend?"

"Eventually. I guess." Now he's broody and disgruntled.

"Man. You can't just keep your siblings from having relationships."

"Do you have a younger sister?"

Sore subject and he knows it. My parents divorced when I was seven. My mom got custody and my dad moved in with his girlfriend, now wife. They got pregnant less than a year later. I do have a younger sister. But she's eight years younger than me, and we didn't grow up together. I don't know what it's like to really be the older brother to someone—not like Kai is to Kalaine.

"Low blow."

"Sorry." He's contrite, but that fierceness hasn't dimmed much.

"I get it. You want to protect her."

"It's my job. And, yeah. I guess I get a little intense about it. If you knew her, you'd understand why."

What's funny is, I feel like I do know Kalaine, even though we've only exchanged a few words and glances. She got under my skin right away—in a way most women don't. She's intriguing. It's not every day you meet a woman who has the drive and determination to take on Mavericks. She still hasn't ridden that spot. I keep checking. But I know she will.

"Is she boy crazy?" Maybe Kai has good reason for this insane level of protectiveness.

"Not exactly. She's just so trusting. And she's a total free spirit. Like, she'll stop and pick up a caterpillar and talk to it, then she'll move it somewhere safe if she thinks it's in danger. If a bee lands on her arm, she's more likely to sing it a song than to scream like most girls. She's just … soft, tender-hearted. I never want to see that side of her crushed. It's not exactly childlike, but there's something so pure in how she sees the world.

It's a sweetness that you don't see in most people. And it's my job to protect that—and her."

I listen to all Kai's words, soaking them in. I've been dying to know more about Kalaine. I want to tuck away and treasure every single tidbit. He's noble, wanting to protect her. I admire it. But also, he's a bit much. And it's my job as his friend to help him face reality.

"Dude. You know she's going to date. Right? I mean, that's what young people do. And she's beautiful and fun. Guys are going to want to take her out."

A prickle of the same possessiveness Kai must feel zings through me after giving him my speech. And I have no right or claim to Kalaine. It's just, the idea of her dating another guy doesn't sit well with me.

"Not you, though. That would be awkward."

"So you'd rather her date some random guy you don't know or trust?"

"I'd rather you agree with me and we jump into the pool and enjoy our time in Bali."

I don't know what possesses me to say what I do, but I throw my towel onto a lounger and say, "Okay. No problem. She's off limits."

~

The first week in Bali drifts by until I don't really know what day it is. We have yoga on the beach, occasional photo shoots and other obligations with our sponsors. After all, they're footing the bill. Sometimes our commitments include a few of the other surfers here if we are repped by the same brand. We surf morning and evening. Our meals are provided by the resort, but we also venture into town and enjoy local dishes. At night we hang out, dancing or talking around a firepit or on one of the beaches.

Kalaine and I have been doing a dance of our own. We make eye contact, smile, study one another. If we're in the same area, we always find each other, even if we don't talk. We have talked a few times, but it's always been cut short. Ever since my conversation with Kai, I've been keeping my distance, but his warning only serves to intensify my curiosity and the temptation to ask Kalaine out so we can spend some time together—just the two of us.

I finally find my opportunity one night at a beach bonfire the next resort over. A bunch of us decided to go pull up these giant bean bags they lay out all over the sand around a firepit where they roast s'mores on the beach. This young woman from Portugal has been chatting Kai up the past day and a half. The two of them are walking ahead of the group like they're in their own bubble.

Kalaine and Leilani come up from behind me and start walking with me, one on each side. "Hey, Bodhi," Leilani says. "How's it going?"

"Great. How 'bout you?" I answer Leilani, but my head turns toward Kalaine like a compass drawn north.

"Oh, I'm great too." Leilani giggles. "And I think I hear someone calling my name. You two have fun."

I turn back toward Leilani, but she's already walking off to talk to a guy they call Minnow. "Huh? Yeah. You too. For sure. Have fun."

Leilani just giggles from up ahead like she's in on some joke I don't know the punchline to. My attraction to Kalaine is so blatant. Leilani's probably laughing at how completely obvious I am. I've lost all capacity to even pretend I'm cool around this girl.

"So, great week, huh?" Kalaine looks up at me through her lashes, her head tilted slightly.

"Pretty great. I haven't done everything on my bucket list yet, but we've still got the rest of the trip, right?"

"Oh? What's on your bucket list?"

You. You basically are my bucket list.

I don't say that, of course. The more Kai has talked about Kalaine and the more I've observed her this week, the more I agree. She's rare, pure, special. That's obviously why she got under my skin. I don't want to do anything reckless with her. She's not like other women. I sensed it the first time we met.

"I want to ride the elephants. Definitely visit the famous temple. Grab a bite to eat at Bingin Beach, and I can't call this trip complete if I don't hang with the monkeys on Padang-Padang beach."

"Yes, please." She smiles up at me. "All of the above. Sign me up."

"Yeah?"

"Definitely. We don't know if we'll ever be here again. We need to do it all, don't you think?"

"I do."

I pause and stare into her eyes. She stares right back. There's this fizz of energy between us. It's been there since that first day at Mavericks.

Way back in high school chemistry I learned how some elements clash—even causing dangerous explosions when mixed. But other elements are compatible, making something more amazing when they combine. Kalaine and I seem to have both things going for us. A lot of combustion, but also some serious compatibility.

I know Kai warned me off, but he didn't say I couldn't take Kalaine to a meal or hang out with her. And I'd never disrespect Kai or endanger our friendship. I look up the walkway where part of our group has already turned into the resort where we're going to hang out. Kai's busy with his new friend, Andreia. I know my intentions with Kalaine. He's over-the-top in his concern for her. I just want to get to know her better.

"I haven't spent enough time with some of the surfers here

either," I say, pinning her with a meaningful gaze—one I'm hoping says everything my words aren't.

"Me either." Her smile grows and her eyes crinkle at the edges. "Maybe that should be on your bucket list too."

It is. Believe me, it is.

14

KALAINE

Any true champion can bounce back.
That's what being a champion is:
being able to deal with adversity
and being able to bounce back.
~ Floyd Mayweather, Jr.

Bodhi takes another wave. A few other surfers sit on their boards at a distance from him, but he's the one I'm watching. I walked down here this morning, like I've been doing every morning this week since I got my boot off. It's my third week on Marbella. I'm doing virtual physical therapy online to strengthen the muscles around the area I broke in my ankle. And I'm wearing a brace when I take walks for the next few weeks.

I'm making progress. Toward what? I don't know. But at least my body is healing.

The early morning air is misty and cool. I snug my hoodie around me and watch Bodhi from my spot on the sand where

I'm mingled between the rows of sun beds. I'm not fully camou-flaged, but I'm far enough from the edge of the water to avoid drawing unnecessary attention to myself.

Two resort employees move up and down the rows of large wooden recliners, placing cushions on each set of loungers for the day. Other than them and me, the beach is basically deserted. I don't know why I come here, morning after morn-ing. Watching Bodhi is a dangerous habit. Even now, he presses his foot onto the board, shifting his weight and propelling himself into a backside snap, sending an arc of spray off the lip of the wave. I'm aware of my own foot pressing into the sand and my body shifting on instinct as if I'm performing the trick, not merely spectating.

Bodhi moves like poetry, athleticism, and sexy masculinity, every line of his body fluid and arching with the water. Surfing is dance, sport, and art. And I'm living vicariously through Bodhi, but each wave he takes reminds me how I'll never do what he's doing again.

He takes a final wave, getting just inside the tube for a few seconds and then shooting out long and clean with a straight ride toward shore. He stands, grabbing his board, and I can see his satisfied smile from here. Time to go.

I should leave before I'm found out, but I can't take my eyes off him as he shakes his head like a dog, water droplets flying to the left and right, and then lifts his free hand to rake his hair back off his face. My heart begs me to go to him. My mind knows better.

He's been nothing but kind and respectful to me—maybe occasionally flirty, but mostly he's stood by his word to befriend me since I moved in. I'm having a hard time hanging on to the grudge I held for so long. He's different. I'm different. Holding on to a resentment isn't my style, and it's not serving me anymore.

I start to turn, unsure if Bodhi sees me. We always did have that acute awareness of one another. That much hasn't dimmed between us.

His face lights up. He sets his board on the sand and starts making purposeful strides in my direction. Maybe he didn't see me. In a burst of what I'll later call temporary insanity, I duck behind the back of a lounger—as if that could change something if he's already seen me. Hopefully he didn't. I grasp the back of one of the chairs, contemplating my escape. Dropping to my knees, I start army crawling down the sand behind the line of loungers, being careful to keep my ankle elevated.

I'm crawling along, without a plan except the deep need to keep my morning surf-watch a secret. My eyes aim downward at the sand and I lift my head every few crawls to check the area ahead of me. I have no idea how I'm going to make a getaway when I get to the end of the row, but I'll deal with it when I get there. My abs are screaming at me for not doing a core workout in ages.

At least Bodhi and I have done yoga four other times since that first session. I'm getting stronger. My physical therapist says it's one of the best things I can do for my healing as long as I don't push it too hard. He has no idea what I go through watching Bodhi stretch and pose. Who knew I was such a glutton for punishment? But I can't find it in me to say no to Bodhi whenever he invites me. *Yoga sesh, Kalaine?* Um. Yes, please.

I take a few more measured crawls and come crashing into two legs, clad in neoprene. My eyes trace the legs up, up past the torso to the smirking face of the man I loved for over two years—maybe I still love him. It's so hard to know my own mind right now.

The entertained expression on his face stokes a fire in me.

"Mornin' Mavs."

He doesn't stutter or cut my nickname short.

"Morning," I say, looking around on the sand like I dropped something besides my dignity.

"Like the view?" He smiles a crooked smile at me and my stomach gets all bubbly and gooey.

"The view? From down here?"

He chuckles. "No. The view you had back there." He points to where I had been standing.

I'm so busted. But I'm not going down that easily.

"Huh? The view. Yeah. It's beautiful out here. A good day for catching some solid waves."

I hoist myself up and end up nearly face to face with a post-surf Bodhi.

He smiles this unguarded smile at me and I give up fighting. Whatever. So, I was watching him. It doesn't mean anything.

"You look great out there."

"I look great, huh?" His eyes crinkle at the corners and he lifts his eyebrows the slightest. It's a look that gets me every time.

"You know what you look like. Stop fishing."

"I like hearing what you think I look like."

"Because I'm your friend." I remind us both.

"Because you matter." His face is dead serious. The teasing is gone.

"You can walk now—and crawl." He chuckles. "How long til you're allowed out on a board again?"

"We will not speak of my crawling ever again."

"Got it." His smile doubles. "No speaking of how you dropped down when you saw me and crawled along the back of these loungers as if I hadn't been aware of you coming out here every morning this week. Sounds about right."

I feel my face flame. "I said, no speaking of it."

"Right. I was just clearing up what we aren't speaking about." He winks that infuriating wink. It should be illegal, or registered. He should have to register his wink like a man registers a lethal weapon. Maybe he should have to get it licensed. And there should be signals. Like a wink stoplight. Red ... don't wink. Green ... bring it on. Yellow ... take caution with your winking.

"Mavs?"

"Huh?"

"When do you think you'll be allowed to get back on a board?"

Oh. That.

"I don't know. My therapist said to take it slowly building in activity that taxes my ankle. It could be a while." As in, *never.* I can't tell Bodhi that, though. He'd fight me.

"Walk with me?" He tips his head in the direction of the shore where he laid his board on the sand. His towel is in a rumpled pile there too.

"Or crawl," he adds under his breath.

I jab him playfully with my elbow as we walk side by side. "I said to drop that."

He looks over at me and raises both hands in innocence. "Dropping ... like you dropped down onto the sand ..."

"Bodhi!"

"Okay. Okay." He chuckles and I can't help smiling along with him.

Neither of us says anything else as we walk toward his board, but I look at him occasionally and he turns his head to meet my glances. No one knows me like Bodhi. There's no hiding from him. Kai knows me like a brother knows a sister. He knows my past, where I came from, the things only family knows. Leilani knows me nearly as well. But she doesn't see certain parts of me. She's usually so busy pushing me or enjoying our friendship. She doesn't stop to study me the way Bodhi does. I'm exposed in his gaze.

"You know," Bodhi's voice is soft and careful. "I didn't want to get back in the ocean after my accident."

"I know."

"But even after I got through the initial healing, I was sure I'd never surf again."

I nod again, unable to find words or say anything around the lump forming in my throat. Bodhi grabs his towel off the ground and starts ruffling his hair. Then he reaches behind himself and unzips his wetsuit, freeing his torso from the soaking neoprene and revealing his chest and arms, freshly pumped from paddling in the water.

He picks up his board and starts heading toward the water-sports shack. I follow along, wishing I had something to hold or carry. The urge to grab his hand and clasp it in mine nearly overpowers me.

"After I got through the initial hell of my accident, I started trying to force myself to imagine a life on land—a life without the two things I loved most in the world."

Bodhi stops in his tracks and stares down at me.

I don't ask him what the two loves of his life were at that time. We both know.

Bodhi starts walking again. "Your brother asked me to surf one day. I had a brittle attitude, so I gave him the brush off. I told him, 'I don't do that anymore. It's not who I am.'"

"And in his wisdom—you know that way Kai always has of cutting through everything and getting down beneath the surface—he said, 'Surfing never was who you were. But it's what you love. And you can love it again.' Then he looked me in the eye and said, 'You can choose to live a half-life or choose to reclaim a part of what you lost. It's up to you. No one can keep you from giving up. I was just hoping you wouldn't.'"

"Then he took off for the morning and came back with that afterglow of a good session in the water. Day after day he'd extend the invitation whenever he went out. His words pinched at me like an ill-fitting wetsuit. I couldn't get comfortable in my resistance. Here I was, living on an island, surrounded by the ocean, working the watersports shack, but never getting in the water."

I nod at Bodhi, certain where he's headed with this story, but still craving a small glimpse of what he was like after we broke up. I need to fill in the gaps. Maybe that will help me move on.

We climb the wooden steps to the dock and Bodhi walks behind the shack to prop his board on a rack. Then he starts removing his wetsuit so he's only wearing his swim trunks.

He keeps talking while he turns on the outdoor shower head. "One day, I couldn't take it anymore. I went to a different part of the island where there's a good evening break—all perfect lefts. I sat on the shore in my wetsuit, staring at the ocean as the sun started to drop low." He looks at me. "I cried like a baby, sitting there, alone on the sand, facing down the ocean, the force of nature that had taken everything that mattered away from me. I had barely cried since the accident. Something unhinged in me and I let it all out in the privacy of that cove."

He steps under the shower head, and I try to figure out where to put my eyes. He's oblivious as to how he's taunting me right now, running his hands through his hair so the water rinses away the residue of the ocean. His biceps and triceps flex and I turn my gaze to check out the surfboard rack. Yep. There are the surfboards ... one ... two ... three ... four ...

The water turns off, and Bodhi smirks at me when I glance back in his direction. "Sorry," he says. "I wasn't thinking that would bother you."

"Not bothered." I lie.

"Hmmm." He hums. "I'd be bothered into next week if that were you under the water and I were standing there watching you."

He always did speak his mind. It's one of the qualities that drew me to him in the first place.

"Anyway," he says, picking up his towel and rubbing his hair with it, and then draping it over his shoulders as he walks toward the back door of the shop. "I sat on that shore, waiting for some magical insight or nudge. Nothing really came, but I walked to the edge of the water and put my feet in. I hadn't even dared to do that. I didn't want to have an inch or two of the ocean when I had experienced all of her in the past. So I never even dipped my toes into the shorepound.

"I stood there with her lapping at my feet, the foam was like the kind of kiss you get on a first date—careful and sweet."

Bodhi's eyes meet mine and I can't even look at him for more than a second before memories of all our kisses flood me. What is he doing? Does he even know?

"I can barely describe what happened without sounding like a lunatic, but you'll understand." Bodhi moves inside toward the dressing room where he's stashed his clothes. But he pauses and looks at me. I'm only a few feet from him, following along like a little puppy ever since he asked me to walk with him. No one is here in the shop. It's still early. The solitude feels decadent and dangerous.

"She called to me, Mavs. The ocean invited me back. I know how nuts that sounds. But before I knew what I was doing, I had turned and grabbed my board and started making my way into the low waves breaking at the shore. And I felt like I was making peace with her in that moment. Like we were getting our second chance."

I'm hanging on every word, living through this experience as if I'm right there, on the sand, watching him share this intimate healing experience with the ocean.

"And I got just past the mush and lay on my board, belly down, letting my hands swirl in the water with no intention of getting up and riding. Even going that far was huge. I could have paddled back to shore and called it a win. But then a swell came, and my instinct kicked in. I paddled into the wave, turned and popped up like I'd never missed a day."

He's smiling now. And I smile with him.

"It wasn't even that great of a wave. But I rode it. And when I bailed, I had to have more. Something broke in me—something broke through to me. I got back on the board and rode and rode and rode for hours until the sun was gone past the horizon, and my arms were burning and my body made me quit."

When I got home, Kai asked where I'd been. I just said, "Surfing." And he nodded with this slow, knowing bob of his head, and smiled. He never said another word about me turning a corner. But he asked me out to surf whenever he went, and I started going out with him. And I've been going out ever since. About six months after that evening on the sand, Kai asked me to start teaching lessons. But that's a whole other story."

Bodhi steps into the dressing room and pulls the curtain shut behind himself. "I never would have gotten over this if Kai hadn't pushed me. I owe him so much."

I stand next to a rack of T-shirts bearing various surfboard brands. My mind swirls with everything Bodhi said, and what he's implying. If he were anyone else, I could chalk his story up to a great redemption rising up from tragedy. I'd be inspired, but I could walk away unchanged.

"I'm so proud of you," I finally say.

The curtain to the dressing room opens and Bodhi emerges holding his wadded up towel. He's wearing a T-shirt and shorts with flip flops, and he's never looked better. I have an urge to go to him and hug him. I start to move in his direction despite my better judgment.

There's a bark outside the back door.

"Ah. Breakfast time." Bodhi winks at me. "Better feed my little buddy."

15

BODHI

You can't buy love, but you can rescue it.
~ Unknown

I'm playing with fire. And I might get burned. I can't seem to help myself, though.

I've seen Mavs there on the shoreline, hiding among the loungers every morning. As if she could hide. This morning I had to show her I saw her—that I've been seeing her. I had to get close to her. I couldn't go one more day, resisting the pull to look at her when I came in off a wave, acting like I believed she had been back home, snug in bed. Not when I knew she was there, watching me surf every single day.

Something made me push the limits. I've been itching to tell Mavs that story about Kai, and how I returned to the water. I see it in her eyes. She thinks she's finished—thinks she'll never ride again. She's wrong. I'm going to show her how wrong she is. If I could bounce back from my tragedy, she definitely can. She's always been more buoyant than me—more full of life and beauty. Kalaine's zest for living is a part of her essence, and I'm going to help her remember who she is and what she's made of.

There's this sadness clinging to her that's new. It's totally understandable. I know. If anyone knows, I do. But I can't let her stay stuck in a spiral of resignation.

It's killing me to be around Mavs without touching her. But I have to respect her—and Kai. I wasn't kidding when I said I owe him everything. I don't know where I'd be without his persistence and devotion. He knew just how to push me. He always left the final move up to me. His gentle relentlessness finally wore me down. And I intend to return the favor by paying it forward to Kalaine.

We walk out of the shop, and I grab a small ziplock full of shredded chicken and rice I saved from last night. I cooked the meat in salsa for our bowls, but I kept a portion unseasoned for my buddy.

"He needs a name," Mavs says while I dump the contents of my baggie into the bowl out here.

The dog goes to town, scarfing down the food like it's going out of style.

"You think?" I lean back against the wall of the shack, watching the dog lick the bowl he just emptied. "You said feeding him makes him mine. The way I figure it, feeding him makes him my friend. Naming him makes him mine."

"Would that be so bad?"

Mavs walks over to join me and the dog. She squats down to rub his head. It's a movement she wouldn't have been able to do a week ago. She's healing. I bet in a week she could try to get out on a board. Maybe two weeks tops.

"It wouldn't be bad for me." I smile down at Mavs. "It's Kai we have to think of. I share that house with him fifty-fifty. And he's always been the more practical of the two of us. I think we could handle a dog. He thinks it's too much work. And you already know his thoughts on how much we're out and about."

"This dog is different," Mavs says, looking up at me with an expression that makes me want to raid the pound for her. If she wants a dog, or twenty, I'm going to get her what she wants.

"He is," I agree. "The way I figure it, my little buddy already hangs out here without causing a fuss. What's the difference if we give him a cozy place to stay at night? If he likes living with us, he can stick around. If he doesn't, he's a nomad. I won't force him."

"You won't have to," she says, looking up at me again. "He wants to be with you."

The look in her eyes could make me imagine the dog's not the only one who wants to be with me. But I know better than to read too much into this situation with Mavs. Besides, she needs to heal. Then we can see what she wants—when the playing field is level and she's not leaning on me for a place to stay or a tether to the life she lost.

"I'll talk to Kai," Mavs says, giving the dog another scratch behind the ears. "What about Barney?"

"No. What? You want to name my dog Barney? Like after that purple dinosaur that sang that song that could drive a sane person nuts?"

"No. Not that dinosaur." She smiles up at me. "You know. A Barney."

"A surf Barney? No. Not my dog. He's no Barney. He just might get on a board one day."

Her smile flickers just the slightest and her gaze drifts out over the water.

"How about Shaka?" I ask.

She makes the sign, sticking her pinky and thumb out and tucking the other three fingers in toward her palm. "Like Shaka?"

"Yeah. Hang loose. All's well. We could use a little shaka, don't you think?"

"Yeah. We could." She smiles. Then she turns to the dog. "What do you think? Do you like the name Shaka?"

The dog looks right at Mavs and pants this happy smile.

She smiles up at me. "He likes it."

"We're keeping him."

"What about me asking Kai?"

"A formality. We'll ask him so he doesn't raise Cain. But this dog? He's yours. Well, technically, he's mine since I named him. But, you know, I've always been good at sharing. Especially when it comes to you."

"Thank you," Mavs says with the softest, sweetest look in her eyes. "I don't think I'll mind sharing."

"Good thing." I smile down at her. "I'd hate to have to thumb wrestle you."

I know I stepped over about fifty tripwires just now, but Mavs is making me crazy, her honey-gold eyes looking up at me, her hair all wild and wavy, the morning sun glinting off her skin. I'll be her friend. I will. It might kill me, but I will.

Mavs decides we ought to try to see if Shaka will follow us home. Like me, it turns out he'd follow her anywhere. At least, now, I would.

I should have followed her then. Begged her to stay. Gotten my head out of my rear and seen further down the road. She seems to have forgiven me with ease over these past few weeks. I can't forgive myself, though. Every day, I'm in the house with her, moving around one another like a couple, only without any of the romance. A taut band of tension stretches between us, but there's a comfortable ease there too. Whenever she accepts my invites, we do yoga together.

And now this. She's beaming down at that adorable mutt, talking away to him like the old Mavs while we stroll along the edge of the sand. And he's smiling up at her like she's the only person who matters in his world.

Buddy, I feel you.

The dog pauses and sits when we get to the end of the road that runs alongside the beach. Mavs walks ahead calling, "Shaka! Come on, sweet boy. You're going to love this."

He's not so sure. He looks back at me and up at her, but he doesn't budge.

"I'll have to carry him," Mavs says, some of her old resolve seeping into her words.

If Kai could see her like this, he'd override any objections he had to her bringing a dog home.

"I don't think your PT would approve of you hauling a thirty pound dog for three blocks. I'll carry him."

"You will?"

"Anything ... Sure." I almost said, *anything for you*. But I've said enough today. My mouth seems to lose its filter around her these days. Everything my heart longs for and lost is within my grasp, and yet she's still so out of reach.

I bend down and give Shaka a few soft strokes down his back. "Hey, buddy, I'm going to carry you. Okay?"

He just sits there, turning his head toward the ocean and then looking at Mavs and then me.

I decide he'll be better off if I act with confidence, so in one swift move, I sweep him up into my arms. He surprises me by leaning into me and resting his head over my shoulder.

"Awwww. Look at him." Mavs beams at me. At me, not the dog.

Her smile triggers mine. I'm smiling so hard my cheeks feel tight. She's happier than she's been since she got here, and I had a little something to do with it.

Mavs leads the way back to the house where Kai is getting ready for work. The timing may not be ideal, but I'm not worried about that. When Kai sees her with this dog, he'll say yes. Ben's opening today, so we have a little bit of time to talk to Kai before he leaves.

Mavs opens the gate to the front yard and walks up the porch steps ahead of me. She's taxed from the exertion of walking to the beach and back and also standing for so long while I surfed. I can tell by the effort it takes her to make it up the stairs.

"Are you hurting?" I ask.

"A little. Just sore. I've probably been overdoing it now that the boot is off. I'll put my leg up for a while after we're settled inside."

"Okay."

Mavs gives me a shy smile. Yeah. I'm still protective of her, and now she sees it. At least she hasn't told me to leave her alone or to stop caring. I couldn't if I wanted to.

"Hey, Kai?" Mavs shouts from inside the front door.

I'm still holding Shaka, walking in behind Mavs. I'm not sure what he'll do once he's out of my arms. Plus, my buddy needs a bath something fierce. I'm not letting him down until he's cleaned up.

"Yeah. What's up?"

Kai comes around the corner from the hallway into the living room. His hair is wet, but he's dressed in shorts and a T-shirt—in other words, our work uniform. We take business casual to a whole new level.

Kai looks from Mavs to me to the dog. "What's going on? Why is there a dog in here? Is that the dog that's been hanging around the shack?"

Mavs squares her shoulders. When Kai's gaze travels over the three of us, I realize how close Mavs and I are standing to one another. We look like a couple. Lines blur so easily with her. It would take nothing—and everything—to slip back into our old relationship. Only, that's dead. Whatever we're doing, it has to be new. We're like Pompeii, buried under rubble. Even if we dug up the remains of what we were, it wouldn't be of any use.

"That's Shaka," Mavs declares with a tone that she only takes with her brother, and only when he's challenging her capabilities or trying to cage her in.

"Shaka?" Kai looks confused.

"He's my dog now," Mavs says.

She reaches over and scrubs the dog behind his ears. Shaka turns toward her and places his cheek in her palm.

"If you don't want me to keep him here, I'll look for another place to stay—with him."

Mavs thumbs over at me and the dog and it almost looks like she's saying she'd move with me. Kai's brows draw in a little.

Mavs squares her hands on her hips like she's ready to take her brother on. This is not exactly what I pictured when she said she'd ask Kai. But, okay, this works too. I'd be lying if I said I wasn't impacted by seeing this fierce side of Mavs return to the forefront. She's gentle and free—one of the kindest souls you'd ever want to meet—but when she sets her mind to something, she's a force.

"Whoa. Whoa." Kai holds his hands in the air. "I just asked what the dog was doing here, Kala. He can stay. You're a grown woman. If you want the dog, he's yours."

"Really?" She nearly squeals, dropping all defensiveness and softening immediately at Kai's words. She runs over—well, it's a sort of a wobbly hopping kind of run—and gives Kai a huge hug. "Thank you! Thank you!"

Shaka's tail thumps against my abs as if he knows he just got the go ahead to become the fourth roommate in this odd configuration we've got going on.

"What about me?" I mutter quietly into Shaka's fur. "I don't get a thank you hug? I'm the one who kept you around long enough for her to fall for you."

Shaka just licks my jaw. It's not a substitute for an exuberant hug from Mavs, not even close. This dog's breath needs whatever dogs use for Listerine. It's nearly toxic.

"I'm going to give him a bath," I tell Kai. "I'll meet you at the shack at ten."

"We'd better get him food," Kai mutters. "And whatever else he'll need."

Mavs shoots me a secretive smile. "Bodhi's got that covered."

I smile back at her and Kai looks between the two of us with an expression of confusion and concern.

"Okay." He turns to grab his sweatshirt. "I'll see you tonight." Kai nods toward Mavs.

Then he turns his attention to me and the dog. "And I'll see you in a few hours. Make sure that thing doesn't poop in here."

"His name is Shaka," Mavs scolds.

Kai looks straight at Shaka. "Don't poop in my house, dude."

Shaka's tongue lolls out of his mouth and he pants.

KALAINE
(OUR SECOND WEEK IN BALI ...)

Good first dates are more than short stories. They are first chapters.
~ David Levithan

Bodhi and I walk toward the beach with a big group of surfers who are all here for these nine weeks. He's been making conversation with me our whole walk over here. The glances he keeps sending me are making me giddy. He's the right balance between playful and serious. The air around us feels magical, and it's not just Bali. It's him. And us. He seems as curious about me as I am about him.

"Want to grab a couple of bean bags and cozy up near the fire?" He smiles down at me.

"Definitely."

I know he has friends here, and I also know most of the single women on the trip have been checking him out. But he's made it clear that he's intent on hanging out with me. I'm definitely not complaining.

We walk over to the spot where a few resort employees are handing out these oversized bean bags I'd expect to see in a college dorm room. Bodhi grabs one and then moves out of the way so I can take mine. We look around and find a spot not too close to the fire, but close enough to enjoy the view of the flames leaping high above the firepit, with the ocean off in the distance.

Leilani's across the way, sending me meaningful looks I hope Bodhi doesn't pick up on. Subtlety is not her strong suit. When Bodhi's not looking I roll my eyes at her and stick out my tongue. Something about being around my life-long bestie brings out the high school antics.

My brother's off with a girl from Portugal. I've seen them chatting over the past two days. I should send her a thank you note for keeping Kai occupied so I can actually get within ten feet of Bodhi. I swear, if Kai could wrap me in bubble wrap and caution tape and station armed guards around me, he would. He means well, I know he does. Unfortunately, his good intentions don't make him less annoying.

Bodhi grabs some s'mores fixings for us when a resort employee comes by with a tray full of graham crackers, chocolate squares and marshmallows.

"So, here's the question. And how you answer this will determine whether we're meant to be friends or not." Bodhi smiles and winks. "Burnt, brown, or somewhere inbetween."

"Easy. Brown. Perfectly brown with a light crisp. Cooked with patience, and rotated regularly so the inside gushes out at the first bite."

"Hmmm." He runs his hand down his jaw and I follow the movement, enjoying the way his end-of-the-day stubble reflects the firelight.

"I'm a little more on the burnt side, but for you, I'll make an exception."

"So I didn't ruin our friendship?" I tease him.

"With anyone else, that would be a deal breaker, but I'm thinking you have enough other qualities in the plus column to outweigh your need for a gourmet chef to toast your marshmallow."

I giggle. "Okay. So I should roast my own, yeah?"

"No way. I'm here to impress. Just kick back and let me cook for you."

I smile as he hops up and walks toward the fire with the typical grace of a man who rides the water on a regular basis. He's gorgeous and flirty and magnetic and I want to spend the rest of this trip getting to know him better. I instinctively look around for Kai. He's usually circling like a vulture whenever a guy shows interest in me. I don't see him, so I relax back into my beanbag and watch Bodhi stick two skewers into the fire pit. I allow my gaze to lazily drift around the beach and the cliffs, and then back to Bodhi.

Bodhi returns with two s'mores. "Just right," he declares before plopping into his beanbag and handing my dessert over to me.

"We'll see," I tease.

I take a bite and pull the treat away from my mouth. A huge string of melted marshmallow goo stretches between me and the cracker, and crumbs fall all down the front of me. Great.

I look over at Bodhi and he's grinning with amusement. "You've got a little something ..."

He points at my mouth and then his finger trails down through the air to point where crumbs are scattered on my shirt. His face looks positively mischievous and thoroughly entertained by my inability to eat s'mores without making a mess of myself.

Meanwhile, I'm trying desperately not to get the goo in my overabundance of hair while attempting to wrangle the sticky strand into my mouth. I lift my other hand and pull the string of melted marshmallow away from the cracker, then I work it into my mouth in a very unglamorous move.

Bodhi's finger swipes out and snags a bit of the fluffy strand before I get all of it into my mouth. He sticks his finger into his mouth and licks it clean and then lets out a hum of appreciation. Oh. My.

My tongue darts out to lick my fingertips and lips and Bodhi fixates on the movement. His eyes are on my mouth and his gaze heats. He's not hiding anything from me—not even trying to make it appear like he wasn't just studying me and thinking about my lips and his.

"Not the best first date food," I murmur through my bite.

"Oh. Is this our first date?" His eyebrows lift suggestively.

"Um. Not. No. You know. I'm just saying if you ever want to take a girl on a first date, this would not be the choice of what to give her."

"I dunno." He shrugs. "I beg to differ. Watching you eat s'mores might be my new favorite thing."

I feel myself blush, and I'm not usually prone to blushing.

"And this isn't our first date," he clarifies. "This is definitely our pre-first date. I plan to take you somewhere without so many of our friends around when we go out."

"On a date?" I ask like a dork.

"I'm assuming. Yeah. Would you go out with me? Maybe we could tick off some Bali bucket-list items together."

"I'd like that. A lot."

My eyes rove the area around the firepit for Kai. Who cares? He's not my boss. I'm allowed to say yes if a guy I'm interested in asks me out.

As if he could read my mind, Bodhi asks. "Looking for your brother? Or your friend?"

"Kai. He's always getting in the middle of things when someone wants to ask me out."

"I get that. He wants to take care of you."

"So his overprotectiveness doesn't bother you? Or scare you away?"

"Nah. He's not the boss of me. He's a good friend. But I'm

not out to hurt you. I just want to get to know you better, and for us to enjoy one another like we are right now. I admire Kai's desire to protect you. You're his sister. But you're also free to make your own choices."

He's not the boss of me. That's exactly what I think all the time.

"So, you'll go out with me?" Bodhi clarifies.

"I'd really like that."

"Good. I've been wanting to spend more time with you ever since the last time I saw you."

"You have?"

"Yeah." He nods and smiles this slow, sexy grin. "I've even been stalking your heats whenever they're televised. I wanted to see if you made it to Mavs yet."

He's been tracking my career? Wow.

I've been tracking his too. The idea of him keeping tabs on my progress means more to me than I'll tell him for now.

"Do you always say everything so plainly?"

"Why not? I'm not into games. I figure it's better to just say what you think."

"I like that."

"I'm glad. Because I like you."

16

KALAINE

Feelings are much like waves:
We can't stop them from coming,
but we can choose which one to surf.
~ Jonatan Mårtensson

"Hey, Lei!" I answer my phone on the first ring.

"What's got you so peppy?" she asks. "Not that I'm complaining. I'm all for your happiness. I'm basically your happiness hype girl."

"You are."

It's been five days since Leilani and I spoke to one another —one of the longest stretches we've gone in our lives. Between her competitions and me avoiding talking with her about Bodhi, calls just didn't happen. When her caller ID showed up on my phone just now, I answered so quickly, Shaka jumped.

"I'm just sitting here with our new housemate." I smile down at Shaka and rub him behind the ears.

"Your new whaaa?"

"Housemate."

Turns out Shaka's coat is white and light tan. I thought he was brown and gray. Bodhi wasn't kidding when he said our dog needed a bath. Shaka's still naturally wiry, but he's so much softer, and he follows me like a little furry shadow wherever I go. I took him back down to the dock yesterday, and he stayed even more closely on my heels the whole time, as if he was afraid I was going to leave him there and let him return to his old life. Not a chance.

"We got a dog."

"Oh! Whew. And ... we?"

"Yeah. You know, the guys and me."

"The guys."

"Kai and Bodhi."

"Sounds cozy."

"It's ... better than I expected it to be."

A smile I can't contain blooms across my face. I am probably crazy, but my heart is coaxing me down paths I'm not sure I should wander. Between watching Bodhi surf, doing yoga with him, cooking meals together, and then rescuing Shaka, I'm feeling a swell of emotions for Bodhi. Mostly everything warm and tempting—but also a little overwhelming.

Those feelings are all tangled up with my uncertain future. It would be easy to fall into Bodhi's arms. I'm not even sure he'd want that to happen. At times, I think he might, and then I just can't tell. I'm nearly positive he's not seeing anyone. There's no sign of texts or calls or visits. And I know Bodhi. If he's dating someone, he's laser focused on her.

"You sound like you're falling all over again."

"What? What makes you say that?"

Leilani makes her voice sound all dreamy and says. "It's better than I expected it to be." She adds a wistful sigh at the end for dramatic effect.

Then she shifts into straight-up girlfriend mode. "Kalaine, do you know the last time I heard you use that tone of voice?"

"No. When?"

"Over two years ago. Before Bodhi's accident. Before that hottie broke your heart."

Talk about a bucket of ice water to the face.

"He's not the same. I can't explain it, Lei. He's come through the trauma and built a new life. He's even surfing again. And, he's being so thoughtful and careful with me. He hasn't pushed me or made any moves, but he's been here for me."

"I get that. And I thought this might happen. I mean, it's like the worst sort of science experiment. You take two people who were madly in love with one another—the kind of love most people only dream of finding. Then you throw them into a trauma where they reevaluate their own lives and also remember how much they meant to one another. And then you stick them in the same little beach cottage where they're in one another's personal space at all hours of the day? No one could escape that sort of setup."

"Wow. Just wow. I never took you for such a cynic."

"Forgive me for not buying a ticket and hopping on the Bodhi Merrick fan club express. I'm just your voice of reason."

"I have a voice of reason in my head. She sounds a lot like you, come to think of it."

"Good. That's what she should sound like."

"You should see Bodhi now."

I try to force my voice to sound more like I'm talking about a kitchen chair than the man who makes my heart rate spike like he always has, only maybe even more so now that we've both faced tragedy.

"Do you need me to fly there when the competition's over so I can see what's what?"

"No. I definitely don't need that."

"Okay. I would, though. In a hot minute. I'd love to see you anyway."

"I'd love to see you too, but give me some time. I'm doing well, but I just need ... a little time."

"I know. And that's why you need to watch yourself around *him*. Promise me you'll be careful."

"I will."

"Talk to me about what you think you want here. I'm actually way more objective than you are when it comes to the subject of your ex."

I'm not really sure Leilani is more objective, considering how fiercely defensive she gets on my behalf.

"I don't know. My body and heart want him. My head is all over the place."

"This is worse than I thought."

"Worse?"

"You've only been there three weeks and you're already ready to open the doors wide and go back to what you had with him."

"Not back, Lei. Forward. Whatever Bodhi and I do, it's not going to be what we were. We'll have to build something new. And we're just friends anyway. Just friends. Nothing else is happening. Don't worry."

Leilani's kind enough to drop the subject.

She fills me in on the competition. I tune out at times. As much as I want to focus on all she's sharing, it's a bit much, hearing about all the waves and surfers, and who's topping each heat so far. I had almost forgotten what I would have been doing if I hadn't been thrown off that wave at Mavericks.

Mavs.

That name.

I let Bodhi call me Mavs. I haven't stopped him. It doesn't mean Leilani's right. Nothing's happening between me and

Bodhi. We're just building a friendship, and he's trying to make up for abandoning me when everything blew up two years ago.

~

IT'S the second night Shaka's been in the house. He curls at my feet during dinner. He sits quietly on the floor behind Bodhi and me while we rinse dishes and load the dishwasher together. Kai took off right after dinner to help fix a plumbing issue on the other side of the island.

Aren't there plumbers on the island? I had asked him.

She called me, was his answer. She who?

Bodhi and Kai had exchanged a look. Now I'm dying to know who *she* is that has my brother taking off after a long day working at the watersports shack so he can help with a plumbing issue.

With Kai gone it's just me and Bodhi and Shaka.

"Want to watch a movie ... or something?" Bodhi hangs the hand towel on the hook on the wall.

"I could watch a movie."

Bodhi walks into the living room and settles into the couch. Shaka jumps up next to him. Kai's not too pleased that Shaka's helping himself to the furniture, but Bodhi and I outvoted him.

I stand across the room from Bodhi and Shaka, staring at the two of them. He's leaned back, one leg is propped on the other. His arm is draped across the back of the couch. He's casual, comfortable, gorgeous. Everything about him is so familiar—like coming home.

"Come over here, Mavs. I won't bite."

I laugh a little too hard. "Didn't think you would."

"What sounds good? Comedy? Drama? Action?" He looks me right in the eyes. "Romance?"

Romance sounds so good. I could get lost in those bright gray-blue eyes.

"How about comedy." I force myself to hold his gaze even though it's like a portal into our past.

"Great, now get yourself comfortable while I find a movie."

I could choose the overstuffed chair to the side of the couch. Or the love seat on the other side of the room, though I'd have to crane my neck to see the screen. Nope. I go straight for level ten torture and plop myself on the couch next to Bodhi. The only thing separating us is my fluffy defender, Shaka.

Bodhi cues up a movie. He hits another button on the home remote and the lights dim. Another tap and the lamp next to Bodhi on the side table turns on, casting a soft yellow glow across his face.

If this were a game, he could be penalized for cheating.

The movie starts and the first thing I notice is Bodhi's arm —it's still draped across the back of the couch which means every time I lean back, my neck hits his hand. I could sit upright like a girl who has been schooled in perfect posture. I try it for a second and it's just weird. No one sits like they've got a pole running straight from their backside up through the top of their head. I lean back a little to try to see if I can look relaxed while not accidentally bumping Bodhi's hand. Even the slightest contact feels like touching a live wire, sending a frisson tingling through me.

Bodhi's staring straight ahead at the movie, completely oblivious to my struggle. Meanwhile, I'm worse than a kid being told the back of the sofa is lava. It may as well be.

Bodhi shoots an amused glance my way. "You okay over there?"

"Yeah. Just ... getting comfortable."

"Your ankle bothering you?" His forehead bunches in concern.

"It's a little sore at the end of every day. Not bad. It's getting better all the time."

"Here." Bodhi says the word so softly I barely have time to process what he's about to do.

Bodhi gently lifts Shaka so the dog is on the other side of him, and then he bends down and grabs both my feet and places them on his lap, causing my whole body to rotate so that my back is toward the armrest. AND MY FEET ARE IN BODHI'S LAP. Gah.

As if this moment didn't just put us into some sort of Twilight Zone time warp, Bodhi starts using his thumbs to rub the sore arches of my feet. It feels so good. I should make him stop, but I'm not crazy ... sane? ... no, definitely it would be crazy ... enough to make him.

"Lean back," he says, stopping his massaging just long enough to toss me a throw pillow to prop behind my head.

I don't say a word. I should. But this is fine. It's not like we're making out. He's just rubbing my feet. Friends give one another foot rubs. It happens.

A soft moan of appreciation leaves my mouth without warning.

"Good?"

"Mm hmm."

"That's good. I had regular massages as a part of my PT routine while I was regaining my full range of motion. Best part of PT, if you ask me."

"I do PT online."

"I know."

Of course he does. Only, the pressure he's applying to my feet is short-circuiting my brain so I can't remember what he knows or doesn't, or for that matter, why I haven't spent the past three weeks trying to catch his eye again. He rubs circles on my heels and then moves up to the balls of my feet.

"Ahhh." I close my eyes. "So good."

I think I'm having an out-of-body experience—which

would totally explain why I'm allowing my ex to give me a foot massage while we're alone in the house.

The movie drones on in the background. I could pretend to watch it, but why bother?

I decide to give in and just enjoy this since it will be the only time I allow it to happen. Obviously, we aren't making foot massages part of our routine friendship protocol.

"You're really good at this," I say. "I had forgotten."

Drool nearly leaks out of the side of my mouth. Yeah. I'm bringing sexy back. Way to ensure everything stays in the friend zone.

"It's the least I can do. You've been overextending yourself to come watch me surf. I'm glad to help you relax those muscles after a long day."

Time for a subject change!

"So ... that text you got the other day. Are you going to go to San Diego?"

Bodhi's hands still. But then he starts massaging again.

"I haven't made up my mind." His voice is clipped. "You want to try to stick these feet in the ocean tomorrow morning?"

Okay. So that's how this is going to be.

"I haven't made up my mind."

I sit up just the slightest to make eye contact when I repeat his words back to him.

"Fair enough." Bodhi gives a final rub up and down each foot and then he lifts my feet off his lap and sets them onto the ground.

I'm sorry I ruined the mood. But then again, fair's fair. If he's going to push me, shouldn't I be able to push him in return? For the first time since I got here, the thought occurs to me: Bodhi might not have healed as much as I thought he had.

17

BODHI

Just the way it never rains
when you have an umbrella,
you'll never run into people if you look fantastic.
But go outside in pajamas,
and you'll run into every ex you have.
~ Tim Gunn

"I'm actually a little wiped out," I tell Mavs.

We both know better. She pushed my buttons and I don't want to deal with the pressure from one more person. Not her, especially.

I'd do anything for her.

Maybe I shouldn't have been rubbing her feet. No. I definitely shouldn't have been touching her with such familiarity and warmth. Mavs makes me crazy. One minute, I'm dead set on building a friendship with her, repairing what I broke. The next, I want to haul her onto my lap and kiss her until we both remember what we lost and resolve to do anything to get it back.

She looks a little sorry that she pushed me. I probably should say something to relieve her of that weight. But I don't want to give her license to nudge me and hassle me like everyone else has been doing. I'll sleep this off. It's not about her. It's me. People don't understand what it took to get as far as I've come. I'm comfortable. I don't need an in-my-face reminder of how much I've lost. Seeing all those guys and riding waves with them could send me spiraling. It's a risk I can't afford to take.

Contentment. I think Ben Franklin or Abe Lincoln ... maybe it was MLK Jr ... whoever it was, said, *be happy with what you have*. Something like that. Maybe it was Shakespeare. Though it doesn't sound flowery enough to be Shakespeare. He would say, *If thou are not in the happiest way with thine own life, get thee to a contented place*. Yeah. That works too.

"What's so funny?" Mavs asks.

I guess I've been standing here looking down at her thinking about Shakespeare.

"Nothing. Just ... Shakespeare. And contentment. Nothing. I think I'd better call it a night."

Mavs' confused expression is the last thing I see of her. I turn and head down the hall to get ready for bed. The dog slept with Mavs in her bed last night. He's latched onto her and decided she's his person. I don't mind. She needs him more than I do right now. And he's still my buddy. I kind of like the idea of him being in there with her.

I wake in the middle of the night needing to use the restroom—like, big time. I walk from my bedroom to the bathroom Kai and I share. The door is locked.

"You in there?" I ask quietly.

"Yeah." He seems barely awake if his raspy voice is any indication.

I don't have the bandwidth to wait. So I walk down to Mavs' bathroom. She's asleep. The bathroom door is partly open and it's empty. I step in and start to relieve myself. With my back to the door, I'm staring at the wall behind the toilet and the curtains covering the small window looking out toward the alley behind our house.

The next thing I know, the bathroom door pops open and slams back against the wall.

Shaka bounds in, trotting right up behind me and licking my calf.

Then Mavs starts screaming "Oh!" "Oopsie Doopsie!" "Yikes!" "Um!" "Well, this is awkward!" "Sorry!"

I adjust my pajama bottoms, and turn to see Mavs with her eyes scrunched shut and her arms flailing around to grab at the door jamb and the counter.

She brings her hands up to her eyes as if she needs the extra layer of protection and shouts, "Shaka!" "No!" "Bodhi, I'm sorry!" Her voice lowers just a little as the blush rises up her cheeks. "Um ... Okay ... I'll just ..."

Shaka starts barking at Mavs' dramatic reaction. He's yapping at a high pitch and running back and forth between the two of us.

"Everything okay?" Kai's stern but sleepy voice comes from down the hall.

"Fine!" Mavs and I both shout in unison.

Mavs' hands look like they've been glued in place with Gorilla Glue. Her blush is so strong her skin looks a shade darker. So I take a moment and wash my hands.

Mavs stands there, frozen in place with her eyes covered.

The sound of Kai's bedroom door shutting echoes down the hallway.

I can't help but grin at the sight of Mavs. She's freaking adorable.

"Coast is clear. I'm decent." I assure her. "No harm. No foul."

She doesn't drop her hands. "Just ... go back to bed. I'll just ..."

I chuckle again. I step toward her, conflicted as to whether to draw her into my arms to help her relax, or to just clear the room. Better to give her space. But there's no way to pass by and squeeze out the doorway without brushing against her.

"Bodhi! What are you doing?!" Her voice is a whisper, but it's shrill and slightly crazed.

If she'd drop her hands and back out of the way, this would be so much easier. Not that I'm complaining about a chance to be near her.

"I'm heading back to my room. Sorry, sweetheart. I didn't mean to cause a fuss. Your brother was in our bathroom. You were asleep."

"Shaka pushed the bathroom door open." She's explaining this with her heels of her hands still pressed firmly into her eye sockets.

"Okay. Well, it wasn't a big deal. I'm going back to bed. Sweet dreams."

"Like I'll have sweet dreams now," she mutters, still barricading her eyes with the heels of her hands.

I smile and place my hand on her shoulder from where I'm standing behind her in the hallway, intending to give it a reassuring squeeze. But she's warm and soft, and my feelings for her are all pinging off at a high frequency. My defenses are down. I'm half-asleep. That's the only excuse I can find for what I do next.

I brush Mavs' hair back from her shoulder, then I lean down and place a soft kiss on the skin between her neck and her sleep tank.

"Oh." She gasps.

My throat tightens and my heartbeat quickens. I'm a runaway freight train. Before I do something even more reckless than kissing her on the shoulder, I turn and head back to my room.

"Goodnight, Mavs."

"Goodnight, Bodhi."

With my door nearly closed behind me, I turn and glance out into the hallway. Our eyes catch. We stare at one another, silently asking unanswered questions until I shut the door and return to bed.

I toss and turn the rest of the night, the memory of Mavs' skin on my lips, and thoughts as to what I'm going to do now, haunting me until dawn.

∽

I'M BLEARY-EYED, standing in front of the coffee machine with a thousand conflicting emotions and thoughts still bombarding me the next morning. Shaka scratched to be let out of Mavs' room when he heard me passing by. I warily opened her door and he came bolting out. After taking him into the yard to do his business, the two of us took parallel spots in the kitchen, waiting for my morning dose of caffeine to finish brewing. He's a better pet than I imagined he'd be. Maybe he's just thankful for this second chance at living a life he might have had before. We probably make quite a picture: a man and his dog side-by-side waiting for the coffee to brew.

"What's going on with you two?" Kai's voice surprises me.

I turn to see him standing at the kitchen entryway, his arms crossed over his chest.

"Me and Shaka? Nothing." My voice is scratchy from lack of sleep. "Waiting for my first cup of coffee."

"You and Kala. Didn't sound like nothing from my vantage point. I heard a commotion last night. And I don't even want to know what all that was about. I've been meaning to ask you all week. She's at the beach with you every morning. The glances you give one another are heavy with something I've seen before."

Is Kai right? I know I've been sitting on a powder keg full of feelings for Mavs. I don't know where she stands, and my biggest concern is not pushing her or taking advantage of her vulnerability. Would I like a second chance? I'd give just about anything to be with her again—to give us our shot at forever. Am I going to take that risk when she's coming off such a massive lifequake? No. I'm not.

My mind flashes to the moment when I kissed her shoulder last night.

Not my brightest hour. Maybe she'll have been so drowsy and out of it that she won't remember it happened.

"You always saw things that weren't there." I look Kai in the eyes.

"I saw things that were there. Before you did, if you recall. And I warned you off. And then you broke her heart."

Wow.

If my face shows the impact of his words, he's going to know that was a straight shot to my heart. Not that I didn't earn it.

"Sorry," Kai backpedals. "I shouldn't have said that."

Kai's lips pull in and his brows raise into a furrow.

"Really. I'm sorry. I just get so protective when it comes to her. I guess my need to see her come out of this with some semblance of hope and purpose makes me twice the over-bearing brother I've ever been. That comment was uncalled for."

"Not completely. But, trust me, I didn't want to hurt her then. It kills me to think of what she went through after the breakup. And I'd never hurt her now. You've got nothing to worry about."

Kai studies me. I turn and pour my coffee. Shaka sits on the floor looking between the two of us. His ears are tucked back just the slightest and his brows are raised.

Kai surprises me by bending down and ruffling Shaka under the chin and saying, "You're a good boy."

When he stands, he looks me in the eyes and says, "I hope you're right."

I don't head out to surf like I usually would. I probably should, but something in me wants to be here when Mavs wakes up—to get a read on where we stand after our awkward middle of the night rendezvous. Shaka and I sit on the couch while I sip coffee and sort through the myriad of thoughts rolling through my head. The contest. Mavs. Kai.

I've been settling for a certain kind of life. It's a good life, but I'm still settling. It's like taking the bronze and walking away. You still got a prize, just not the gold. And I always went for the gold before my accident.

Ever since I witnessed Mavs take that drop over the falls at Mavericks, I've been off center. A strange sense of restlessness has taken hold of me.

I had resolved to let Mavs go, resigning myself to life here on Marbella. My focus centered on healing and moving on from my past. But I've been fooling myself. I thought I was good. I thought teaching surfing and being the fun single guy would be enough. Ever since Mavs stood at my doorway with her paisley bag and her one crutch, staring into my eyes and making me remember everything I had lost, I discovered my glass has been half empty, or cracked ... unable to provide enough to quench the thirst rising up in me.

I miss competing.

I miss her.

She's right here, only fifteen or twenty feet away from me. Sometimes only mere inches separate us, and yet I miss her with an ache that threatens to consume me.

I used to be a risk-taker. I was known as one of the few men on the planet who put his life on the line regularly to go for what he wanted most. When did that change? When did I become this guy who settles for good enough?

Shaka looks up at me and cocks his head. I run my hand down his neck in soothing strokes.

"Wanna be my emotional support animal?"

He rolls over and shows me his belly.

"Gotcha."

The sound of Mavs' door opening causes both me and the dog to look up expectantly. He flips onto his front, and his tail starts wagging furiously. Then he's off the couch and running in her direction. She rounds the corner and looks up at me through sleepy eyes. Her hair is wild. She's wearing that sleep tank and sleep shorts.

I sip my coffee which is down to the bottom of the cup now. I'm basically slurping air like some actor on a show. Anything to give myself a buffer when all I want to do is walk over to her and pull her into my arms. Maybe I should have hit the waves after all.

"You're still here?"

"I was ... uh ..." *Man up, Merrick.* "I was waiting for you. You know? In case you wanted to talk about last night?"

"Which part? The part where you gave me a foot rub? The part where I pushed your buttons by bringing up the contest? The part where Shaka decided to burst into the bathroom? Or the part where you kissed my neck?"

"Um ... any of the above?"

"Nope. I don't want to talk about any of that. I do want coffee, though."

"Let me get it for you."

"Okay." Her voice comes out more subdued.

I stand and walk toward the kitchen. When I pass by her, I pause and look her in the eyes until she returns my gaze. "Are we good?"

"We're good, Bodhi. Confused. But good."

"Yeah." I smile down at her. "Definitely confused."

"At least that's both of us."

I head into the kitchen to pour her coffee. "I still might hit the waves. I've got a night sail tonight, so I start work late. Wanna walk down with me?"

"I'd love that. Let me get changed."

KALAINE
(OUR THIRD WEEK IN BALI ...)

I like a man who can come out and say he's nervous on the first date.
I think that would be really cute.
~ Sarah Shahi

The knock at our door sends Leilani into a fit of squealing giddiness. "He's here! He's here!"

"Shhhh." I give her a glare. "Can you act normal for just the next five minutes? Then you can go back to being your same crazy self."

"Normal? What is this normal you speak of?"

I smile despite myself, and then glance in the mirror over the desk. I'm wearing a tropical print, halter-neck, backless jumpsuit with flared pant legs. It's not something I'd usually choose. Leilani picked it out for me. She was all, *Ooooh. Bodhi will love this!*

"You look hot, and he's going to love it." Leilani's face fills the mirror from behind me. "Now answer the door."

"Shhhh."

I take a deep breath and walk to the door of our room, pulling it open to reveal Bodhi leaned against the door jamb, wearing khaki pants and a linen collared shirt that's unbuttoned at the top.

"Wow," I say without thinking first.

Bodhi chuckles. "Wow to you too."

"This should be interesting," Leilani says from her spot on her bed.

"Oh, hey, Leilani."

"Hey, Bodhi. I hope you have a night planned that's worthy of my bestie's time."

"Of course."

I grab Bodhi by the elbow and turn him out of our room "Okay! We're going. Goodnight, Lei. Don't wait up."

"Oh, I'm waiting up. Don't you worry."

I shut the door before I can hear the rest of whatever she wants to say to embarrass me. It's a wonder I even have this date between her running her big mouth and Kai's overbearing interference.

Bodhi pauses right outside the door. "You look amazing tonight, Mavs. I'm pretty sure I'm the luckiest guy on the island."

"Mavs? Like in Mavericks?"

"Yeah. It fits you."

I grin. No one besides my family and Leilani ever bothered to give me a nickname.

"I don't have a nickname for you."

"You don't need one. I like when you call me Bodhi."

I know I'm blushing again, and I thank my ancestors for a skin tone that keeps my blush camouflaged at least a little.

"Where are we going?" I ask.

"You said you like surprises, so it's a surprise."

Bodhi puts his hand on my back as he steers me down one of the paths on the resort property. With the top of this jumpsuit being open at the back, his hand hits my skin. Warmth and tingles erupt where he touches me.

"Unless you want me to tell you."

"No. You're right. I love surprises. Surprise me."

"I got us a car."

"You bought me a car!" I laugh. "On the first date!"

Bodhi laughs too. His laugh is deep and rich and full. Bodhi on the waves is a sight to behold. Watching any surfer is a thing of beauty. But Bodhi, walking next to me, laughing at a joke I just told—that's something I'll never forget.

"Here we are," Bodhi says, waving at a sedan. The driver exits the car and introduces himself and then Bodhi and I climb into the back seat.

"To the temple?" he asks.

Bodhi nods and then he looks at me and says, "Surprise!"

"We're going to the Uluwatu Temple?"

"I thought you might like watching the fire dance."

"It is very sacred," our driver informs us. "The temple faces southwest. We have nine directional temples in Bali. They ward off all evil spirits. You will wear a sarong or sash when you come onto the sacred grounds. Because you have long pants, only the sash. They will give it to you when you pay your entrance fee."

We chat with our driver for the short eight minutes from the resort to the temple. Bodhi asks him about his family and good places to eat around Uluwatu. The car pulls up to the temple grounds. Before we exit the car, our driver says, "And watch out for the monkeys."

After Bodhi pays the driver, we walk onto the temple grounds. Bodhi pays the equivalent of about seven dollars and then we are each given an orange scarf to tie around our waists.

"Lookin' good, Mavs. That's just the finishing touch to your outfit."

"Be careful with the monkeys." One of the workers tells us. "They like to steal."

We walk along large stone patios with various stone

pergolas and pavilions to the sides along the way. Some are decorated with solid-colored fabric banners. We're barely onto the property when I start to see the monkeys.

Bodhi takes out his phone and starts filming.

"Look at these monkeys," he says into his mic while he films. "They're everywhere. Hey! Look at that one. He's got a water bottle!"

Sure enough, one of the monkeys along the edge of the path is twisting the cap off a water bottle and chugging the liquid. Then he bores of drinking and literally tosses the bottle so it goes sailing through the air with an arc of water spraying out in its trail.

A crowd is gathered a little way down. When we reach them, we see a monkey holding a cell phone. A man is talking to him in a British accent. "Here, fella. You can have a sweet. It's my last one. Trade, would ya?"

The monkey bares his teeth. Those are some very sharp teeth, and he looks like he knows how to use them. When his mouth is closed, this monkey looks like a little old man, working at a phone repair shop. Because, yes, he has decided to dismantle the phone, starting with adeptly removing the case.

Bodhi puts his hand on my back and guides me away from the crowd. We walk down another stone path that overlooks the limestone cliff leading to the Indian Ocean below. The sun is still up and the water in the cove is a shade of turquoise that makes it look as if someone dumped food coloring into it. I've never seen any part of the ocean so clear and blue in my life—not even the Caribbean.

The driver was right. Monkeys dominate the landscape—sitting on stone pillars, crossing paths, up in trees, on walls. Their gray coats and long tails and tiny human-like faces pop out of nowhere. And they aren't afraid of the tourists at all.

We're walking toward the amphitheater when Bodhi shouts, "Look out!"

I turn just in time to see a monkey literally jumping out of the bushes right at me. He's flying like Batman, arms outstretched and a wild look on his face. He lands on my back with a thump, instantly gripping my hair and the part of my jumper that goes over my shoulder.

I'm freaked out but also laughing hard.

The monkey obviously has no intention of releasing me. In an instant, I remember those sharp teeth of the monkey we saw with the cell phone, so I start shouting, "He's on me! He's on me! Get him off!"

The monkey isn't bothered in the least by my reaction to him. He hangs on to my hair and bends toward my waist. He begins pulling at the flap on my crossbody purse which is resting on my hip.

I love animals. Love them. I'm not loving this monkey clinging to me like I'm his wild monkey mama.

Bodhi's eyes catch mine and when I see he's not freaking out, we both burst into cackling laughter. Bodhi's cracking up so hard, almost to the point where he can't breathe.

I spin in a circle and the monkey hangs on. He starts making this screeching noise while I turn. What does the screeching mean? Is he having fun? Or is he getting dizzy? I come to a stop and he's still attached with a determined grip on my jumpsuit, purse and hair.

A Balinese woman walks up to Bodhi and hands him this fruit that looks like a short, green, fat banana. "Offer him this and he will jump off your girlfriend."

Bodhi's eyes crinkle with his smile. I heard it too.

Girlfriend.

"Are you ready to ditch your hitchhiker, Mavs?"

Mavs. Gah. I love that he gave me a nickname. But there's no time to think about nicknames or the way they make me feel because other monkeys are starting to approach us now that Bodhi has the fruit in his hand.

I glance over my shoulder at my clinging monkey and he looks up at me with a face that could be captioned, *Get used to me. I'm not leaving anytime soon.* He's still got a death grip on my hair. And he's laser focused on trying to unfasten my purse like one of the actors in *National Treasure* sitting in front of a vault. Another monkey leaps off the stone wall across from us, aiming for Bodhi now that he's holding that piece of fruit. The monkeys around us start to screech and shriek in some sort of *There's a banana among us* chant.

Bodhi hurries over next to me and holds the banana thingy toward the monkey on my back. My monkey reaches for the fruit while the other monkey on the ground jumps up at it. Now we're the setting for an official banana war. And my body seems to be the central arena.

People around us start taking their cameras out and filming.

"Walk toward the wall," Bodhi says, his voice focused and serious.

The monkey on my back leans out while perilously balancing on my back and purse and using my hair to stabilize himself like he's the second mate on a catamaran and we're taking a sharp turn. He's reaching for Bodhi's hand, but refusing to dismount his perch—and by perch, I mean me.

The other monkey is jumping up repeatedly at Bodhi's hand trying to get that squatty unripened banana from him. And the chorus of primates around us are still screeching the *happy to see a banana* song.

Bodhi looks me in the eyes and says, "Get ready to run for it!"

He quickly sets the fruit on the wall. Both monkeys jump for it, the one on my back, propelling off my purse and flying toward the fruit. We take off running until we're a short distance away.

"Oh my gosh!" I say through my laughter. "I didn't think he'd ever let go!"

"Are you alright?"

"I am. Really. I think. I'm sure my hair looks like I electrocuted myself."

Bodhi steps behind me to check me out. He lifts my hair and runs a hand up my back. "Your skin is a little pink back here. But you look okay."

Oh man. His touch makes me wish a whole troop of macaques would jump on me, just so he could run a soothing hand over the spot afterward.

Bodhi doesn't lift his hand when we start walking again. He strolls next to me, looking over with a tenderness I know I'll always remember, even years from this night.

"I'll confess I was nervous about you having a good time tonight." His voice is uncharacteristically reserved. "I didn't ever factor in attacking monkeys. Either that was the most memorable date ever, or the most disastrous."

"Can it be both?" I laugh again.

"The night is still young." Bodhi laughs too. "But we might want to get some supplies at the canopy over there, just to have something to barter with the monkeys on the way out."

He points to a pop-up where flip-flops, sarongs and water bottles are being sold. Smart vendors, they know what we'll need most. I guess the monkeys don't only take phones and water bottles when they're pillaging.

Bodhi takes his hand off my back and clasps my hand in his. Our palms connect and there's an unexpected comfort between us. Bodhi interlaces our fingers, and leads me toward the open-air amphitheater. We're seated a few rows up from the cement floor at the center of the theater. The ocean is just beyond the cliff's edge. A short time after we're seated, a large group of men dressed in black and white tartan plaid wraps come out chanting.

"My mom has napkins with that pattern," Bodhi whispers into my ear.

I giggle softly. "Shhh."

He grabs my hand and holds it in his. His thumb rubs over my knuckles in a soothing rhythm.

The men in the center of the amphitheater chant repetitively while swaying and pulsing in the dance movements of what's called the Kecak dance. Other performers enter the arena at various times: women dressed in silks, a guy with his face and body painted white, another guy with what looks like a feathered kabuki mask and outfit on. At times these extra performers mingle into the crowd, rubbing the head of a bald man and making the crowd laugh, or putting an arm around the shoulder of another guest, making faces at us and then returning to the center of the theater with the group of chanting men.

Toward the end of the show, a few performers scatter dried brush on the ground in a circle and then light it on fire and a guy dances through it, kicking it in all directions. Growing up in Hawaii, I'm used to seeing tribal dances and ceremonies. The temple dance we're watching is nothing like what I've ever seen before. All the while, Bodhi holds my hand and occasionally softly brushes his fingers over mine.

When the show is over, we walk out of the amphitheater with a crowd full of people. A group of guys passes us, mimicking the chants we just heard for an hour. The monkeys must have retreated into the trees along the path for the night. The same car is waiting for us when we come out of the temple grounds. Bodhi asks our driver to take us to Single Fin, a surf bar and restaurant that's perched on the pinnacle of a cliff. We order a salad and a pizza to split.

Bodhi and I stare out at the ocean and then back at one another throughout the meal. I could stare at him forever. He's beautiful, and there's this ease and kindness in his eyes that turns playful at times. The way he looks at me—focused on me as if I'm the only person in the room—it's intoxicating.

Bodhi asks me about my childhood in Hawaii. I get him talking about his life growing up in a beach town in California. We share about contests we've ridden in and waves we caught so far since we've been here. We never run out of topics or hit a lull. And we laugh. Not one moment feels awkward between us. It's the perfect date.

When dinner is over, our car takes us back to the cottages at our resort. Bodhi pays the driver and then it's just the two of us on a path lined with tiki lights.

"Let's go look at the stars from the cliff's edge," Bodhi suggests.

His hand is clasping mine again and my heart is light and free, like life could go any direction right now and they'd all be good ones.

"Do you say that to all the girls?"

"I don't. I've been saving all my cheesy lines for you. How am I doing so far?"

"Great." I look up at him.

His features are muted in the darkness of the evening, but the light of the tiki torches and the moon illuminates the cut line of his jaw and the whites of his eyes. "You're doing really great."

"I don't know if I can beat attacking monkeys, but I'd like to try."

Bodhi pauses at the cliff's edge. The Milky Way stretches out across the sky from the horizon, arching over our heads, a pinkish-purple hue radiating off the countless stars clustered amid what looks like clouds. The rest of the sky is black with pinpricks of light scattered as if someone threw a handful of confetti in the air and it stuck there. The sound of the waves beneath us lapping at the shore is the only noise outside my heartbeat, which feels loud and full.

"Come here," Bodhi says.

He extends his arms and I step into them, resting my head

on his chest. He wraps me in his embrace and we stand there, staring out at the ocean together. My breathing evens out and my heart rate settles. I don't know how long it's been since I've been held like this. Maybe I've never been held like *this*.

"This is nice," I say, tilting my head to look up at Bodhi.

"Mmmm. It's very nice." His hand draws a lazy circle on my back and goosebumps rise across my skin where he touches me.

"Kiss me, Bodhi."

His eyes go soft and his lids drop just the slightest. He cups my chin in one of his hands and tilts my face so I'm looking directly into his eyes.

"I've wanted to kiss you for nearly a year." His voice is gravelly and full of emotion. It sends chills through me to hear him so affected by my nearness and words.

"Well, then?"

Bodhi chuckles. But then his mood grows serious. "I really like you, Mavs. I'd like to take you out again. Do I get a second date?"

"You can have a fifth date. Probably even a tenth. Now, kiss me."

His head tips back in laughter. He's still cupping my chin in his palm with a gentleness that makes me feel cherished. When his eyes meet mine again, I watch them shutter closed. Then he's leaning toward my mouth and I'm standing on tiptoes to meet him halfway. His lips touch mine. This kiss is like nothing I've felt before. He's soft and careful, brushing across my mouth, then he's back for more. His hand slides across my cheek to the nape of my neck. His other hand is on my back, pulling me toward him. I loop my hands around his shoulders and hold him to me. He's not the only one who's been waiting for this kiss.

Our kiss carries me away. I'm lost in Bodhi. And I'm pretty sure I never want to be found again.

Bodhi pulls away, leaving one more soft kiss on my lips and then resting his forehead on mine.

"Elephants," he says softly into my hair. "Next time we're riding the elephants."

I chuckle softly. "Yes. Yes to elephants and anything else— anything but monkeys."

He laughs and tugs me near.

I'm basically floating on air when I quietly open the door to my cottage after Bodhi walks me home and kisses me again on my doorstep. I watch him walk away, and he turns and catches me watching. I don't even care that I'm busted. We both just smile big, goofy smiles at one another and then he turns and walks away for the night.

I carefully shut the door so as not to wake Leilani.

I'm about to duck into the bathroom to get ready when the bedroom lamp comes on.

Leilani sits up in bed. "So? How was it? I want to hear every juicy detail! Spill the deets!"

18

BODHI

You can take a surfer out of the surf,
but you can not take the surf out of a surfer.
~ Bob McTavish

Mavs and I walk side-by-side down the street leading to the beach. She's walked with me every morning this week. An entire week has passed since I kissed her shoulder in the middle of the night. I can't shake the way she smelled, the feel of her skin on my lips, the little "oh" sound she made when I stepped over the line—a line I can't risk crossing again. But I'll never forget the sweetness of what passed between us, like a stolen piece of chocolate melting into my urchin heart.

I may mark the rest of my life by that kiss. Before shoulder. After shoulder.

Shaka follows along behind us, sometimes to one side or the other of us, but he never ventures ahead. You have to spend months training most dogs to walk in a pack formation, following their leaders. Not Shaka. He's so aware of where he came from, he'll never risk being left behind, and he'd rather stay home than consider outrunning us.

He's still sleeping in Mavs' bed every night. We've got a little routine going.

He whines when he hears me walk through the hallway each morning. Mavs sleeps through his plea to come out. I crack her door and he trots out to join me in the pre-dawn darkness of the hallway. I let him out to do his business, and then he and I take our spots in the kitchen staring at the coffee pot while I brew enough for me and Mavs.

Once the coffee is ready, I crack Mavs' door open again, and Shaka leaps onto her bed, smothering her in kisses until she rouses and joins us for the morning surf.

No. She's not surfing—yet.

Yes. I ask her every day.

It's gotten nearly comical and slightly frustrating—our little exchanges. I ask. She declines. I playfully push. She pushes back.

But I'm relentless for her. She needs this. Maybe what I needed was Kai leaving me alone just enough so I would make the decision to get back in the water on my own. But Mavs isn't me. She needs me to annoy her until she gets so riled up she faces the ocean just to spite me or to shut me up.

I'm switching it up on her today to make things interesting and to keep her on her toes.

"I'm not going to ask you this morning."

"To ask me to surf?"

"Yep. Not asking."

"Why?" She narrows her eyes at me.

"I'm sick of being a pain in your tush. You'll ride when you're good and ready."

"Or not."

She's feisty. That's a good sign. Better than the hopeless resignation I've seen her slip into on occasion.

"Or not. But the way I figure it, you wet your feet in the shower. You even soaked your feet in that little foot massaging tub Kai got for you. What's the difference between that and the ocean? You might want to put your feet in the shorepound—especially today."

"What makes today so special?" Her expression is curious, or skeptical, I can't tell.

"I'm thinking of taking Shaka out."

"What? Bodhi! No! He's not a surf dog. He could get hurt."

This is not the answer Mavs would ever have given before her accident.

"I'm not going to let anything happen to him on my watch. I'm just going to play around with him in the shallow stuff. Let him stand on the board, get a feel for whether he'd like it or not."

Mavs' brows raise high, her eyes go wide and her mouth turns down.

"Mavs." I stop walking.

We're right at the edge of the sand. Shaka stops right beside us and looks up.

"I won't let anything happen. I promise."

Her face softens. "Okay. I know. You won't. Sorry."

I put my hands on her biceps and stare down into her eyes. "I get it. I've been right where you are, only I dragged my feet a heck of a lot longer, and I couldn't get a foothold strong enough to move forward. You're already rocking this stage of your recovery. And I'm not rushing you. I know how it feels. If you really don't want me to take Shaka out into the water, I'll just go out myself. I can try this with him another day—or never."

"No. You're right. This isn't the same."

Mavs' unspoken meaning hangs between us. The ocean still feels universally dangerous and unpredictable to her. It's gone from playground to death trap in her eyes. And she's not sure she can ever trust it again. Trust is a delicate thing—so easily shattered, and painstaking to repair. I should know.

I ache to lean in and hold Mavs—to comfort her and let her know she's not as stuck as she feels. I smile at her and step back so I don't follow through with my urge to place a reassuring kiss on her forehead. As if I could keep it at that. Even the thought of kissing her forehead makes me think of kissing her lips.

"Okay, then. Let's go have some fun in the shorepound."

We stop at the watersports shack and grab my board. I throw on a wetsuit, and then we head down the wooden steps off the dock onto the sand. Mavs leads the way to the same spot where I usually put in, dropping our bag onto the sand. She's walking as if she never injured her leg now that the boot is off. Summer's even planning a celebration of some sort for Mavs this weekend down here on the beach. We don't have as many bonfires in the winter months out here, but her healing definitely calls for one.

I'm about to head into the water when I am stopped in my tracks. Mavs is slipping off her flip-flops and setting them by the pile of our towels. I stand stock still like a statue titled, *Man Holding His Breath*. Even if I wanted to move forward, I wouldn't be able. This moment feels sacred and precarious.

Mavs walks toward the edge of the water and stares out at the ocean as if she's looking for Mavericks in the distance. A smaller wave comes up, folds, and sloshes onto shore, spreading out in a curved, foamy tide only less than an inch deep. One of Mavs' feet is enveloped by the gentle uprush of saltwater. She glances down, watching the sand sink just the slightest in the shape of her footprint on the water's edge.

She always made her mark in the ocean, then the ocean left its mark in her. And now, together they are marking off a new beginning. It may seem like nothing. To any passerby, this would be a surfer and his girl, waiting for the early break. She's just another woman with her foot in the swash.

A tear forms in the corner of my eye as she steps forward, putting both feet in until she's ankle deep. Shaka must sense the potent meaning of her decision because he walks up right next to her, getting all four of his paws wet a third of the way up his legs, and then he just stands there with her in this canine show of solidarity.

Not a surf dog? He's definitely a surf dog. I'm half wondering if he's an angel.

Mavs looks over at me, her face a combination of wonder and pride. My smile breaks free and I drop my board and stride toward her.

"That's what I'm talking about, Mavs! You did this!"

"I put my feet in some slush, Bodhi. Let's not get carried away here."

"Right. No big. You're just wetting your toes. Gotcha."

I look down at her and she smiles up at me.

I pick her up by the waist and spin her around.

Her hands grasp my shoulders and she squeals. I'll never forget the look of unbounded joy in her eyes. I know I'm smiling from ear to ear. Shaka jumps around at our feet barking and leaping.

"Bodhi! What are you doing?"

"Nothing." I set Mavs down. "Nothing at all. Just getting super carried away over absolutely nothing."

Mavs dips her head down, looking at her feet—where they are both covered in the incoming low waves. Then she looks back up at me.

"Why was I making this into such a big deal? What's so big about this?" Her brows bunch together.

"Everything." I pin her with my gaze. "Everything."

I pick up my board and head into the waves, needing to work out this adrenaline, and to put some space between me and Mavs. She feels like she's mine again. My schedule, my thoughts, my heart all rotate around her now. I don't have any right to make that claim. I told her I'd build a friendship—that I'd repair what I'd broken. She's making strides, but she's not finished. She's barely taking her first baby steps. I need to keep myself in check—for her sake.

When I finish about an hour's worth of riding, I take a wave in. Mavs and Shaka sit on the beach. He's wet from head to toe, and she's got a towel around her shoulders and another underneath her to keep the sand away.

I place my board in the shorepound, far enough onto the sand that it won't get tugged out to sea. Then I call Shaka over. He comes right away. I sit cross-legged on the back of the board and slap the nose.

"Come on, boy. Come on up here."

Mavs smiles over at us. The fear from this morning evidently washed away in the saltwater.

Shaka steps onto the board, standing right in front of me and licking my face while his tail wags. He thinks he's just greeting me after I've been gone out on the waves. I know better. I'm getting him used to the board. Everything worth having is worth the incremental steps of getting there. I'm learning exactly how patient I can be these days.

"Sit." I lift my finger and Shaka sits.

It's become obvious he learned some basic commands from someone at one point or another. Kai insisted we put a listing on *Island This-N-That* on the web. No one claimed Shaka. Still, he was someone's dog at one point. But now he's ours. Mine. Mavs'. Hers, I guess.

"Stay." I stand slowly, keeping my body language loose and confident.

Shaka stays on the board when I stand. I walk to the side and he looks up at me with expectant eyes. He's waiting for my next command. I let him sit there a little bit and then I call him off the board.

He runs over to Mavs and she loves all over him. "Good boy! You're such a good boy."

He's doing so well, I decide to push things just a little further. I turn the board so the nose points into the surf.

"Come 'mere, Shaka. Come." He trots over to me.

I sit on the board and then I call him. He comes willingly. When he's on the board again, I pull him into my lap between my spread legs so he's facing the ocean with his back toward me. Then I stick my leg off the board and use my foot to push us just the slightest so we're bobbing and moving in the low water. Shaka leans into me, but he's not freaking out. We bob like that for a minute and then I let go of my grip on his chest and he immediately dives off into the water, and makes a bounding run through the low waves to safety—aka Mavs.

She takes the towel off her shoulders and rubs it all over him, all the while telling him how brave he is. She ought to know. I've never met anyone braver than Kalaine.

"So, what am I supposed to dry off with now?" I tease as I lug my board onto the sand.

"You'll figure it out." Mavs smirks.

"I see how it is."

She smiles at me and grabs up the towels and our bag while I lift my board. We walk toward the watersports shack in silence.

When we're up on the dock, I stash my board, lower my wetsuit zipper and rinse off.

I'm about to head in to grab my clothes when Mavs says, "I'm not fully ready to make peace with the ocean, Bodhi."

I stop and turn toward her. "I get it. You don't make peace with something that broke you all at once. You did a big thing today. Huge. It might seem like nothing. We both know what it took. I promise I won't push you—much. You'll get there. I'll just wait til you're ready."

"What if I'm never ready?" Her voice is small again.

"You'll do whatever you decide is right. In your time. Don't ruin the joy of what you accomplished today with worries about what's next. One person's inch is another person's marathon. Give yourself some credit. 'K?"

"Yeah." She smiles shyly over at me. "And thanks, Bodhi. I wouldn't have done this without you."

"That's what I'm here for." I smile and wink at her. "Certified watersports instructor at your service."

I have to make light of things. If I don't, I'll mess it all up. And I already did that one too many times with her.

19

KALAINE

I don't want to dream of you anymore.
I want you for real.
~ Unknown

"Okay. So, let me get this straight," Leilani laughs so hard she has to take a break from talking. "At your beach house there's a new day of the week?"

"What? What do you mean?" I'm confused, but I can't help but smile at the way Leilani is cracking up.

She laughs some more. "Friday, Saturday, Sunday ... and MOONday!"

Now she's cackling.

"He didn't moon me. Lei. Calm down." I wait. "Lei. Seriously." She's still laughing at her own joke. "I said he didn't moon me. The dog popped the door open."

"I know. I know! And you were shouting and covering your eyes and flailing around ... and then. Whew, girl. This is my favorite part."

"Let's not."

"Oh, no. Let's. Then he brushes past you while you're acting like all three of the emoji monkeys—trying to cover your eyes, ears and mouth all at once! And then he smoothed your hair off your shoulder and placed a soft kiss on your neck? Oh, sweet friend. You are in trouble with a capital T and a final letter E and all the letters in between. I am so buying my ticket to California. Hold the phone while I pull up my travel app."

"Stop it." I'm grinning despite her teasing.

She's so ridiculous I have to smile.

"So? What is the upshot? Are you two pursuing something again, despite my best attempts to warn you not to go there?"

"No. That's the end of the story—the story you can tell better than me now, apparently. Nothing more. We're just going through the motions."

"Mm hmm. And what motions are those exactly?" I can almost see the mischievous glint in her eye.

"Get your head out of the gutter. The motions of living in the same house as good friends who used to date."

"Let me check something. Hold that thought." She pauses, so I wait. "Oh. Yeah. I checked. The last time my friend softly brushed my hair away from my shoulder and kissed my neck was ... um ... let me see here ... yep. The twelfth of never."

"It was nothing. He was half asleep. It was probably an automatic reaction—him acting on a memory. He didn't put two and two together. He was basically sleepwalking. I shouldn't have even told you."

"What? No—no, no, no. You don't start holding out on me. Promise me. You need me. Remember, I'm the voice of reason."

"If you're my voice of reason, I can only imagine what my voice of insanity sounds like."

"Ha. Ha. Truthfully, though. You sound good. Lighter."

"I feel good. The boot is off. I walk to the beach every morning. I even put my feet in the water."

"That's awesome! Does that mean you're getting ready to get on a board again?"

"I'm ... I'm not sure. Not yet."

"Okay. That's fine. No rush. You can take your time getting back into things. You'll get yourself built back up eventually. We're all here when you're ready. Dan's here. He's working with a team for a while, but you and I both know he'll take you on privately as soon as you say the word. Your sponsorships are all on hold, but they'll support you when you come back."

"That's all great. Thanks, Lei."

I stare out the window of the kitchen. I've been mindlessly chewing a cuticle while Leilani gave me a rundown of all the people who are eagerly awaiting my return to surfing. Shaka's running through the yard chasing a seagull who landed there a minute ago. I watch him make a half-baked attempt at a jump toward the gull. Then he trots toward the back door and I walk over to let him in.

"I better go. I'm meeting someone for coffee."

"A hot guy?"

"No, not a hot guy. A friend of Kai and Bodhi's ... Um. Actually, it's Summer Monroe."

"Shut the front door! You are having coffee with Summer Monroe?"

"Yeah. Her boyfriend works for Kai. We've been hanging out a little since I got here."

"Kai is the boss of Summer Monroe's boyfriend. Man. Your brother just went up a notch in my book."

"Like he needed to go up a notch. You always had a crush on him. Don't promote him too far. He's still an overbearing pain at times."

"I *had* a crush. I'm over that. Though, I'd love to officially be your sister. But that's not reason enough to throw myself at your brother. I'm finished chasing men who need to be convinced

I'm awesome. And, you might gripe about him being overbearing, but you love him."

"So much."

"Okay. Well, call me tomorrow or Friday."

"I will. Love you, Lei."

"Love you too, Kah."

We hang up. I get ready, put Shaka back out into the yard, and then I grab the used bike Kai got for me and ride over to C-Side coffee to meet Summer. There aren't words for what it feels like to be on a bicycle. My life's still aimless and far too dependent on my brother. When I'm on a bike with the breeze in my hair and the sun in my face, I can forget how stuck I am. At least for the short ride from Kai and Bodhi's to C-Side, I'm carefree and adventuresome again.

Summer's sitting at the coffee bar, chatting with Riley when I walk in.

"Kalaine!" Summer shouts. "You have to try this new drink Riley made."

"Okay. I'm game." I slip onto the stool next to Summer.

"It's called the Monroe. I personally hate the name, but the drink is worth the humiliation."

"Why would having a drink named after you be humiliating?" Riley asks Summer.

"I don't want to be that person."

"You're not that person. I am. I named the drink after one of my closest friends who happens to be a local celebrity."

Clarissa, the owner of C-Side comes in from the patio. "Oh, hi, Kalaine. Look at you! No boot."

"Yep," Summer says as if she healed me herself. "We're planning a party ... a bootless bonfire. Boots-off? Buh-bye bootie? I like big boots? ... I'm working on the name."

The four of us laugh.

"We don't need to name it," I offer. "And you don't need to throw a party. I don't really know that many people here."

"Oh. We need the party. And we need to theme it, shugah."
Summer's voice takes on that soft southern lilt. "Besides, what
better way to get to know people than at a party in your
honor?"

"Don't even try to dissuade her," Riley says.

She sets a drink in front of me. "The Monroe. Let me know
what you think."

The drink is beautiful. Caramel drizzle lines the inside of
my glass. There's a cold foam topped with more caramel drizzle
and what looks like a sprinkling of cinnamon and these little
brown sugar crystals.

I take a sip. "Mmmm. That's so good."

Riley beams. "It's cinnamon and caramel with vanilla cold
brew. It encompasses both the sweet and sassy sides of Summer
Monroe. It's gorgeous and complex, but surprisingly your
favorite once you give it a try."

"Awww," Summer smiles at Riley. "That's almost a compliment. And so so true. I'm an acquired taste."

"I never got sassy vibes from you," I tell Summer.

"Me neither," Riley agrees. "But I've seen Summer in action.
Trust me. You're just glad you weren't the sad puppy dog trying
to win her heart."

Summer laughs. "He won it. So ..."

Riley just smiles.

"Oh!" Summer turns to me. "Did Phyllis get a hold of you
yet?"

"No. Why?"

"Her niece Mila runs a bed and breakfast. I think Phyllis
told you about her. Anyway, Mila needs someone to work the
front desk at her place part-time. There's no physical labor
involved. It would be something to do. A way to make a little
money ... I thought of you."

"Wow. Okay."

"Okay, you'll do it?"

"Okay, that's totally random, and I don't know what to say."

"Well, Phyllis is going to call you. I gave her your number. Once she gets an idea in her head, it's pretty much going to happen. So, unless you don't want to work right now, I think you've got yourself a new job."

I grew up on an island. And locals on the North Shore all know one another or know someone who knows someone. We're separated by one or two degrees of separation. There are only around sixteen thousand permanent residents on our side of Oahu. I know how island life can be similar to any small-town. But this way of doing things is next level, to be sure.

The air in the coffee shop feels charged. That's the only way I can describe it. I turn to look toward the door and realize why. Bodhi just walked in, his wavy hair tousled, a big smile on his face, and his gaze focused on me. I'd be lying if I said he didn't affect me.

"What's up, people?" His casual air makes everyone in the place smile.

I haven't seen him around a group for a while. I almost forgot how charismatic he is with everyone, not just me.

"Hey, Bodhi!" Summer beams at him.

If I didn't know she was engaged, I'd be jealous.

I can't be jealous. Bodhi's not mine. He's free to date and draw in whatever female attention he wants. But then his eyes drift to mine and his smile grows. He walks over to the stool where I'm sitting.

"Mavs." He winks.

My responding smile is automatic. And then I'm thinking of him kissing my shoulder and the way he spun me around after I put my feet in the shorepound.

He leans his arms on the bar, placing himself right between Summer and me, and looking Riley in the eyes. "Tell me what's good."

Riley's married, I remind myself.

Leilani's right. I'm in trouble.

"I just made a Monroe for Kalaine."

"No way! You got your own drink?" He smiles at Summer. Then he looks at Riley and says, "Make me a Bodhi."

Riley laughs. "Okay. Challenge accepted." She studies Bodhi for a minute, and then it's like a little light bulb goes off over her head.

Bodhi turns toward me, tilting so his back is facing Summer. "What are you up to today?"

"Just meeting Summer here for coffee."

"And considering her job options," Summer unhelpfully adds.

"Job options?" Bodhi asks, still aiming those blue-gray eyes at me. There's a touch of green in them today, making him all the more alluring and possibly mischievous.

Bodhi's too near. His charm feels too potent. My hand could simply raise from the bar and drag along his jawline, or rest softly on his chest. I could wrap my fingers in his.

We used to constantly touch one another when we were a couple. We're physical people—athletes, both affectionate by nature. When Bodhi was mine, I'd never have gone this long after he entered a room without touching him. He's driving me crazy.

I look over his shoulder at Summer. "Tell Mila I'll consider the position."

"Yippee! That's such good news. She's going to be so happy."

"You're taking a job at Mila's? That's great, Mavs. It will be so good for you to have something to do. A job gives a person a reason to get up every morning."

"I do have a reason," I pause and look at him, aware of what that sounds like. "Shaka. I'm up for Shaka."

"Shaka, huh?"

Bodhi looks down into my eyes and straight through to my

soul. He knows what gets me up every day. And that's why I need a job, pronto.

He chuckles, and turns so he's facing the bar again. Then he tilts his head in my direction. "Getting up for Shaka's not the same as having a job, and you know it."

Nothing is the same. Nothing.

Riley sets a drink in front of Bodhi. It's iced and the colors bleed together in liquid layers: a translucent minty green, then light yellow with a red layer on the bottom.

"Give it a stir before drinking," Riley says. "The layers are just for show."

Bodhi spins the straw in the drink and it turns a peachy orange. Like magic.

"What's this called?" He looks up at Riley.

"It's the Bodhi. If you approve."

Bodhi takes a sip. "Riley. You are pure genius. What's in this? It's the bomb."

"Green coffee extract, lemonade, and cherry syrup, all over crushed ice. I make the syrup from scratch here at the shop. This drink's chill and beachy and fun—like you."

Bodhi smiles at Riley. "Mavs. You gotta try this."

Bodhi holds the drink up to my mouth and I take a sip through the same straw he did. Our eyes connect. I close mine, but it doesn't help. I can't shut him out anymore. I don't even know if I want to.

"Delicious," I tell Riley.

"Right?" Bodhi smiles triumphantly. "I got a drink named after me. Man. I can retire in peace now."

He seems playful, but a note of wistfulness trails behind his words. I'm probably the only one who notices. There's no hiding the nuances of what we're feeling or thinking from one another.

Bodhi sips his drink, chatting comfortably with the four of us while he rests between me and Summer. He's so close, and yet completely off-limits. When he sets his empty glass on the counter, he thanks Riley, and then he heads back out to the watersports shack.

I watch him go, completely lost in my own thoughts while my head swivels in his direction.

"So?" Summer looks at me pointedly when I turn my head back toward the coffee bar.

"Hmmm?"

"Your thoughts on Bodhi ..."

"My thoughts?"

"How is it going? You're looking at him like he's a steak and you're one of the guys on Dude Perfect."

I chuckle. "It's complicated."

"Oh, girl."

Riley and Summer share a look, and then Clarissa says, "Complicated is the touchstone of all good romances. Imagine a simple romance? Boy meets girl. They fall in love. The end. Bo-ring."

"That was us, though." I shock myself by sharing so easily. "We fell quickly and easily, and never had an ounce of drama—unless you count my brother being none too happy about his best friend dating his baby sister."

It's just the four of us at the bar. The other patrons are all engaged in conversations around the room or out on the patio.

I tell them all about how Bodhi and I met and started dating. I wrap up my story by saying, "When I met him, that piece of me recognized him as my missing counterpart—like a ship pulling into the harbor and finding its slip. I've never felt so drawn to anyone in my life. It sounds crazy when I describe it out loud."

"Soulmates." Clarissa nods in an understanding way.

"I don't know if I believe in soulmates," I confess. "But I definitely know we had something special. I've never felt anything near what we had with anyone else."

"You're talking in the past tense," Riley notes.

"Yeah. Well. We're building a friendship now. We went through a gnarly breakup." I don't elaborate. My face probably tells enough of the story anyway.

"If my *friend* looked at me the way Bodhi just looked at you, Ben would take him out back and have words." Summer puts air quotes around the word *friend*.

"Bodhi's like that with everyone. You all know him well enough to know that. He is my friend. Trust me. That's all we are now."

"Um. No. Nope." Riley smiles at me. "Sure, he's got that easy way about him and he looks directly at anyone and everyone with those soulful eyes of his. Not to mention his charming smile which he freely flashes whenever he enters a room. He's definitely winsome and has a special magnetism. The best part is, he's sincere.

"But I've never seen him so into someone. It's like the whole world disappears when he looks at you. You might be building a friendship, but I see a man fighting hard not to push you even though every cell in his body wants you back."

I just stare at Riley.

Summer looks at me with a smirky smile on her face.

"Sometimes, Kalaine, a man needs a stop sign. Then there are times he needs a green light. And I think I know what we're going to do in your case."

I'm not sure what Summer has in mind, or if I'm even fully on board with it. But if it means giving me and Bodhi a chance at a relationship again, I might be willing to try whatever she suggests.

BODHI

(OUR SIXTH MONTH OFFICIALLY DATING LONG DISTANCE)

For the two of us, home isn't a place. It is a person.
And we are finally home.
~ Stephanie Perkins

I reread Kalaine's last texts to me as the plane slowly rolls toward the terminal. After hours over the open ocean, the shoreline of Oahu came into view. I haven't stopped smiling since I saw the green hills and palm trees of the island out the airplane window.

> **Kalaine:** *I'm so excited you're coming to Oahu! Only six more hours til I see you!*
> **Bodhi:** *Can't wait. You're the best part of this trip. By far.*
> **Kalaine:** *Not the contest?*
> **Bodhi:** *What contest?*
> **Kalaine:** *Good one. You've only been preparing for this since we left Bali.*
> **Bodhi:** *Right. That contest. Well, I'm stoked for that too. But not half as stoked as I am to see you.*

Kalaine: *I wish you could see my smile right now. You always make me smile, Bo.*

Bo. Kalaine decided I needed a nickname. I've never had one, which is slightly peculiar considering how many surfers end up being known by some random name like Gull or Spaz or Howler. I know three guys with those exact names. I don't even know Howler's real name since he doesn't do contests. Sometimes that's the only way we learn one another's given names—the competition rank board gives them away. But since surfing is the coolest sport on the planet, they always include our nicknames on the board in the middle of our actual names.

The passengers around me rustle in their seats. As soon as the pilot turns off the seatbelt signs, everyone's up and grabbing their carry-ons, restlessly looking at one another and shooting glances toward the front of the plane. After our early six-hour flight out of LA this morning, we're all ready to stretch our legs and get on with whatever we've got going here on the islands.

I've only got a backpack with me. My duffle and board are checked.

I follow the rest of the passengers to baggage claim and wait for my stuff to drop onto the carousel. I'm standing with my bag at my feet when a pair of hands comes around from behind me, enveloping my face and covering my eyes. I feel the press of her body on my back, and I inhale the smell of sun, tropical flowers and pure joy.

"Guess who!" Kalaine's cheerful voice surrounds me like a dream I never want to wake from.

"Is it Kai?"

Kalaine giggles. I pivot around and grab her by the waist, picking her up and spinning her once and then dropping her slowly so she slides down my chest until her feet hit the floor.

"I couldn't decide if I wanted to greet you that way or with a running leap into your arms."

"Want to do both?" I offer.

"No." Kalaine softly shakes her head. "Not now that I'm already here with you." Her arms loop around my neck, and she says, "Kiss me, Bodhi."

I've teased her ever since that first date for being the one who demanded a kiss from me. As if I wasn't going to make sure I kissed her that night, and any chance I got after that.

"Why don't you kiss me?" I tease.

"You don't have to ask me twice."

Kalaine stands on tiptoes. When our mouths finally connect, I'm home. I run my hand down her hair. A hibiscus flower is tucked behind one ear but the rest falls down her back in long, full waves. Kalaine grips the back of my neck like she's trying to keep me in Hawaii and never let me return to the mainland. My hands rest on her hips, holding her with equal intensity and need. This kiss is better than riding the winter breaks at Point Conception. She's exhilarating, a rush, consuming. And our kiss is about to move from *Welcome to Hawaii* to *cover your children's eyes*, so I pull away, brushing one last soft kiss across her lips. Kalaine looks up at me and then she wraps her arms around my waist and rests her head on my chest.

The luggage starts to drop, so I reluctantly release Kalaine to collect my bag and my board. She grabs my duffle from me so I can carry my board more efficiently.

On our way out the sliding glass doors, Kalaine spontaneously twirls, her head tilted back, the arm not gripping my bag outstretched. It's like the scene in that old movie, *The Sound of Music*. Kalaine's completely unconcerned with anyone watching her. And people are, of course, stopping to stare at the beautiful Hawaiian woman spinning in the middle of an airport like she's got exactly zero cares in the world. Her bliss is contagious. And addictive. I can't get enough of her.

After nine weeks of nearly constant time together in Bali, Kalaine and I have only seen one another once for the Mobile Gold Coast Pro event back in May in Queensland. Since then, it's been four months of not seeing one another face-to-face. Four months trying to exist on the poor substitute of video chats, phone calls, and texting. No touching her, no holding her, no hanging out together on the beach. Long distance sucks. It's something I plan to fix as soon as I'm able. Living miles away from Mavs only did me one favor. It showed me she's the most important person in my life now. I've had time and perspective to convince myself of what I really want with her.

I'm not the type to settle down. As a child of divorce, I know it's natural I'd be gun shy. But no matter my circumstances, I was born with the spirit of a nomad. My mother always said that. She'd say, "Bodhi, you're going to leave me one day to go explore the world, and I'd be cruel to stop you." Mom's the only thing keeping me tethered to California. But she's met Mavs over some video chats, and more importantly, she's witnessed me falling hard for the beauty walking out the doors ahead of me right now.

Kalaine slows to allow me to catch up with her. She smiles up at me and all's right in the world.

Two wild chickens strut on the ground between us, pecking at random things on the sidewalk.

I look down at Kalaine. She's gotten even more beautiful over the past four months. How is that even possible?

"How did I ever stay away from you for four months? You're like the sun."

"Hot?" She wags her eyebrows at me and winks.

"So hot. And I think you've also become my center of gravity."

Kalaine stops right on the sidewalk between the terminal

and the street, while passengers and locals shuffle past us. She leans in and places a kiss on my cheek. "I like that."

"I love ... it." I nearly spill all my feelings for her right on the spot.

The words have been on the tip of my tongue a hundred times. More like thousands. But I want to say them when the time is right, not over a phone call. And not the second I land for this visit. I'll find the right time.

But leave it up to Kalaine, my free-spirited, light-hearted girl. She looks up into my eyes and her voice softens. "Me too, Bodhi. I love it. I love you."

She says it so easily I almost miss it.

Is it too soon to feel this much?

I never knew love could be so wholly consuming. The only other thing on earth that ever gripped me—mind, body, and soul—has been surfing. I've given my life to it, regularly risked my life for the biggest and best waves on the planet. Now, I'd give all that up just to know I could have her. Thankfully, I don't have to choose. I can be a pro surfer and have the love of the most intriguing, delightful, beautiful woman on earth.

When I look at her, there's no doubt. "I love you too, Mavs ... Kalaine. I love you."

"I know you do." She smiles that full smile of hers—the one where her whole face gets in on the action—and then she grabs my hand and drags me further into the balmy Hawaiian air.

"Aloha, Bodhi." She smiles up at me. "Welcome to Hawaii."

"Aloha, love." I kiss her on the forehead and wrap my free arm around her, shifting so I can still tote my board in the other. Then I look toward the parking spaces across the airport street to see my best friend standing on the driver's side of a Jeep staring at the two of us with a pensive expression on his face.

When we approach Kai, he smiles warmly at me.

"Hey, dude! Glad you made it. Welcome back to Hawaii."

"It's good to be here."

I prop my board on the side of the Jeep, and Kai and I give one another a bro hug.

Once my board is on the roof rack, I take the back seat so Mavs can sit up front next to Kai while he drives. It takes a little over a half hour to drive from the Honolulu airport to the North Shore where Kai and Mavs live with their parents. We talk about the competition, who's already here, and the forecast. Surfers watch the weather more than the local meteorologists. We need to know when to expect a swell or a riptide. The moon cycle, wind currents, even storms halfway around the world all impact conditions.

Outside the Jeep, the big city gives way to more wide open spaces and mountains off in the distance. Thick clusters of Bana grass and trees line the roadside. Before long we're in Haleiwa, a small town on the North Shore just before all the major breaks.

I'm the houseguest, staying with my girlfriend's parents the same day I meet them. And with my best friend, who acts happy to see me, but also, like he wouldn't mind drowning me for dating his sister when he told me not to. No big.

The Kapule family's home is on a side street off Kamehameha Highway. The yards are filled with palms and mango trees and low growing tropical plants. A waist-high stone wall runs along the front of the property and their house sits back, elevated with a porch wrapping around the front and sides. Kai pulls the Jeep up the driveway that runs alongside the house.

Mrs. Kapule comes out through the front door. She's a short woman with a round figure and one of the broadest smiles I've ever seen. She's wearing a flowered Hawaiian sundress and her hair is pulled up with combs on both sides.

"Aloha, Bodhi! Welcome to our home!" She steps off the porch and approaches the Jeep.

"We should have warned him," Mavs says to Kai in a low voice.

"Nah. He asked for this when he started dating you." Kai looks at me through the rearview mirror and smiles a smile that reeks of sweet vindication.

I brace myself for whatever they think they should have warned me about. As soon as the door opens and I step out of the backseat, Mrs. Kapule rushes me with a force that would knock me off my board if I were in the water. She wraps her arms around me and hugs me tightly. My arms are pinned to my sides, so I stand stock still while she holds me in a vice grip hug with strength I wouldn't have guessed she had.

"Okay, Mom. That's plenty," Mavs says from behind her mom.

Mrs. Kapule steps back and looks me over. "Yes. Good. He's good."

"Oh my gosh. Mom. Stop."

"No. Mom," Kai says with mischief in his tone. "Go for it. Bodhi loves hugs. Don't ya, Bodhi?"

He's testing me, and maybe getting even for the fact that Kalaine and I are growing so close. It has made my relationship with Kai a little awkward, to be sure. But I'm counting on the fact that we'll work through the initial discomfort in time.

"Yep. I'm a hugger." I chuckle and wink at Mavs.

"I'm so glad you are here," Mrs. Kapule beams up at me. "Kalaine's father will be home later. He's at the shop now. You will have to visit him at his work while you are here."

Kalaine's dad owns a surf shop in town and is known by locals for shaping boards.

"I'd love that," I tell Mrs. Kapule. "I've been wanting to learn more about shaping someday. Maybe when I retire from the circuit."

"You should learn now. If you're like most surfers, you'll say you're retiring, but you'll keep on going until the ocean tells you she is finished with you. And even then you will pout like a baby losing his favorite toy. It's always the same no matter when it happens. So, learn now. Don't put things off until when you stop surfing in competitions."

I nod. She's probably not wrong.

We carry my things inside and Kai shows me to my room. Then Mavs borrows the keys to Kai's Jeep and the two of us take off for Waimea, only five or six miles up the coast from where Kai and Mavs grew up. The waves aren't huge right now, but we're expecting the results of a tropical storm at sea over the next few days, so we should have impressive waves for the competition.

Mavs and I park the Jeep and walk to the shore. We find a spot on the sand and I sit. She nestles down between my legs and leans back on me. We stare out at the water, my chin resting on her shoulder, her hair blowing into my face and getting tangled in my beard at times. I've grown it out a little because Mavs said she liked it that way. Anything for her. Anything.

"I can't believe you're here." She tilts her head so she can look up at me from over her shoulder, swiping her hair to the side over her other shoulder so nothing separates us.

"I can't either. And you're right here in my arms. I never want to leave you again."

"You don't have to leave for seven days. So, let's just not think about it, okay?"

"Not at all?"

"Not at all. I want to pretend you're here for good. That way we don't waste any of this week being sad about you leaving."

"Okay." I place a soft kiss on the top of her head.

Mavs swivels and kisses my lips. We sit there, on one of my favorite beaches in the world, kissing and talking until we have to head back to her family's house for dinner.

That week, Mavs, Kai and I all ride in the competition. I

come in second in the men's contests and Mavs takes first place among the women. When we're not in the water, we take hikes, lay on the beach, or hit a few local hotspots. The three of us hang out together: Mavs, Kai and me. Sometimes Leilani joins us, but Kai makes it clear he's not on a double date. I don't see the two of them being a match, but Leilani seems intent on pressing her luck anyway. Kai and I even take an evening to go out for fish tacos together just the two of us. After that, he begins to warm up to the idea of me dating his sister. It's not full-blown acceptance, but it's progress.

Mavs and I steal away alone whenever we can. She asked me not to bring up the fact that I'm leaving, but it's never far from my mind. I spend time at her dad's shop a few afternoons during the week I'm in Oahu. He even lets me try my hand at shaping a board. I don't finish it by the time I have to head back to California, but I got the feel for the process. He says I'm a natural. The day before I fly back to Los Angeles, I approach Mavs' dad in the back yard.

"Do you have a minute, Mr. Kapule?"

"I told you, call me Kahiau."

"Okay." I don't call him Kahiau. "I wanted to talk to you about something important."

"About Kalaine."

It's a statement, not a question.

"Yes." I take a big breath and barrel forward in my usual blunt style. I don't see any use in skirting an issue when you have to bring it up eventually. May as well cut to the chase.

"I'm in love with your daughter. Madly in love. I know that might seem over the top or irrational. But it is what it is. And I want you to know I will do everything in my power to make her happy and protect her, but also I will respect her independent spirit ..."

I'm rambling, so it's probably good when he cuts me off to ask, "And you want to marry her?"

"No." My eyes go wide and a breath wooshes out of me. "No. Not now. Someday. But we're still new."

"I knew I wanted to marry her mother the moment I laid eyes on her. In kindergarten."

"Wow."

Mavs' dad bursts into laughter. "I'm kidding ... Bodhi. You should see your face. I did fall fast for my wife, but not that fast, and not that young. In kindergarten, I was more interested in catching lizards than girls."

I laugh too. Not as hard as Kalaine's dad, but I laugh.

"Well, I do love your daughter. I just think we need time—preferably in the same state."

"Ah. Yes. I agree. But I don't want Kalaine to live in California. She belongs here, with her mother and me and Kai. Hawaii is her home."

"I know. I was actually thinking of moving here. But I need to coordinate a lot of pieces to make that happen. I'll need a job. A place to stay. Transportation. My mom is all I have back home. I don't have any siblings."

I don't go into the convoluted reality of my family. For all intents and purposes, I am an only child of a single mom.

"And you would leave your mother?"

Knowing the little I do about Hawaiian culture, I understand the look of concern on Mr. Kapule's face right now. Family comes first—always.

"My mom has her sister a few blocks over, and she has a good group of friends. She knows I live to travel the world and surf. It's always been an understanding between us—a sort of an agreement in two parts. One is that I'll be an adventure seeker. The other is that I'll always come back home to her. I mean, she's my mom."

At this declaration, Mavs' dad smiles a deep and satisfied smile.

"But my life is at a point where I ..." How do I say this to Kalaine's dad?

"Where you want to settle down? And you met my daughter and you think she's the one for you. Your ku'u aloha."

"I know she is."

He nods. "I've watched you this week, Bodhi. You do love my daughter. And she loves you too. I think you are wise to try to be closer to her. Distance teaches us some lessons, and it can serve a young relationship in certain ways. But you need time together so conflict can grow and you can work through it. You need to learn about one another in ways only living in close proximity will allow you to do." He pauses, and then he offers, "If there is something I could do to help you with this move, please, let me know."

"Thank you. That means the world to me."

"What kind of work do you want to look for? I might know someone who could give you a job, depending on what you want."

"I just need to pay the bills. And I need something flexible enough so I can still keep up my training. I'm in the water every day. I need to be able to take time off to compete too."

I start to feel defeated as soon as the words are out of my mouth. Where am I going to find a job that will allow me that kind of flexibility and still pay me enough to live in one of the most expensive places in the United States?

"So, you could work in a surf shop?"

I look Mr. Kapule in the eyes. "I'd definitely work in a surf shop."

Is he asking me what I think he is?

20

KALAINE

Meet me where the sky touches the sea.
~ Jennifer Donnelly

The weather is starting to stay a little warmer in the evenings instead of cooling off unbearably. The sun isn't quite setting, but it's late afternoon and the signs of evening are starting to blow in off the water.

I'm on the shore, watching Bodhi teach a lesson to a teen boy who's here with his family on a week's vacation. Shaka's lying in the sand next to me.

I haven't put my feet in the shorepound again since that first day, but the tug is ever present. The ocean is a relentless lover, wooing me, reminding me of our past, telling me things will be different this time. I'm not so sure I can trust her or give her the second chance she's begging me for. When you've taken a fall as hard as I did, losing everything in one fell swoop, the idea of going back isn't merely intimidating. It's incapacitating.

And dipping my toes in the water was ironically akin to

Bodhi's lips on my neck in the middle of the night. Seemingly harmless, yet oh-so perilous. So little and yet not nearly enough. These teasers of loves I experienced so fully feel promising—promising enough to make me forget my sense of self-preservation. I can't imagine going back after being hurt so deeply. And yet, I can't imagine my life without Bodhi or surfing. It's nothing I need to decide today.

I rub Shaka on the neck and he flops his head onto my lap. If he were a cat, he'd be purring loudly enough for people to hear him up on the dock.

"You won't ever let me down, will you Shaka?"

He doesn't move. It's just the sign of solidarity and faithfulness I need right now.

Bodhi and his student ride a few waves. His student is obviously athletic, and only takes one fall. For the most part, he's learning to shift his weight, to pop up on time, and to ride once he's up. It's exhilarating to watch. Tempting.

They ride a wave all the way in, and Bodhi instructs the student to leave the boards on the beach. I stand and brush the sand off my shorts and legs and follow the two of them up to the watersports shack with Shaka at my heels.

I don't get too close to Bodhi and his student, instead, I wander inside the shop and chat with Ben and Kai and the part-timer, named Jamie, while Bodhi and the teen boy rinse their wetsuits and change. Shaka waits on the dock. Kai made it clear the dog wasn't allowed inside the shop and Shaka knows where he's not welcome.

"So, I talked to Mila today," I tell my brother and Ben.

They're folding shirts and reshelving them after customers riffled through them and left wrinkled clothing cattywampus on the display tables. Jamie's manning the register.

"Mila?" Kai asks, looking up at me with his brows drawn together.

"Yeah. She told Summer she's got a part-time job opening

for a receptionist at the bed and breakfast. I even met her son, Noah. Anyway, I'm thinking of taking the position."

Ben says, "That's awesome, Kalaine," at the same time as Kai says, "Mila asked for your help?"

I smile at Ben and answer my brother. "Yeah. Do you know her?"

"I do."

"What's that look?" I ask Kai.

His face looks concerned, and there's something else there I can't pinpoint.

"What look?"

"You look like you've got a job with the CIA and you're keeping state secrets no one could even waterboard out of you. What aren't you saying?"

"Nothing. I've done work over at Mila's Place. Minor repairs. Stuff like that. She's good people. You ought to take the job if you want it."

"Yeah. Okay."

I try to study Kai, but he dips his head and averts my gaze while he straightens more merchandise.

Bodhi enters the shop. His student follows behind him, thanking him profusely.

Once the teen leaves, Bodhi turns to me. "I've got to carry the two boards in from my lesson. Want to help me?"

"I've got it," Kai offers.

"I've got it, Kai." I tell my brother. "Please stop babying me. My PT said to use my foot and leg normally as long as I don't overdo it. I know what I can handle."

"If you say so."

"I do."

Bodhi looks between Kai and me, and then he heads out onto the dock, wisely dodging any potential crossfire from the Kapule siblings when they are in the middle of something tense.

Bodhi and I walk in silence down to where the boards are on the sand. Shaka trots behind us.

I grab a board and tuck it under my arm. The motion flows like second nature. How long has it been since I held a surfboard? That final day at Mavericks. I haven't touched one since. The weight and curve of the stick feel so familiar I'm almost tempted to walk into the surf and lie down on the board without a wetsuit or any forethought.

"Want to sit in the foam with Shaka? I could hold the board steady and you two could just bob for a while."

"On a board? No." My answer comes out in a rush and with some force behind my words.

I backpedal. "Sorry. Just, no."

"Okay. Your call."

Bodhi's natural ease and the way he goes along with the flow still surprises me. When things ended between us, this version of him had been so far gone, I never knew if it would come back.

"I'll put my toes in, though."

I offer a compromise. Besides, I want to. I wouldn't mind another kiss on the neck, either, but I'll settle for the feeling of the saltwater on my skin. I slip my sandals off and walk toward the edge of the water. Shaka's alongside me, his tail wagging. Maybe he is a surf dog.

I put my toes on the sand where a wave just receded. The next one's rolling in. Bodhi's right next to me. Maybe a foot or two separates us, at most. He's far too happy watching me get my feet wet.

I'm staring out at the horizon, enjoying the wash of the waves up over my feet and ankles and then tugging back out, again and again. A splash from my left side surprises me and snaps me out of my reverie.

Bodhi's wearing a mischievous grin.

"Did you just splash me?"

He shrugs.

Then he swishes his foot in the water as if he's innocent.

At the end of another swish, he puts a little more force behind his movements and water sprays in my direction.

"Hey, what was that for?" I act miffed, but I'm not and we both know it.

"What was what?" He taunts.

I lift my foot, step in a little further to get a good amount of water on my side, and then I kick a spray of water back at him. "That."

"Did you just splash me?" His grin is nearly devilish now. "You know I've got to retaliate."

"You started it!"

Bodhi goes deeper, where the water is at his calves and he kicks a shot that sends enough spray my way to get my shorts partially wet.

I go in a little deeper and kick back, soaking his board shorts and the edge of his T-shirt.

We're lost in the moment, in the competition, in one another.

Now it's a full-on splash fight. "Bring it, Bo!"

His old nickname slips out and I barely notice because now he's bending and using his hands as well as his legs to propel water in my direction. As in all things, we both bring our A-game when it comes to a contest, and I'm not going down until Bodhi is soaked through. His hair is still wet, falling in reckless waves around his face from his surf session. But I'm not going to let the water he voluntarily took on be the marker of my champion status. I will soak his face and hair.

We're thigh deep now, using our forearms to send arcs of spray at one another. I have to jump the waves as they hit me, and I don't care. My sole focus is on getting Bodhi drenched with my shots of ocean water.

A bigger wave rolls through and hits me waist-high. I jump

and nearly fall because I'm scooping a big armful of water in Bodhi's direction at the same time.

Bodhi reaches out and loops his arms around my waist, catching me and holding me up.

"You good?" he asks.

His face is right there, looking down at me with the sunset at its golden hour glow. Sparkles of light reflect off the water onto his skin. He hasn't released me. And I don't want him to. I lift my hand to ... I don't know what ... but it lands on his cheek and I rub my thumb across the short whiskers on Bodhi's jaw. The hair is wet with saltwater, and smooth under my fingertips. We're staring at one another as if someone froze time. The water sloshes around us, making us sway. Still, he's holding me.

Then it happens. He leans in almost imperceptibly. I tilt my head just the slightest. And before either of us can think or protest or change our minds, his mouth is crashing down on mine and he's dragging me toward himself, holding me against him while we kiss. This isn't the careful kiss on my neck from that night outside the bathroom. This is two years of hunger unleashed. This is waiting and wondering and grieving. Our kiss is a reunion, a reconciliation, a rebirth. We are coming home and moving on. I grip the back of Bodhi's sopping wet T-shirt for dear life. Nothing terrifies me more than what we're doing. Maybe not ever doing this again would frighten me at even greater levels. All I know is I need him. And I never want to lose him again.

He's kissing me, and I'm returning his kiss with everything I am. What if this is only one kiss—our last kiss? I banish that thought and throw myself into telling Bodhi all he means to me through the way my lips meet his, the way my hands hold him so he can't get away this time, the way my heart beats nearly out of my chest at every brush of his mouth, every satisfied hum, every caress of his hands. I can't say the words. But I can show him.

Shaka's bark penetrates the moment between us and we pull back from one another, nearly panting from the kiss that came out of nowhere like a summer squall. Our faces hold mirrored stunned expressions.

"Bodhi." My voice cracks as I say his name.

"Don't tell me you regret that." His eyes plead with me more than his words. He's still got me wrapped in his embrace. "Even if you do regret it, don't tell me. My heart won't take it, Mavs. If you don't want me to kiss you again, I won't ..."

"Kiss me, Bodhi." I cut him off and stand on my tiptoes, using the phrase that drags up memories, but also invites us into whatever might come next.

Then I silence Bodhi by kissing him again.

21

BODHI

Because, with the right person,
sometimes kissing feels like healing.
~ Lisa McMann

"What happened to you two?" Kai's question catches me off guard.

Was he watching us in the ocean just now? Nah. He would be fuming and pulling me aside.

"We ... uh ..." Mavs looks up at me.

"We got in the water and it ended in a splash fight," I supply.

There's residual fire in the confidential glance Mavs sends me. I want to haul her off somewhere private. But I'm not even sure where we stand, or if I should have kissed her. She's still healing, even though her ankle is basically back to normal. The deepest injuries aren't those we can see with our eyes. And those take the longest to heal. I promised myself I'd give her time—until the playing field was level. But I couldn't help myself out there. Things got carried away.

When I look at her now, though, I'd do it all again in a heartbeat.

"Let me get you a towel." I walk toward the supply closet at the back of the shop.

"You got in the ocean?" Kai's voice has a note of awe in it.

"Yeah. I actually stuck my feet in a few days ago. And today I felt like ... more."

"I'll say." I quietly mutter the words to myself, facing the closet.

My smile is for me alone, but it breaks across my face. If I were facing Kai right now, I'd be so busted. The memory of that kiss will be all I think of for the foreseeable future.

"You two want to grab tacos?" Kai asks. "Or maybe get a pizza? I had planned on cooking up some salmon but I'm not feeling motivated."

"I've got to throw in a load of laundry," I say. "I'll put the salmon in some marinade and fire up the grill. Unless you're totally in the mood for pizza. Summer's hosting that boot-scoot bonfire for Mavs tonight."

Her nickname slips out and the look on Kai's face would seem neutral to anyone who doesn't know him. It's far from neutral. His eyes squint just the slightest and I catch the movement.

"Salmon? What do you say, Kai?"

"I ... yeah. Salmon. If you're willing, that would be great."

"Are you coming to the bonfire?" Mavs asks Kai.

"Yeah. I'll be there. Of course. I just need to lie down for a minute when I get home. I'm wiped out."

"Two scuba lessons and a three-hour sailing tour will do that to a man." I smile at Kai.

Maybe I'm not smiling at him. Maybe I'm just smiling. Mavs walks past me, grabbing the towel from my hand. I nearly pull her in toward me. I need to get home and do something besides hanging out in close quarters with her and Kai so soon after that kiss. And I need to talk to her, but not before I sort out my own thoughts.

"I'll take off then. See you two at home."

"Wait up!" Mavs shouts, giving one last squeeze to her hair and then tossing the wet towel into the hamper we keep at the back of the shop. "I'll walk with you and Shaka. I can make a salad while you prep the fish."

"Okay. Sounds good."

"See you two at home. I'll lock up here and be there in thirty or forty minutes."

I walk ahead of Mavs out the front door of the shop. She follows behind me, catching up and putting her hand on my bicep.

"Are you going to start acting weird now?" She twists her lips and narrows her eyes at me.

I stop and turn toward her, covering her hand with my own.

"No. I'm just up in my head, to be honest. I had told myself to give you space. I promised you we'd be friends. I didn't mean to kiss you. The splashing was done in fun. And then it escalated, which was awesome—probably the most fun I've had in a long time. I couldn't believe how deep you went into the water. I've got all these feelings ... I ... I don't want to mess things up for you. You're still healing. I should probably sort this out first before I open my mouth. That was the plan."

"You had a plan? Because I have no plan, Bo. None. I don't know what I'm doing past tonight's bonfire. I know I'm going to work for Mila for a bit. But that's not what I'm doing long-term. The only thing I know is ... I don't regret that kiss. And I don't need time to think that through. If you do ..."

"I want you, Mavs. All I ever wanted was you."

She crosses her arms and looks up at me. The fire in her eyes isn't about our kiss now. We both know who ended things between us. She thought I didn't want her. That wasn't ever the issue. I've always wanted her. There won't be a day that I'm living that I won't want her.

I pull Mavs in toward me and she collapses into my embrace. Relief floods me, being able to hold her like this. My lips brush across the top of her head. I probably shouldn't be doing this right here, such a short distance from the shack. If Kai walked out front for any reason, he'd see us.

My words are muffled in Mavs' hair. We're both still wearing damp clothes and her hair is wet and curlier than usual. I tug her nearer to warm her up. "I want to explain where I'm coming from. But if my thoughts come out messed up, it's because I haven't had time to sort through everything. Promise me you will give me a chance to clear things up if I get something wrong here."

"I promise, Bodhi."

I smile, even though she can't see my face right now. Those three words, and the way she says them, send a shot of hope through my system. Maybe there's a future for us after all. I'm getting ahead of myself, but I've always been like that with her. No brake pedals, only wings. At least, that's how it was before I blew things up.

"Okay. So. I'll tell you where my head's at. Ever since you showed up on our doorstep that first day, I've been at war within myself. I'm fighting the urge to touch you—to hold you —every single minute. I'm doing that for you. I've been where you are. I know what it takes to move forward. I didn't want to be a distraction or hindrance. At first it was because I knew I didn't deserve you. And I probably still don't. But I want you, Mavs. I want you with everything I am. That's never changed for me. I'll always want you."

Mavs' eyes soften when she looks up at me. "You are not a distraction or a hindrance. Without you, I might not even have put my feet in the water."

I lean down and kiss her lips, softly and just for the briefest instant. She wraps her hand behind my head and draws me in again for more. Our kisses are sweeter, more tender and thoughtful this time. Still, everything crackles and hums between us. She's so familiar. The way we move is like a practiced dance between partners who have been together for years.

Mine. Something in my soul roars out the word.

I ignore the rush of thoughts about where this might lead. Instead, I place one more soft kiss on Mavs' lips and then her forehead. And then I separate from her, because we are out here in public where anyone could see us. And we still haven't decided what we're doing. And Kai would probably kill me if he saw us together.

We may want one another with the same urgency and sense of belonging we always had, but we haven't thought about what a relationship would really mean for us at this time—for her, especially. It would be so easy to slip back into this familiarity, the rush of our emotions, the tug of our chemistry. But I refuse to wreck Mavs' life again—ever.

Once we're back at the house, Mavs retreats to her bedroom and then I hear doors opening and shutting and the sound of the shower turning on. My mind is like a hamster on a wheel, only if that hamster decided he was going to try to run on the outside of the wheel and he ended up flying off the top and landing in a pinball machine during that last round when ten balls fire off and you can't hit the buttons fast enough to fling those suckers at all the targets. Poor hamster.

I need to be on the water, which is crazy because I just came off the water. But I was teaching a lesson then. I desperately need to find a night break and ride until my thoughts become dull murmurs instead of rapid pings.

I busy myself putting together a marinade of oil and balsamic with herbs and lime juice. Then I lay the salmon in a baking dish and pour the marinade over it. Food prep isn't surfing, but it's at least an outlet. I leave the fish in the fridge and go out back to light the grill. Shaka trails behind me. I'm putting my load of clothes into the laundry machine when Mavs comes into the garage.

"Are you okay?" She knows me too well.

Her face is etched with concern, but she's not rattled. She looks like she just got a massage, or took a nap, whereas I probably look like I'm standing on thumbtacks while a rabid animal gnaws at my ankle and someone drops ice cubes down my back.

"I'm a crazy man, aren't I? I blew it with you. You were everything to me, and I blew it. And then you showed up here, and all I could think about was how much we had, and how we'd lost it all because of me."

"It wasn't completely your choice, Bodhi. There were circumstances." She doesn't meet my eyes.

"Maybe not, but it feels like a better man would have found a way to make things work."

She smiles softly "I'm probably not the person to tell you what you should or shouldn't have done back then."

"Yeah. You're right. No matter how you slice it, I foolishly threw away what we had. It wrecked me even more to know I was hurting you."

"That's all in the past. We're trying to move on. Or ... I think we are. Am I wrong?"

"We are. And I should be ... I don't know what I should be. But confused isn't one of the things topping that list. Why am I so confused? I should be stoked out of my mind."

I look over at her. She's got that peaceful, easy-going look on her face—the one she always had before life ripped us apart and tore our dreams to shreds.

"I am stoked. Don't get me wrong." I run a hand through my still damp hair. "Kissing you ... I never thought I'd get to kiss you again. I just don't want to mess this up. I meant what I said on the walk home. You need to heal. I need to stay out of your way. And I'd like it a whole lot if your brother didn't kill me."

"Forget him."

"I can't. He was there for me when everything went down. He stepped in, even though he knew I had hurt you. He's my best friend. And I know you wouldn't want me to just ignore his concerns or him."

"Maybe not, but he's always had too much say in our relationship. This is about us, Bodhi. Not him."

"You're probably right. Why aren't you freaking out?" I lean back against the washing machine, studying her. As usual, I fight the urge to reach out and pull her toward me. You'd think a kiss would resolve all this tension and the need for such rigid boundaries between us. Instead, our kiss seems to have only amplified everything.

"Am I not freaking out? I'm a little freaked out." She smiles like the most un-freaked out person I've ever seen. "But mostly, I'm buzzing with a sweet sort of anticipation. It feels like Christmas, when you're sure your parents couldn't afford the gift you really wanted. You stare at the box under the tree, hoping, but telling yourself not to hope, trying to talk yourself down from the possibility so you can accept whatever they actually gave you. More than anything, you want to show them you appreciate what they chose for you. Your fingers nearly tremble as you tug the ribbon and rip through the paper. A corner of the package shows underneath. Your heart rate kicks up. Are you really getting what you wanted more than anything in the world? When you tear through the rest of the paper and see that gift, you're alight with joy and gratitude."

She steps toward me, placing her hand gently on my jaw and staring up into my eyes. It's not a romantic gesture. She's grounding me, like I'm this live wire and she's the completion to my circuit. A flicker of something passes across her expression, but then it's gone and the sweet assurance is back in its place so quickly I wonder if I imagined it.

"Bodhi, up until today out in the water, I didn't even know if you wanted anything but friendship with me. I had my suspicions. But I wouldn't ask you. I couldn't. If you rejected me, I didn't think I could take it. Not now. Not after all we went through. Not with my future being so uncertain."

She smiles up at me and I want to have my head examined. Why wouldn't we just get back together? Nothing else makes sense but her. She's everything.

"But when you kissed me, you said it all—all the thoughts and longings you hadn't been expressing to me were in that kiss."

Mavs' eyes search mine. She steps in closer to me and stands between my legs while I lean back on the washing machine. She's not hesitating, instead she's backing up everything she said with an expression that looks like the Mavs I fell for years ago: so very free and yet, intently focused.

"Kiss me, Bodhi." The words are a whisper.

She's not asking. She's inviting me to let go of every thought but her, of every path but the one that involves the two of us moving forward together. At least I think that's what this is—an invitation for us to try to make a go at something romantic between us again. I hope I'm not misreading her.

I cup the back of Mavs' neck with my hand and draw her toward me. She places her palm on my chest and dips near to brush her lips across mine. As soon as our mouths connect, all bets are off. I want her. She's mine. She's always been mine. And I've always belonged to her. Since the first day we flirted at Mavericks, no other woman could compete with her. I'll do whatever it takes, face whatever obstacles, give her whatever space she needs.

I love Kalaine. That's all that matters.

There's a noise from inside the house—the sound of the

front door shutting. Mavs jumps backward, nearly tripping over the pile of my next load of laundry. Next thing I know, she's dodging away from me and ducking behind the workhorse where the board I'm shaping sits like a table top. Her eyes are wide and wild.

"Kai's home!" she whisper-shouts.

"Duck!" she calls over to me in that same nearly-silent rasp.

Under any other circumstances, I'd probably think, "Why?" But instead, the panic on Mavs' face, the thought of Kai catching us, combined with the swirl of thoughts and emotions I've been experiencing ever since our kiss ... well, I freak out.

"Where?" I ask, frantically in a hoarse whisper, looking around for a space like I'm that one kid who always got caught first in hide-and-seek because he debated his spot for too long.

Mavs points to the shelving along the side wall which ends about two feet before the garage door. I duck into that small nook between the end of the shelves and the front of the garage, and maintain eye contact with her.

"Why are we hiding?" I whisper across to her.

Kai obviously knows we're home. The grill is on. My laundry is running. The fish is marinating in the fridge.

This can't end well.

Somewhere in my brain the words, *Act natural,* flit by. Unfortunately, we've long since forfeited the opportunity to act natural. Natural's not even remotely an option at this point. I can only stand here in this cranny and hope for something akin to an alien abduction. I'd gladly have my brain probed right now instead of facing my best friend when he figures out I'm hiding because his sister and I have been kissing all afternoon.

"Shhhhhh," is the only answer I get from Mavs before Kai's voice booms through the house.

"Guys? Kala? Bodhi? Where are you?"

I'm ready to step out of this ridiculous hiding space and face my best friend, but the look Mavs sends me keeps me glued in place. She talked a big talk: *Forget him.* When it comes down to it, she's as nervous about his reaction to us reconnecting as I am. I'm not quite sure how hiding in the garage will solve that issue, but I'm not about to go all logical on her when she looks like a feral animal hunkered down in her ineffective den made of eight workhorse legs.

"Guys?" Kai's voice booms again and then the door leading from the house to the garage opens.

Shaka comes bolting down the stairs and runs straight to Mavs, tail wagging wildly when he sees her. Mavs stays ducked under the workhorse, hidden in plain sight, as if she can evade her brother even though he's looking straight at her now.

"Shaka!" she says, standing, bonking her head on the board, and ducking down again to rub the point of impact. "There you are!"

Okay. So we're going with *the dog was missing and you were on all fours under a workbench looking for him.* Totally believable. No problem. We all crawl around when we're searching for Shaka. All day, every day. Yep. She's got this. Kai won't suspect a thing. In other words, I'm a dead man walking, or hiding—in an equally ridiculous spot, if we want to be honest. I'm pretty sure Kai sees me by now too.

"Kala, what are you doing?" Kai asks. He folds his arms across his chest and his voice takes on that stern older-brother tone that annoys Mavs to no end.

Shaka's not finished with his role as private investigator. He trots from where Kalaine is still hunkered down straight over to me. His tail wags and he jumps so his paws land on my stomach in a gesture that very much says, *Here's Bodhi. I found him.*

"Bodhi?" Kai's confusion is evident—and obviously valid.

"Yep," I say, stepping out from the odd nook where I'd been hiding. Then I turn to Shaka. "There you are, buddy! We were looking for you."

In for a penny, in for a pound.

Kai looks from me to Mavs and back. "Looking for the dog? That's what we're calling it these days?"

Mavs stands from under the workhorse slowly, craning her neck a little to avoid another collision with the surfboard. When she's at her full height, she props her hands on her hips.

"Do you have a problem with that?"

"With you looking for the dog under the workhorse?" Kai asks with a smirk on his face. "And Bodhi looking ..." Kai gestures to where I'm standing, now just outside the little nook where I had sequestered myself. "Over there?"

"Right. With me and Bodhi ... uh ... looking for a dog ... together."

"You're consenting adults. Look for a dog together however you want. Just don't get hurt in the process." Kai turns his full attention to me. "And don't hurt my sister ... while ... dog hunting. Or you'll wish you never started that hunt."

Kai turns and heads back into the house. "I'm going to lay down. Can we eat in a half hour?"

"Half hour's good," I say.

Once the door shuts behind Kai, I let out a long breath. Mavs waits a few beats to make sure we're alone, and then she says, "Well, that went well, don't you think?"

"Yeah. It went great."

Mavs smirks over at me, and then her face breaks into a full smile.

"Looking for Shaka?" she says. "What was I thinking?"

Her laughter fills the garage, and I join her.

"Beats me," I say, drawn to her like filaments to a magnet.

I pull her into my arms and kiss her forehead.

"Want to *look for the dog* with me now, while Kai sleeps?" She winks up at me.

"I'm all about the hunt."

KALAINE
(ONE AND A HALF YEARS INTO OUR RELATIONSHIP)

Stay true in the dark and humble in the spotlight.
~ Harold B. Lee

Surfers call it dawn patrol. It's when we hit the waves before the sun is fully up. In the gray-blue light of pre-dawn, we pull into the parking lot at Banzai and wordlessly don our wetsuits at the backs of our respective trucks, cars and vans.

We greet one another with a dip of the chin or a smile. Sometimes a few people talk on their way to the water. But we're all focused, and here for a reason. The surfers willing to get out of bed to ride before the day gets rolling are serious about surfing. And today, we've had a swell that even hit the news. When these kinds of storms at sea come our way in the form of massive waves, people travel from around the island or even fly into Honolulu to come ride.

Bodhi and I have been waking early every day for months to hit the waves before he heads into my dad's shop to shape boards and serve customers. Every morning, I drive my little red VW Beetle over to Bodhi and Kai's apartment—a back house on my uncle's property. And then the two of us jump in his truck and drive to whatever spot is breaking best.

Kai joins us occasionally, but his passion for competing seems to be waning, so he's not always eager to trade sleep for time in the ocean. Whereas, Bodhi and I are only getting hungrier for bigger waves in more exotic places. Many nights, we're snuggled together on his couch or mine, trolling the internet to watch videos of people surfing around the world. Mostly these days, it's Nazare in Portugal, Mullaghmore Head, Ireland, or Belharra, France. We're dreaming up a European surf tour and talking with our coaches and sponsors about what it will take to make it happen.

I ride my last wave in, carry my board up the sand, and tug my wetsuit zipper down my back. My eyes are on the water, watching Bodhi weave along a wave and turn into the perfect off-the-lip before he rides toward shore, hops off his board and turns to paddle out for another.

Surfers dot the waves here at Banzai Pipeline, even at this early hour with the sun just cresting the hills across the road. Five lifeguards man the tower next to the path leading to the beach. Their Sea-Doos line the sand close to the shorepound. Being a lifeguard on the North Shore means constant diligence, especially in waves as big as the swell rolling in today.

I'm drying my hair with one of our towels when Bodhi comes up behind me. He drops his board in the sand, steps in front of me and slips his arms around my waist. Then he shakes his head like a drenched dog, spraying me with droplets of saltwater.

"Hey!" I shout, but I'm smiling.

He rests his cheek right up against mine. His skin is cold even though the water stays relatively warm here in Hawaii.

"Mmmm. You're so toasty, Mavs."

"You're like a disobedient puppy."

"Train me." He tilts his head back and wags his eyebrows mischievously.

My smile grows. He's still so flirtatious, and the feelings he elicits from me haven't dimmed in the slightest over the past year of him living on Oahu.

Bodhi leans in and kisses me. Then we grab our boards and our beach bag and haul everything back to Bodhi's truck. Bodhi straps our surfboards onto the roof racks. We do a quick surf change into our shorts and shirts.

Bodhi turns to me. "Are you ready for today?"

"Sure. Are you?"

"Yeah. I'm getting used to reporters, I guess. Anytime I get to talk about you is fun."

He steps in front of me and brushes a lock of wet hair away from my face, smiling down at me with that post-surf, sated look in his eyes.

"You know how much I love you?" The corner of Bodhi's mouth tips up in a lopsided grin.

"Enough to buy me an açaí bowl at Sunrise Shack?"

"Hmmm." He pretends to run his hand along his jaw in a contemplative move.

I smack his bicep and look up at him through my lashes.

He runs his hand down my hair. "I'd say my love is big enough to treat for açaí."

"Such a romantic," I tease him, turning to jump up into the passenger seat.

Bodhi stops me, catching my elbow in his hand. He pivots me toward him.

"I'm so crazy about you, Mavs. You're my forever."

He says that all the time, and it doesn't get old.

"You're my favorite disobedient puppy."

"Whom you love with undying devotion." He says this while his fingers find the most ticklish spot under my ribs. I fold over laughing.

"Stop! Bodhi! Stop!"

"Say you're madly in love with me." He lessens his assault, but not by much.

"Uncle! Uncle! I love you—madly."

"Get a room, you two!" Someone taunts us from across the parking lot.

"One day, man! One day!" Bodhi shouts back.

I shake my head at him. Bodhi always blurts out all his thoughts. My man has no filter. It's one of the things that drew me to him after the initial physical attraction. He's just so guileless and forthright. I love that about him. Fearless: that's my Bodhi.

"Kiss me, Bodhi."

"Always this." He makes a show of rolling his eyes as if I'm the biggest pain in his tush. Meanwhile, his dimples pop and his eyes sparkle with mischief. "Always demanding my kisses. And açaí, and surf trips ... Who knew you'd be so high maintenance?"

I poke him just below his armpit—where he's ticklish. He grabs my wrist and then his eyes turn from playful to serious.

"I love you, Mavs. I'm not really sure there are words to express how much I love you. You're the perfect woman—and you're mine." The note of reverence in his voice floors me.

We're pretty affectionate—almost obnoxiously so. At first I thought it was the newness of our relationship. Then, when Bodhi moved to Hawaii, I thought it was the fact that we finally were in the same place after so much distance separating us. But he's been here a year, and we're still "over the top," at least according to my brother. My mom says it's a gift to find a man who loves me like Bodhi does. I'm going with Mom on this one.

I'm about to answer Bodhi—to tell him how much he means to me—but he bends in and kisses me with the same heat and urgency he always does. It's like we have to keep reminding ourselves how rare this love we share is—and our kisses seem to be the most thorough reminder.

Bodhi pulls away from me and runs the back of his hand down my face while he looks me in the eyes. "We'd better get a move on. It will be time for the interview before we know it. I want to feed you and then I have to stop at the shop for a few hours. Then I'll meet you and that reporter at the restaurant. What's her name again?"

"Megan Woodruff. From *Surfer* mag."

"I know she's with *Surfer*. I just forgot her name."

"That's why you have me." I jump up into the passenger seat.

When Bodhi climbs into the driver's seat, he says, "That's why I have you? I was wondering." Then he looks over and winks at me before turning the key.

I stare at him, because I can. He's truly one of the most gorgeous men I've ever seen. And he's always a bit ruffled, even when we dress up. I love that he never looks completely put together. That casual air of sexiness fills every space he occupies.

I'm sitting here thinking how precious he is and how lucky we are when this odd rush of fear washes over me from out of nowhere.

"Will it change, do you think?" I look over at Bodhi. "Will we feel less ... urgent, less like we've got to grab up all the goodness between us?" I tug at a cuticle and pull it off my thumb. "I mean, will there come a day when we take one another and everything we have for granted and get bored with one another?"

He smiles softly at me, pinching his lips slightly and shaking his head. "Nah. Not a chance."

"I'm greedy for you, Bo."

He turns left out of the parking lot to take me to my favorite little roadside stand for a quick breakfast.

"Babe, you cannot say things like that to me when I have to leave to get ready for work. And, no. I don't think the feelings we have for one another will change. If anything, they'll just get stronger and deeper with time. I've seen plenty of marriages go south. And I know enough guys who sadly don't appreciate what they have. We're not them. I think we're more like your parents. You know the photos of them around your house? The ones from when they were dating, or when you and Kai were little? Your mom looks like you in those—or you look like her, whatever. Yeah, your parents have aged. But they still have that connection, like they know they found their person. Their love has mellowed, but in a good way, and it's still strong."

"I always wanted what they have."

"Well, now you have what we have. I hope it's what you want."

"You're everything I want, Bodhi."

I pause before saying the next sentence. We've talked about our future a lot, but sometimes it feels like we're overshooting the mark with all we hope we can grab out of life. We're already two of the top surfers in the world. And we have one another.

Still, I muster up the courage to say what I need to say. "I want a bunch of little Bodhis running around on the beaches with us one day."

He smiles. "And little Mavs. We'll take them around the world with us."

"I don't know if I can picture traveling with kids. Something about that puts a big wet, soggy blanket on the dream. Diaper bags. Crying. Tantrums. Overtired and hungry children in strange places."

He chuckles. "We'll make it work. This is our life. Our kids will be born into it. We'll adjust and so will they."

Bodhi entwines my fingers in his, resting our enjoined hands on the seat between us. "Lots of people travel with kids. And they have a home base—or not. Oahu is our home base.

And you know I'm working on talking my mom into relocating here. I don't think we have to give up the life we love to have kids. We'll make changes—we'll have to. But we can still be surfers. And we can raise our little Bodhis and little Mavs to love all the places we love and to ride the ocean—like your dad raised you in the water."

Bodhi pauses to focus on finding a parking spot. He pulls the truck to a stop along the road. The Sunshine Shack is right on the other side of the fence, painted a bright yellow, the awning up telling everyone they're open for business. You'd almost drive right past this place if you didn't live here. It's small and nondescript with chickens wandering around the dirt surrounding the shack and the green mountains in the background.

Bodhi looks at me. "It nearly blows me away to think of a little girl who looks like you, spinning in circles with flowers in her hair. I don't know if my heart could take it."

Thinking of Bodhi as a dad fills me with a new warmth. "I want it all, Bo. Everything you described."

"And I'm going to give it to you. All that and more. I just have to get a little more saved up so I can move out of the place I share with Kai. I've got a lot socked away from my sponsorships and contest earnings, but I don't want to touch that. Give me a few more months ... I'm not going into details ... just know I've got plans."

"And you think I'll say yes?" I tease him.

"Nothing's guaranteed in life. But I'm a risk taker, and I'm willing to take a risk any and every day when it comes to you."

I smile over at Bodhi, and nearly whisper, "Yes."

He didn't ask, but he might as well. And I'm his. He knows that. There will never be another man for me. I don't care if we make it official today or next year. My future is only happening with Bodhi Merrick at my side.

~

We're sitting on the top deck of the Haleiwa Beach House Restaurant. The view of the ocean from up here is spectacular. A breeze is blowing through, taming the warmth of the midday sun. Bodhi and I are on a couch, my hand in his. The journalist for *Surfer* magazine, Megan, is sitting across from us. Her photographer, Denny, sits behind her, snapping shots of us occasionally. We'll do an official photo shoot with him after the interview.

The article Megan plans to publish will be titled, *The "It" Couple of Big Wave Surfing*. It still blows my mind that people care about me and Bodhi outside of how we each surf. But, our relationship is more famous than our surfing at this point, drawing interest from people who never even cared about the world of surfing.

Megan continues her questions. We've each already gone into our reactions to our ranking and plans we have for future competitions. She asked us about our rigorous training regimen and now she's getting personal.

"Bodhi, teen girls around the world have posters of you on their walls."

"Yeah. I guess they do." He's so unaffected by this statement I almost laugh.

"Kalaine, does that bother you?" Megan smiles warmly at me.

"No. I have one too."

Bodhi turns to me. "You do?"

"Of course I do. Don't you have my poster?" I tease him.

Megan sits back, watching us. She's done a lot of that. This time with her feels more like a conversation than an interview —a testament to her skills as a journalist.

"I don't need a poster," Bodhi says. "I've got the real thing. But now that you mention it ..."

He lifts my hand in his and brushes a kiss across my knuckles.

"We'll arrange for you to get one," Megan says.

I'm not sure if she's serious or not.

"So, I'm wondering," Megan looks between the two of us. "Are there plans for marriage? And if so, how will being married and starting a family impact your futures as competitive surfers?"

"Lots of big wave surfers are married," Bodhi tells Megan, even though she probably already knows this. It's her job to know about the professional and personal lives of prominent pro surfers.

"But most of them are married to someone who doesn't surf, so that spouse can stay home with the kids," Megan says. "I know I'm jumping ahead here. But our readers want to know if you plan to step back from surfing in the coming years, or if you have plans to somehow straddle your sport and your personal lives."

Bodhi fields the question again, so I just watch him in action. He's relaxed, leaning back on the couch in that casual posture he always takes whenever he's seated. He's got my hand in his, but his other arm is outstretched along the back of the bamboo sofa. His T-shirt outlines his arm muscles. His eyes are fixed on Megan and he has a congenial smile on his face like nothing in the world could rattle his cage.

"Mav ... Kalaine and I have talked about our future. What our fans need to know is that we'll make it work. We're the type of people who ride big waves. By nature that makes us daredevils, but also we're extremely hard workers. We know how to devote ourselves to something we're passionate about. And when we have a family, we're both going to be passionate about our kids and making life as a family a priority. I don't see our love of surfing diminishing. Do I know what that will look like in a practical sense? Nah. I don't. But we'll figure it out when we get there. We're blessed with a huge support network. Between us and the people who love us, we'll make it happen."

Megan smiles. Then she asks, "What drew you to one another? Our readers really want to know how you two met. Your love for one another is quite an inspiration. Being here with you, I can tell why your relationship has gained the attention it has."

Bodhi tells Megan how we met at Mavericks. He says things like, *I had to see her again*, and *I couldn't get her off my mind*. Then I tell her about Bali. We smile at one another throughout the retelling of our past, and I'm left feeling like I might just be the luckiest girl on the planet.

"Bodhi, one of your best friends is Kai Kapule, Kalaine's brother," Megan says. "How does Kai feel about you two dating?"

"He was a bit protective at first."

"A bit?" I laugh and roll my eyes.

"Yeah. Well." Bodhi smiles over at me. "But he came around. The three of us actually hang out a lot in the water. Kai and I share a place here on the island. So, yeah. We're cool."

"What's next for you two? I heard there are rumors of you riding Mavs this winter."

We smile a private smile. The reporter has no idea that's Bodhi's nickname for me.

"I'm training for that, yeah," Bodhi answers. "Ma ... Kalaine is training too. It's our dream to ride that spot together during the same contest. And we hope to ride Nazare too and a few other big spots in Europe. Details are still in the works. Wherever the waves are massive, we feel called to go test our skills and take them on."

Bodhi looks over at me, so I pick up where he left off. "We've both been training hard for the next big waves— building up our lung capacity and upper body strength, traveling to big breaks so we can keep ourselves in tune with what those sorts of conditions demand of us. Our coaches constantly work with us to get us ready to take on the biggest waves on earth."

"Does it make you nervous to watch her go into the big surf?" Megan asks.

Bodhi doesn't even flinch. "No. I admire her. Kalaine's the bravest, most dedicated athlete I know. And she's got what it takes. I guess a part of me holds my breath when she's pushing her limits, but that's what we do. It's hard to explain, but when you live the kind of life we do, you have to learn to set aside fear and hesitation—for yourself and others."

Megan turns to me. "Does it make you nervous to see him on big waves?"

"I love watching Bodhi surf. Besides the times we share with one another when no one else is around, watching him surf is my favorite thing to do. The bigger the better. I know he's happiest in the water. He's full of grace and beauty out there riding something only a miniscule fraction of the population can conquer. We're blessed to have this life. And we get to cheer one another on, train together, and watch one another soar. There's nothing like it."

"Aww, thanks babe." Bodhi leans in and kisses me on the spot.

"I can completely see why you two are surfing's 'it' couple."

"She hates that term." Bodhi nudges me playfully.

"Really?" Megan looks surprised.

"It's just so Hollywood. We're just us. We're nothing special," I tell Megan.

"You are," Bodhi says.

I smile at him and mouth, *so are you.*

Megan looks over her shoulder at Denny. "Did you catch that?"

He nods. I had forgotten the photographer was even there. It should be odd to think of pictures of me and Bodhi along with all this personal information about us going out to total strangers. Over the past year, I've gotten a bit desensitized to all the publicity. At least around Oahu, we're just another couple of surfers to most people. Everyone knows who we are, but no one treats us differently for it. Hawaii's chill like that. People don't make too big of a deal about anything.

"Well, thank you for your time, you two," Megan says. "It really was a pleasure to meet with you. Denny is going to take some photos of you and then we'll get out of your hair."

22

KALAINE

How we handle our fears will determine
where we go with the rest of our lives.
~ Judy Blume

"Welcome to Mila's Place," I say to the couple who just stepped through the door. The husband is hanging back tugging two rolling bags behind him and looking around at the interior of the bed and breakfast. The wife approaches me and tells me the name for their reservation.

"Jennifer and Matt Wilhelm. This place is darling! Way cuter than the website, and that's saying something."

"Thank you. I hope your ferry ride over to the island was enjoyable." I punch their name into the computer the way Mila showed me. Then I grab their room keys from the drawer.

"We're glad you're here. These are your keys. This one's for your room. And this one opens the front and back doors if you enter after ten p.m. There's a welcome basket on your dresser. You have full access to the grounds, and there are complimentary bikes and kayaks available for your use. Breakfast is served between seven and nine each morning. Picnic lunches are available on request, and we offer Saturday dinner ..." I glance at my computer screen. "... which I see you already reserved. Also, you can schedule a complimentary snorkeling or surf lesson with the Alicante Water Sports Shack on Descanso Beach."

The words *water sports shack* draw my mind to Bodhi and the kisses we shared yesterday.

We ate dinner with Kai and then the three of us walked to the beach for the bonfire. My eyes kept drifting to wherever Bodhi was throughout the night. Sometimes we stood next to one another, laughing and talking with friends. But, as happens at parties, we would invariably be separated. And when that happened, my eyes would seek Bodhi out. As soon as I located him, we'd share a private smile through the crowd.

Before the night ended, Bodhi and I sat together around the bonfire sharing a driftwood log as a chair. He didn't put his arm around me or rest his hand on my knee. I didn't lean my head on his shoulder. Aside from the hum of invisible longing and the memory of our kisses buzzing silently between us, we appeared like two friends enjoying a night on the beach— nothing more. We need to figure out what we're doing, but there hasn't been enough time alone to do that since Kai came home.

I came to Mila's early this morning for my orientation. Most days, she won't need me until mid-morning, so I'll be able to keep my routine of walking to the beach with Bodhi and Shaka, watching him surf, and then coming home to get ready for work.

Mila must have heard the guests arrive, because she pops out from the kitchen area off to my right.

"Welcome to Mila's place. I'm Mila. Did Kalaine get you checked in?"

"She did. We were about to go find our room."

"Let me show you the way."

Mila and our guests walk past the entry desk and through the living room. They pass the large dining room on their way to the stairs going up to one of the six bedrooms on the second story.

This home must have been designed for a family with ten or twelve children. There's a huge front porch where Mila's set up several separated seating areas and a porch swing. On this first floor there's a kitchen that Mila's had upgraded, but it still retains that vintage feel.

My desk sits along the back wall of the living room/family room, facing the double front doors. The back yard is huge. Mila explained that the original owners had built the house on two lots. Apparently, she inherited it, and now she's running it single-handedly, with the support of her three aunts, all while raising her seven-year-old son.

I'm updating the Saturday menu on the inn's website when the front door opens. I look up to see my brother sauntering through the entryway with a familiarity that tells me he knows his way around the place.

"Kai? What are you doing here?"

"I ... uh. I came to see if the ... uh ... Well, Mila had a leak in the kitchen. I fixed it yesterday and I wanted to make sure it wasn't causing her any other problems."

He blushes. My big brother is blushing. What on earth is going on?

Mila comes back downstairs alone, and I look between the two of them.

"Oh, Kai. Hi. What brings you over here today?"

"Hey, Mila. Uh. Yeah. Well, I just wanted to check on the faucet. Make sure it was holding up after that repair."

"It is." Mila ducks her face down slightly and tucks a strand of her long brown hair behind her ear. "Thanks. You didn't have to come all this way just to check."

Oh. My. Gosh. It's like watching Kai in high school all over again. I might be crazy, but this version of Kai usually only comes out when he has a crush. And from the way he looks like he doesn't know what to do with his hands ... or head ... or eyes, I'm guessing he's got it bad for Mila.

"Good. Good. That's good." The blush on Kai's face might even deepen.

It's nearly painful watching my brother, who is usually super pulled together and in-charge, stumble over his words like a prepubescent boy who just literally bumped into the homecoming queen. It would be downright embarrassing if it weren't so amusing.

Mila looks at Kai with an expression that's either compassionate or concerned. It could be something more, but it resembles the face a mom makes when her son falls off his bike, not a woman who can't stop thinking about a man. Which, ewww. That's my brother.

"Would you like a scone? I just baked them." Mila offers. "Want one, Kalaine?" she adds as almost a polite afterthought.

"I'm good," I say, typing a bunch of random letters on the keyboard in front of me as if I'm composing a letter to someone very important. Sakdfjsljfsildjfksl;fjsldfj fills my screen while my eyes continue to observe my brother in his very-not-natural-habitat.

"I'd love one," Kai says. "I was wondering what that amazing smell was."

I nearly chuckle. He's got it *bad*. It's pretty cute.

"Awww. Thank you." Mila smiles over at Kai while she walks toward the kitchen. "They're cranberry orange with white chocolate chips and an orange glaze."

"Mmm." My brother looks nearly dazed, and I don't think it's over the idea of fresh baked goods.

He starts to follow Mila, and when he steps down from the elevated entryway into the living area, one of his feet catches on the lip of the step and he does this sort of superman sprawl forward with both arms reaching in front of himself and his legs trailing behind, followed by what looks like the running man dance, and then this slow motion winding arm flail which is an uncanny impersonation of a human windmill. To his credit, and probably at least in part due to his years surfing, Kai doesn't go down.

I can't help myself. I try to hold it in, I really do. But a snort of laughter flies out of me. Since I'm trying to contain myself, it comes out more like a congested seal bark than a burst of laughter.

"Watch it," Kai growls in my direction.

"I'm pretty sure *you* should watch it," I tell him, still chuckling, but trying hard to restrain myself on his behalf.

Mila smiles shyly over at my big brother. "That step is always something I wondered if I should have removed. It's part of the original architecture and I love it, but it's a hazard."

Kai's all business now. "If you need it taken out, you'd have to do it during a mid-week when you don't have guests here. I could get Bodhi and Ben to cover the shack so I could do it for you. Just let me know."

"You already do so much around here," Mila says.

He does? Okay, then.

Mila walks into the kitchen and Kai follows behind her.

"Watch your step," I mutter with the grin of an annoying baby sister on my face.

Kai shakes his head and brushes his hands down the front of his jeans and then he's in the kitchen alone with Mila and I'm dying to put a cup up to the wall to eavesdrop, but I busy myself deleting the gibberish letters off my screen and then responding to actual emails from future guests about their bookings.

On his way out of the inn, Kai pauses at the reception desk. When I look up, he says, "I forgot to tell you when I got here. A woman stopped by the house a few hours ago. She was looking for you."

"Looking for me?"

"Yeah. She said her name was Megan. She said she'd catch up with you later."

"Megan?"

Kai just nods. "She didn't leave any info. I figured you knew her. She's not a local—at least I've never seen her around."

I scan through faces in my brain. I don't know a Megan.

～

BODHI WAS RIGHT. Having a job gives me a sense of purpose. Every morning I wake and walk with him and Shaka to the beach. He asks me to surf. I decline the invitation. Every. Single. Time. It's a little dance we do. I admire his tenacity. He doesn't even look frustrated or angry. He's just quietly relentless, like he knows one day I'll cave. I'm not sure he's right, but I wouldn't trade these mornings for anything. After we get home, I clean up, go to work for a few hours, and then the hardest part of my day kicks in—sitting at home alone with nothing much to do and no sense of the big picture.

One thing has changed in my morning routine. Ever since that day we had the water fight and ended up kissing one another, I do put my feet in the shorepound before Bodhi paddles in from his last wave. I go up to my knees at times, talking to the ocean, telling her how I miss her, but I can't trust her like I used to. I have this private heart-to-heart, and I don't even tell Bodhi or Leilani about it. What's said in those early morning chats remains strictly between me and the sea.

I was never naive about the dangers of my occupation and passion. Surfers know wild animals lurk in the depths, sometimes even the shallows—sharks, jellies, or other sea life. We know we could cut ourselves on a jagged piece of coral or a rocky bottom. When we surf unfamiliar breaks, if the water is at all opaque, we don't always know the layout of the cove or bay. For big wave surfers, the dangers increase exponentially. We're risking our lives every ride and we know it.

People call us foolish, addicts, thrill-seekers. I understand those sentiments, even if they don't capture the heart of why we do what we do.

Even still, something in me always felt like I had a pact with the ocean—a deep love and respect that passed both ways between us. It went something like this: I'll pour myself into training, and do everything it takes to understand and respect the ocean. In turn, she'll never harm me.

There's a difference between getting hurt and being harmed. Hurt heals over time—like my ankle injury. Harm lodges somewhere deep and untouchable. I'm not really sure, even this morning as I stand ankle deep in the shorepound, if I've been temporarily set back or if I've received the final blow to my relationship with the ocean. Did she hurt me or harm me? Only time will tell.

The irony isn't lost on me. My feelings for the sea are a mirror for my emotions about Bodhi. I thought we would always be one another's safe place. I never expected him to hurt me, let alone harm me. And now, we're kissing and laughing and hanging out every spare minute we get. But we haven't defined what's happening or where we're headed. Aside from Kai's warning that night in the garage, my brother hasn't said anything. Bodhi and I keep things detached and friendly around Kai. Until we're more defined, we don't need to drag my overprotective brother into the mix.

I know Bodhi wants me. He's said so a hundred times if he's said it once. But he's also trying to hold back while I heal from my accident. I want him too—so much. But I just don't know.

I lift my eyes and watch as he takes a wave, carving along the face, tipping the nose of his board to rise up and dip again, and then finding the sweet spot in the curl.

He rides it in, which is a little odd, since we've barely been out here twenty or thirty minutes tops. Usually he's in the water at least an hour, especially on a morning where the waves look as perfect and consistent as they do today.

He lifts his board and walks out through the smaller waves near shore, aiming straight for me.

He's a vision standing in front of me, still knee deep in the water, dripping wet, grinning a roguish smile, hugging his board to his side. His eyes are alight with the thrill of the ride. He's breathtaking—captivating.

"Come on, Mavs," he shouts over to me. "The conditions are perfect this morning. The waves couldn't be more consistent if we secretly hid a machine underwater. And they're just the right height for a reentry. I promised myself not to push you, but I keep thinking this is your day."

I start to shake my head.

Shaka runs out into the waves, paddling the last few feet to reach Bodhi.

"He loves it out here," Bodhi says with a big smile. "Nothing's going to happen on my watch, Mavs."

It's the same promise he made when he was training Shaka. And now the dog will sit on the board while Bodhi takes smaller sets near shore. He's actually a surf dog. Bodhi called it. It's more than we could ask for. A small voice nudges, *even the dog surfs.*

I've always been known for the way I go with the flow. But

people who know me well know how driven I am—and competitive. I'm not going to be out-surfed by my stray dog.

Bodhi walks the rest of the way out of the water toward me and Shaka trails behind him, shaking his fur when he reaches the sand.

"Okay," I say in a voice I'm sure only I hear.

"Okay?" Bodhi whoops. "Oh, yeah! I was right! This is your day! I knew it."

"Calm down, you'll scare the fish."

"Right. No scaring anyone. Let's get you suited up."

Bodhi nearly vibrates with excitement while we walk from the shore to the watersports shack. Shaka seems to sense the weight of my decision. He trots along beside us with what looks like a full smile on his face. My stomach is in knots, but I'm also eager. I know how to surf. My body is healed. There's no physical reason I can't do this. Still, it's like I'm about to take on Sydney's Cape Solander, the giant slab of a wave that ends on a jagged, shallow reef shelf. If that wave doesn't take you, the landing will remind you why those waves were never intended for pleasure. But surfers ride there. Come to think of it, maybe we are actually a bit crazy.

"You okay?" Bodhi's eyes fill with concern as we walk up the steps and he opens the wetsuit locker to pull out a women's suit in my size.

I nod. "This is never going to be easy."

"You never were one for easy. That's not who you are. So, go grab a bikini off the rack and get suited up. Let's go have some fun in the water."

I know what he's doing, and I appreciate it more than I can say, so I do as I'm told. When I come out the shop's back door, Bodhi's holding a longer board than I would have chosen. Longboards are sturdy. You can't really do tricks on them unless you work it hard in the right conditions, but they're steady— like the crash-test approved minivan of the surfing world. Yeah.

I'm about to ride a mom-car in the water when I've been used to high-performance sports cars.

"Ready?" He smiles down at me, barely containing his eagerness.

"Let's not check in on that. I just need to do an out-of-body for the next half-hour or so. This shouldn't feel like going to the dentist for a root canal. But somehow, it does."

"Mavs." Bodhi props the board on a wall.

He places his hands on either side of my arms and gives a reassuring squeeze.

"You are a world-class surfer. You love the ocean. Maybe you're not ready to hit Nazare this week. But I promise you, nothing will satisfy you as much as getting on this stick and riding it into what's rolling in today. It's all going to come back. My prediction: You're going to walk back onto shore feeling invincible. Maybe you'll never ride anything over four feet again. Who cares? Just do this. And maybe even enjoy it."

Bodhi leans in and places the most tender, soft kiss on my lips. His mouth is warm and gentle. He brushes his hand down my cheek when he pulls away.

"This is going to be a day you remember for the rest of your life. I remember the first day I got back on a board. It's a marker. I'm honored to be here to witness this day for you."

"Stop your yammering, Yoda. I'm going in."

He chuckles. "Yoda, huh?"

"Sexy Yoda." I smile up at him.

"Yeah. That's not a picture I can wrap my brain around. Could I be Han instead?"

"Sure." I smile over at him.

Bodhi grabs my board and we walk side-by-side with Shaka at our feet to the water's edge.

When we get there he lays the board on the ground.

A serious expression crosses his face and then he asks, "Will you put your hair up in those cinnamon bun things like Princess Leah?" He's got this smirky half-smile on his face.

I giggle. "You're ridiculous."

"You're right. I like your hair wild and falling down your back in waves. No cinnamon rolls for you."

He's distracting me on purpose. And it's almost working.

I look out at the ocean like I'm facing down a bully.

Bodhi must sense the attitude of my heart.

"The ocean isn't out to get you, babe. You can still have a lot of fun. We just learned to respect her in ways we never did before she turned on us. It won't be what it was. But it will be good anyway."

I wonder if he's talking about the water stretching out in front of us, or the relationship we're easing into. Either way, I made a decision and followed it up with action, so I take a deep breath, let it out slowly, and then I bend to grab the board.

Bodhi grabs his short board—the kind that is best for doing tricks—and follows me into the shallow water near shore. Shaka stays on the sand, watching us go out together.

I mount the longboard, laying belly-down on the surface. Then I dip one cupped hand into the water and drag it backward parallel to the board, followed by the other. I'm slowly pulling myself into deeper waters—waters where my feet won't touch, where I'm committed to riding my way out.

A rush of familiarity and a sense of hope starts to bubble up in my chest as I tug at the water on my right and then my left. Bodhi's tracking with me at a slight distance—giving me space to own this section of the water. He's smiling over at me. I smile back, but then I look and a wave is breaking right in front of us. I hold my breath, and on instinct, I duck dive under. Saltwater covers my head and body and the board, and I pop out the other side.

I've been duck diving since early elementary school. It's a

maneuver we learn so we can make it out to where the waves are really breaking before they fold into something unsurfable.

Bodhi and I make it to a good spot where we can wait for waves. When I sit up on my board, allowing my legs to dangle below me in the water, I look around. Shaka is a small tan blob on shore. The water glistens. The whole town of Descanso looks like a postcard of an island beach town. It's idyllic. Bodhi still doesn't speak. There's something sacred about this morning that words would corrupt.

A set starts to roll in. It will be good. My body knows it. I sense the tug of the incoming waves, so I ready myself. I don't even have to think about it. I instinctively lower myself onto my board in a motion as natural to me as breathing, and I start paddling in. When the moment is right, I pop up, like I've done thousands and thousands of times before.

And then I'm riding along in a sweet line, the ocean breeze blowing my hair back, and this board is already limiting me. These aren't longboard waves. This wave calls for a shorter stick—one I could maneuver to do some turns and even an off-the-lip. Instead, I do some old-school Hawaiian moves, walking toward the front, hanging five, and walking backward. Nothing feels clumsy or out of place.

I'm home.

This is my home.

I've been a nomad, drifting, uncertain. Now I'm home. Everything clicks inside me. One of the biggest smiles ever pulls at my face until my cheeks are taut. A sweet ecstasy courses through me.

I ride my wave all the way in. And then, without a moment's hesitation, I turn and paddle out again.

When I reach Bodhi, I can't believe what I see.

He's crying.

Full blown tears are leaking down his joy-filled face. And the look in his eyes is filled with pride and ... love.

"You did it!" He whoops, throwing a fist in the air. His voice cracks with emotion.

"I did! And now you better grab yours before I beat you to it."

"Is that a dare, Mavs?"

"Mayyybe."

We both laugh as Bodhi turns and sets off paddling for the next swell.

23

BODHI

Success is not final, failure is not fatal:
It is the courage to continue that counts.
~ Winston S. Churchill

We ride wave after wave, and it's like Mavs never fell at Mavericks—like she's been surfing every day without any lapse. My heart and head keep going back in time, remembering Bali, our year in Oahu, the way we believed nothing would ever hold us under.

Mavs sometimes used to ask me if what we had was too good to be true. Maybe it was. But now she's back, and we're reconnecting—maybe even giving our love a second chance. It's like digging through the back of your closet to discover your favorite T-shirt's been hanging in the dark recesses. Then you slip it on to find it only softened with age.

I need Mavs in my life in a way I couldn't allow myself to acknowledge for these past two years. Now that she's back, I'm going to do whatever it takes to keep her.

We take the last wave in. Shaka's on shore wagging his tail in celebration of our return. But something else catches my eye.

"Megan?" Mavs says her name while I'm still trying to figure out what the magazine journalist we met with over two years ago is doing standing here on Marbella Island next to my dog.

"Kalaine! So good to see you." Megan says this like they're old friends. Not like it's beyond weird that she's standing here at dawn on a small California island interrupting a very private moment between me and my ... whatever we are.

"Good to see you too." Mavs' face is still filled with the smile she's had since she took her first wave. It's not as broad of a grin now that we're on land, but she hasn't stopped smiling.

Mavs walks to the spot on the sand where I dropped our stuff when I first went out. She grabs two towels, handing me one and using the other to squeeze the water out of her hair.

"What brings you to Marbella?" Mavs asks Megan casually.

"You, actually."

Mavs stops drying her hair and looks up at Megan. "Me?"

"I know you shunned reporters after the accident," Megan says. "And I fully understand that. But the surfing world is itching to know how you're doing. And ... I didn't expect to find you here too, Bodhi."

My skin prickles. I don't say anything—not really sure what I'd say if I could find the words.

Mavs and I are celebrities in a small way. Some people will never know us, and that's for the better. Neither of us did what we did for fame or glory. Most surfers don't. But we became famous—more famous than most pro surfers—because of our relationship. We were an anomaly, two young people in love with the ocean and one another. Between the inherent risks we took on a regular basis, and the fact that Mavs was one of the top women—and one of the few to take on giants, we became known.

And now we're known for our accidents—the last rides that

ended our careers. And we're known for me disappearing and our world-renowned love affair going up in smoke because of me.

The last thing I want to face right now is a reporter, even one as seemingly mild-mannered and well-intentioned as Megan.

"I'm living here," I say. "And don't quote me on that." I turn to look at Mavs who has a softly scolding look on her face, so I add. "Please."

"I want to tell your story," Megan says to Mavs. "Your way. You control the narrative. I just want to be the one to tell the world how you're doing now. I came here in person because I didn't want someone else to be the one. Also, honestly, reporters don't have much luck getting a story when they use the phone or computer to reach out. Not for this kind of story, anyway. Selfishly, I'd love *Surfer* to be the publication that runs this. And I'd love my name on that article and feature. But personally, I want to do this well. I know you've been through a lot—both of you. I don't want your experiences to be treated with anything but the care you deserve."

Mavs looks at me. I stare back at her. Megan waits. Shaka walks over to Megan and wags his tail. She bends and scratches his head.

"This is ... unexpected," Mavs finally says. "I hate to waste your time, but I need to think this over."

"You didn't waste my time. I'm living in Santa Barbara now. It's just a ferry ride over here. And I was due to get away from things for a few days anyway, so I booked a room at the resort. I'm here through tomorrow. But I can always come back."

"Okay," Mavs says. "I'll get in touch with you."

Mavs fishes through our beach bag and pulls out her cell. Megan gives Mavs her number, and then she turns to walk off the beach, back toward the resort.

I refuse to let Megan's appearance and the idea of a pending interview cloud a perfect morning—the morning Mavs first got back on a board. It's not easy to regain the unbridled joy I felt watching her, surfing with her. But I shove all thoughts of Megan into some remote compartment of my brain when I turn to Mavs and pull her into my arms.

"I'm so proud of you." I look down into her honey-brown eyes. "Not even proud. It's more than pride." I search for the right word. "It's admiration. I admire you. You're braver than anyone I know."

I almost tell her how lucky I am. Today, at least, I'm the luckiest person to have been here with her when she faced her fears and re-entered the water. And no matter what goes down in the future, I'll always have been the one who spurred her on and who got to witness her first ride after the fall.

Her expression turns shy. "Thanks, Bodhi."

I know she's thanking me for more than the compliment.

I lean in and give her a kiss. She holds me in place. And I swear I'll never take her for granted ever again.

We walk up to the shack, rehashing the waves we rode, like any two surfers after a morning sesh. Only, it's me and Mavs.

When we get to the surf shower, Kai's waiting for us. He's got a scowl on his face.

"You went surfing?"

"Yeah." Mavs looks at him with an easy-going expression. "It was amazing, Kai. I rode the first wave and then I kept taking waves. We were out there for an hour or so. Can you believe it?"

"No." His face has softened a bit, but he's still far more stern than he should be.

"I wasn't going to go in, but Bodhi kept asking. Then something clicked. It just felt right. I can't believe it."

Does she not see his face? He's obviously got a bone to pick about Mavs surfing. I can't figure out why for the life of me. I put my board away and come back to grab the board Mavs rode. She'll need something shorter next time.

Kai takes a breath and looks off toward the waves. "You had fun out there?"

"So much fun. More than fun, Kai. It was like ... I don't know. I don't want to say much. It feels like talking about it will ruin the magic. It was a great morning. And I have Bodhi to thank for it. Just like he has you."

That last line seems to snap my best friend out of his oddly broody reaction. "That's great, Kala. I'm happy for you."

"You might want to tell your face how happy you are," she teases.

Okay. So she did see how weird he was being.

"Are you both going home now?" Kai asks us.

"Yeah. I'll be back after I shower and grab a bite. Is that okay?" I ask Kai.

He nods at me. "Sure."

Then he turns to Mavs. "Could I snag you for a second?"

"Uh. Yeah. Okay. I have a little time before I have to get to Mila's."

Kai's face softens at the mention of Mila. I think he has a thing for her, but he denies it whenever I bring it up. He also gets overly defensive about the suggestion, which only confirms my suspicions.

"I'll wait for you," I offer to Mavs.

"I need to talk to my sister alone," Kai tells me.

"Okay. No problem." I look at Mavs. "Shaka and I will see you at home."

I walk to the front of the shop where Shaka's lying on the ground, blissfully unaware of anything but the moment at hand and his chill surroundings.

"Come on, Shaka. Let's get you some breakfast."

Mavs comes out the front door behind me. She approaches me, places her hand on my chest and stands on her tiptoes. Then she kisses me on my cheek.

"Thanks for everything, Bodhi." She smiles up at me.

There's something new in her eyes.

"See you at home." She kisses my cheek again.

I kiss her temple and stare down at her one more time, taking in everything about her.

"See you then."

24

KALAINE

If you have nothing in this world,
but have a loving brother,
then you are rich already.
~ A Japanese Legend

Bodhi walks down the dock with Shaka at his heels and I watch him. You know I do. He might be even better looking than he was a few years ago, or maybe absence made me forget the finer points of Bodhi Merrick. I'm so grateful for this refresher course now. He doesn't turn back to look at me, probably assuming I ducked into the shack as soon as he left, so I watch him for a little while longer, indulging myself in the sweet memories of him riding in and inviting me out, because somehow he knew it was the day I'd finally say yes.

When I walk back into the shop, Kai's face is etched with concern. "You surfed?"

"I think we just covered that fact." I realize my tone is

snappy, but I'm not about to let my overprotective older brother diminish the joy I'm feeling. "It was amazing, Kai. My nerves almost got the best of me at first. But once I got on the board, it was like everything came back, and then some. We have Bodhi to thank for it, too. He kept nudging me daily, and finally today, I caved."

Kai cuts me off. "Are you sure about this? You just got the boot off. There's no need to rush things. Don't let your infatuation with Bodhi pressure you into things you aren't ready for."

"You sound like my ninth grade Health teacher. Bodhi isn't pressuring me. He's just been there, believing in me until I believed in myself. Did you hear anything I just said? It was like I'd never been off the water. I'm not saying I'm ready to take on Waimea. But I surfed." The irrepressible smile fills my face again. "Kai. I surfed."

A tear tracks down my face, and I don't swipe it. "I didn't know if I would ever ride a board again. And now ... now I know I will."

Kai reaches over and swipes my cheek with the pad of his thumb.

We stand there silently processing too many things for words. Everything that led to this moment fills the space between us. Hanging heavy, but also lifting.

"I'm proud of you, Kala. I really am. I don't mean to be a wet blanket. I just take your safety and wellbeing seriously. When you fell ..."

Kai's brow draws in and his jaw tightens. If I didn't know better, I'd say his eyes glisten with unshed tears. Then he clears his throat.

"I stood there, frozen in my living room, powerless to act or do anything useful. I beat myself up that whole day. I should have been there, watching you in person, hopping on a jet ski to try to rescue you."

"Kai? Seriously?"

He stares at me with an intensity I've rarely seen in him. But under that veneer is my brother—the one I ran with through tall grasses and over sandy beaches. The one who let me trail behind him and his friends while he called me a grommie. He's always had an eye out for me. My brother's far more sensitive than I am in many ways. It's almost as though his heart's too soft, so he has to cover it up with bossiness and detachment. But I see him. It's pretty hard to hide from your sibling.

"Kai."

I reach out and put my hand over his. My voice is gentle.

"You're my brother, not my maker. Yes, you have an obligation to watch over me. That's how we were raised. But, man. I wouldn't want to be in your shoes. How are you supposed to keep a daredevil like me from ever taking risks that could end badly? That's not your job. You're giving me a place to stay. You've been supportive and watchful. That's what it looks like to be a big brother. But cushioning my life or being my constant shadow? No. That's too much. Trust me. I'm a woman now. It's time for you to let me be responsible for my own outcomes."

"I just worry about you. I guess it's over the top like you and Bodhi always say."

"No. Well, yeah. You have your moments, but when I imagine life without a brother like you ... I'm lucky to have you."

He smiles at me. I don't tell him often enough.

"I love you, Kai."

"I love you too, Kala. And, I'll try to dial it back a bit."

"Thanks. Any level short of personal armed bodyguard and keeper of my tower will be appreciated."

He chuckles and pulls me into a hug.

His next question catches me off guard. He's still holding me in a brotherly embrace when he asks, "So, you and Bodhi?"

"Um. Yeah. Maybe. I don't know." I pull away from Kai, smiling up at him. "I never stopped loving him."

"I know. I'm pretty sure he never got over you either. I just don't want to see you two crash and burn again."

I nod. Kai took our breakup nearly as hard as we did. I had no idea he'd taken Bodhi in, but that means he never had a reprieve from the reality of our separation.

This whole morning has taken a turn for the serious. I'm glad Kai and I talked, though. We needed this. Still, I want the joy of my time on the water back.

"We're surfing tomorrow morning," I tell Kai. "Why don't you come out with us?"

"Yeah?"

"Yeah."

"I'd like that."

"It will be just like old times."

Old times, when Bodhi and I thought nothing could dim our light.

BODHI
(DATING FOR OVER TWO YEARS)

Sadly enough, the most painful goodbyes
are the ones that are left unsaid and never explained.
~ Jonathan Harnisch

We'd all been watching the Pacific Islands Ocean Observing System live wave observation charts for weeks. A big swell has been expected at Jaws, otherwise known by its official name, Pe'ahi. It's Maui's biggest surfing break. Some friends and I reserved a couple of small chartered planes on standby to take us to Maui as soon as we hear that the big waves hit.

And hit, they did.

I wake before the alarm I had set so I could surf dawn patrol here on Oahu. My phone lights with the image of my buddy Makani, or Mak as we like to call him. He's built like a Mack truck, so the name fits. I tap my screen to answer his call as I roll over and sit up on the edge of my bed.

"What time is it, dude?" I wipe the sleep out of my eyes.

"Bro. It's time." Mak's deep voice bellows through the phone.

"Yeah? What time?"

"Time. Jaws is popping off. We're on. Get your stuff and meet me at the muni airport in thirty."

Mak's words sink in and adrenaline starts to pump through me. The sky outside the back house I share with Kai is still black as night. I don't even know what time it is, but I don't care. If you've ever watched a fireman change when the bell rings at the station, that's me right now. It probably takes five minutes between the moment I groggily answered my cell until I'm seated in my truck, backing down the driveway that runs past Kai's uncle's house at the front of the property. Then I'm on the main road, calling Mavs on my way to the airport. I loaded my wetsuit, board and inflation vest. Then I threw my pre-packed rucksack in the back. It all feels like I'm still half-asleep, but also more awake than I've ever been.

Mavs answers on the first ring, before I even realize I'm calling her at an ungodly hour. She's just getting over a head cold, so she's not surfing with us this trip.

"Bodhi?" Her voice is scratchy from sleep. Adorable. Man, I love that girl.

"Yeah. Sorry. Go back to sleep. We'll talk later."

"Is everything okay?"

"Yeah, babe. It's better than okay. Mak just called and we're heading to Maui. Jaws is going off!" My excitement overtakes me.

"Really?" She's still got that sleep-saturated tone to her voice.

"Yeah. Go to sleep. I'll check in later. I love you."

"I love you too. Always, Bo."

"Always."

We hang up and I'm smiling into the darkness. I'm a month away from my goal of asking her. I've got the ring. I've got Kai's blessing and his dad's. I don't know which means more to me. Nah. That's a lie. Getting Kai to finally approve of me being with Mavs is everything. He actually said, *If she's going to be with anyone, I'd want it to be someone like you. Be good to her.* Being good to Mavs happens to be my life's mission, so he has nothing to worry about. First, I'm going to ask Mavs to marry me, and then I'm going to keep saving so I can buy a place for the two of us here on the North Shore.

Riding a record-breaking set at Jaws is something I've dreamt of doing forever. The timing hasn't been right. Every time this level of waves hit in the past year, Mavs and I were somewhere else, surfing contests or hitting other swells on our bucket list.

The way we ride at Jaws is unique. We're not towing in, we're paddling. The jet skis will be there in the water, but only for rescues if needed. Our riding over the next few days is all prep for two future contests at Jaws and it's a test of a different sort of surfing skill.

It's not normal to paddle into waves this massive—well, surfing waves this massive isn't normal, but it's our normal. And on waves over twenty-five or thirty feet, it's customary to get a tow in. Not at Jaws. Here, we paddle. I've been training my upper body and lungs for this day for months—running under-water holding boulders, doing intense arm workouts, and preparing my joints through virtual physical therapy sessions with this physiotherapist I met in Bali.

The top names in surfing will flock to Maui over the next few days. And many tourists and locals will line the cliffs, hoping to experience the power of the ocean when waves are this high. They're also trekking all the way out to Pe'ahi for a chance at watching us—the few humans skilled, courageous and slightly insane enough to take on waves of up to fifty feet or more.

Mak is already standing next to the six-seater, single-engine plane when I park my truck. I stride over to him and greet our pilot and the two other guys on board. Once all our stuff is loaded, we taxi and then it's less than an hour before we're descending into Maui. Our friend, Griff, meets us at the airport in a 4x4 Jeep. The road out to Jaws is rugged. It's a few miles long, and dirt all the way. If conditions are good you can traverse it without too much trouble, but if it rains, all bets are off. Thankfully, today we haven't had any rain so far.

We head straight to Pe'ahi and gather with a bunch of other surfers. Some are Hawaiian natives or haole transplants like me. Others are already representing the people who are coming from all over the world to surf this break under these conditions. The energy among us is electric as we suit up and board boats or ride tandem on the back of jet skis and head out to where we'll paddle in.

They haven't invented words to describe the force of these waves. Even before I start paddling, this heady cocktail of reverence and awe bubbles through my veins. Between the anticipation and energy of the surfers here in the water, I'm pretty sure I'm literally buzzing as if someone set off a transmitter just beneath my skin.

We whoop and call out to one another. Everyone's amped up. This is our version of Christmas morning. We wait for days like this one—for the chance to gather and ride, to show our skills, to master something insurmountable, to share this thrill with other surfers we respect.

The surfing community is my ohana: my family.

We paddle up the sheer face of the waves in well-spaced clusters of four surfers at a time. I'd estimate the average wave being thirty-five to forty feet high, but some are coming in at fifty or higher. We can only estimate, but since our boards are ten-footers, we have a gauge.

My arms burn. My mind narrows in on each stroke of my hand into the water, the force of the current beneath me, and the sensations telling me when to stand. I pop up and catch this wave and ride it like I'm sliding down glass. They say we speed at around fifty miles an hour on waves like this. Everything diminishes except the rush of wind and spray of water surrounding me. And then I hit the tube and I'm sucked backwards so all I see is the clear, blue-green, glassy water to my right and the foamy wall to my left. When I exit the greenroom, I shoot out, whooping at the top of my lungs, coming to the end of my ride at a spot not far from the cluster of jet skis at the base of the waves, sitting on high-alert off to the south of the main break.

When my next turn comes to face down another set, I paddle up the face like before. But, the wave takes an unexpected turn and starts to fold before I expected it, signaling another wall of water is coming right behind it. It's a creeper set, changing the dynamic of my ride without notice. I shoot down the face of the wave, wobbling a little. I try to maintain my stance, but my knee compresses as I pivot. When I release the pressure in a snap, something pings behind my knee. A sharp pain follows. I'm thrown from my board about halfway down the face, and now I'm in the churn. My board shot overhead, I lost it. Before I can get my bearings the board lands, hitting the side of my skull with a thunk. I clamber for it, but it's ripped away, sloshed and thrown in this turbulent swell of water.

Mavs.

The ring.

I have to survive this.

She's my everything.

I'm pulled up and down as if drawn by a giant underwater bungee. Water presses in on me and then tugs away. My eyeballs feel like they could pop. Everything is being stretched and jolted.

Mavs. I love you, Mavs.

I hear her sweet voice saying the last word she spoke to me, *Always.*

I pull my inflation vest and start to surface, but everything's still upside down and sideways. I'm surrounded and overtaken by a whirling, sloshing, bubbly, surge of white chaos.

I just need a breath. One breath.

And then someone's grabbing for me. A hand comes down into the water at me like an angel reaching through the clouds. I grab for it, my arms barely able to lift. I'm hoisted out and I suck in air, sputter coughing, a burning in my chest. I don't even have the ability to register the face of the jet ski driver who pulled me up. My head throbs. My eyes ache. My knee screams in pain.

I lay across the seat of the Sea-Doo like a wet doll, gasping for huge gulps of air. Only two thoughts circle on repeat through my mind.

Mavs.

It's over. I'll never surf again.

~

When I open my eyes, Mavs is here, sitting in a chair next to me. I'm lying in a bed. A rhythmic beeping catches my attention. I turn to see the monitor displaying my heartbeat.

"I'm in the hospital?"

"Yeah. You had a pretty big fall." Mavs' eyebrows draw up into the center of her forehead and her eyes soften. "How do you feel?"

"Like crap." I close my eyes to avoid the look on Mavs' face.

I did this to her. She's been crying. And her eyes have dark circles underneath them. She's suffering because of me.

Memories flash like a slideshow: driving out to Jaws, getting in the water, the paddle up, the tube. Then things get fuzzy. My body hurts, but not like it did ... was that when I came up from the water? My head feels ... off, kind of woozy and cottony, and that spot behind my knee feels like someone took a machete to my leg.

Most of all, a dark, invisible cloud hangs over me, coating my perception. Nothing is right. Nothing will ever be right again. The word hopeless gets bantered around too lightly. I've never known the depth of that word until today. If I look forward, into what's next, a bleak emptiness stretches out as far as I can see. I won't surf again. The soul-deep truth of what I lost rings through me with the dull clang of a death knell.

I've always been an upbeat, easy-going guy. I know, somewhere deep inside me, I am not that guy anymore. He was washed away at Jaws, submerged and drowned on the rocky shores of Pe'ahi. What remains is only a shadow of the man I was before.

"Bo?" The plea in Mavs' voice tugs me out of my mental spiral.

"Yeah?"

"Look at me."

I do, instantly wishing I hadn't.

"It's going to be okay."

Mavs' words are soft. She touches my arm when she says them. She believes what she's saying.

She reaches out and brushes a piece of hair away from my forehead. Then she clasps my hand in hers.

"The doctors say you sustained a mild concussion. You tore your ACL too. But that will all be temporary. You'll need surgery and physical therapy, but as far as they know, you'll heal and be back to your old life in six months—a year tops."

I muster a smile. "Sounds good."

"What do you need?"

"Sleep. I'm a little thirsty, but mostly I need sleep."

"Okay. I'll get you water."

~

I wake, who knows how many hours later, to a nurse taking my vitals, and Mavs still stationed on the chair next to me. Kai is here now. And my mom.

"Mom?"

"Bodhi, sweetheart. I flew out as soon as Kai called. How are you feeling?"

I don't answer at first. The things I would say are fine to shout out on the water, surrounded by guys who basically eat adrenaline for breakfast. They aren't fit for my mother's ears— or Mavs', even though she's heard it all.

Finally, I say, "I've been better."

My mom's a rock. She's survived a divorce, raised me single-handedly, and has been the kind of mother who never held me back, even when my passion took me into life threatening situations on the regular.

Mom steps closer and looks me in the eyes. "Bodhi Merrick. Don't you dare give up."

A choking noise follows her last word. She's holding back tears for my sake.

"Okay." I lie again.

I should say, *too late*. No one was in that water with me. Not one soul knows what I went through, and how thoroughly an experience can rip you of everything you ever held precious, and more importantly, everything you thought you were.

But these people—Kai, my mom, Mavs—they are everything to me. I've already put them through hell. I'm not going to add to their pain by sharing the depth of despair that, in a cruel twist of fate, has become my new permanent address.

Kai has taken a seat on the other side of me. A few of the guys from the surf trip show up later in the afternoon, or evening. I don't really know what time it is until one of the attendants brings me a plastic tray with some shrimp dish and a sweet potato and taro mash next to rice. There are even two slices of pineapple at the top of the tray.

"Well, that's not usual hospital food, is it?" my mom says in a cheery voice I'm sure is meant to lift my spirits and make me grateful to be alive.

My room feels crowded, and for once in my life I'm not digging being the center of attention.

My surf buddies fill me in on the parts of my story I didn't witness while I poke at the food that should be appetizing. I can't muster the desire to eat. I take a bite or two to appease the women who love me, but I can't do any significant damage to the meal. I finally shove it away and lean back on my pillow.

Griff is regaling us with a blow-by-blow of my accident from his perspective. Surfers generally make great storytellers. When we're not on the water, we're talking up our experiences in the spirit of a fisherman sharing his latest catch.

"... The guys on the cliff were radioing to the guys on the water as to where you were. They kept getting a visual and then losing you. That slosh was insane, man."

Mak chimes in. "Your board went out from behind you. The wave sucked it up and overhead. Then it plummeted like a rocket straight down into the pound at the bottom of the wave. I couldn't tell if it hit you or not from where I was floating."

Griff takes over the story again. "You got so close to the rocks at the north part of the bay. But you averted the worst of it. Once those guys had eyes on you, Jackson took off and went right to where you were. He pulled you out and draped you over his jet ski."

"I owe him," I say, numbly.

"That's what they do, Bo." Mavs' quiet voice draws my eyes back to hers. She's been more reserved than usual, her hand always on mine, or on my arm. She only got up to use the restroom once. I can tell this is wrecking her nearly as much as it is me, and that's nearly worse than being held under a life-threatening wave.

Finally, after hours of visitation, people coming and going

to see for themselves that I'm alive, or to recount their version of the accident, I'm alone in my room. Mavs and Kai and my mom were the last to leave.

Kai just quietly put a hand on my shoulder and looked into my eyes. He squeezed the spot where his hand was resting and nodded his head. Then he walked out. If anything felt like a pinprick of light in this whole dark day, it was that moment, and the way he knew I didn't need more words from anyone. I've had my fill of encouragement and well wishers telling me how lucky I am to be alive.

Mavs left last. She kissed my forehead and then softly kissed my lips. I kissed her back, knowing it will be one of the last kisses I give her. I should have made it count, but I couldn't even muster that kind of pretense. My life is going in a different direction. I need to think of her and what hanging on to me at this point in her career would do to her.

I lie here in the dark, my only companion the beeping of my monitors. A plan starts to form. I run the options through my head multiple times before sleep takes me under. It's obvious what I have to do—for her sake. Mavs would never leave me. She would give up everything that matters to her to stand by me through this. All the while, she'd tell herself and me that this was temporary. She has no idea it's over for me. And I can't be the man who dashes her dreams and pulls her out of the life she loves. I won't be the one thing holding her back when her life needs to propel forward. She's got everything to look forward to. I've got nothing.

The next day, I'm scheduled to be discharged. My concussion is manageable enough that the doctors say I can fly home to California tomorrow. I had to make that call—whether to stay in Hawaii or go home to Cali. My mom and my aunt can tag team caring for me. We have a doctor friend in Santa Barbara who recommended an orthopedic surgeon who can see me for my ACL.

Mavs showed up as soon as visitors were allowed here today. She's snuggled on my good side, curled into me, her head on my chest, tracing patterns on my opposite arm with her free hand. It feels like I'm robbing her by allowing this kind of intimacy. It's a deception, and it leaves a bad taste in my mouth. But I'm grabbing up the last moments with her like a beggar.

"I'm going to cancel the competition," she says softly into my chest.

"No. Don't do that. I'm going back to Cali. You need to stay the course. Don't derail your life for me right now."

"I want to, Bo. I can come with you. Your mom said there's a spare room at her place. I can be there. You'd do it for me."

She's not wrong. I would do it for her. But that's different. I'm a guy. My career would pick right up. She's at a critical juncture. I can't allow her to lose momentum now—not over me and my setback, especially because in my heart I know this isn't temporary.

"Mavs." Saying her nickname nearly guts me. "I need you to go ride in that contest. And dominate. Do that for us—for yourself, for all you've worked for so far."

She shifts so her face is aimed up at mine, but our eyes don't meet because I don't tip my head down to meet her gaze.

"Okay," she relents. "But I'll see you after. As soon as it's over, I'll come to Ventura and stay with you and your mom."

I take a deep breath. I have to tell her. Stalling will only do more damage.

"No, Mavs. You should just ... maybe we need a little space. You don't need me holding you back, and this might never get better. *I* might never get better."

There. I said it.

Her voice takes on a note of panic. "I don't care. I'll stay with you as long as you need me to, Bo. Don't you realize that? You're way more important than surfing."

I knew she'd go there. Just as I suspected she would. She'll give up everything she worked so hard to achieve for me, and I can't let her.

"Don't say things like that." I turn my head and stare out the window, unable to bring myself to witness the evidence of our breakup etched on her face. "If you give up your life for me, I'll only feel worse. I want you to soar. You were made for pro surfing. You are paving the way for other women in this sport. You're living your dream. Don't give all that up for a man who can barely get out of bed in the morning."

"This is all fresh. You don't know what it will be like, even tomorrow. You'll get better, Bodhi. You will."

A fierce determination undergirds her words. It would almost convince me if I weren't so steeped in the color gray. I can taste hopelessness like a bland and bitter film coating everything. I won't get better. The thoughts I have are dreary and weighted, dragging me further into myself. I muster the most lame smile for her sake.

"Go to the contest. We'll see what's next."

I'm lying. We both know it. I never thought I'd lie to Mavs. I've always been someone who said everything he thought without pausing to filter myself. Knowing I'm deceiving her—even if it's for her own good—nearly kills me. I thought I was as low as I could go. Apparently there are new lows to hit.

"Bodhi, don't." Kalaine's voice is weak.

I've reduced her to begging. This is destroying me. But I would never live with myself if we both lost everything over my accident. The ocean might have taken my future and my joy. I won't let it rob her too.

"Kalaine." I don't call her by my favorite nickname. I can't associate that place with her anymore. "I need you to do something for me."

"Nooo." She burrows her head into my shoulder and cries.

I hold her until her sobs abate. She's still sniffling and

clinging to me as if she can reverse time through sheer willpower alone.

"Please, Mavs. I need you to do it—for me."

The taste of her pet name on my tongue feels wrong and out of place. I'm not the Bodhi she fell for. And she won't be my Mavs.

She curls into me and sobs some more. I let her, rubbing my hand in comforting strokes down her back. After a while her cries diminish and she lifts her head to look me in the eyes.

Hesitantly, she asks, "What do you need from me, Bo?"

I stare down at her, questioning my resolve only for a brief moment. "I need you to move on. Go to the contest and show them who the number one women's surfer in the world is. Win that first place for me—for us. And then keep surfing. Go big. Grab it all up. I need to know I didn't wreck you."

"You're wrecking me now." She whispers the words.

"I know." I stare out the window. I'm a coward, unable to even look at her. "But I'd wreck you more if you stayed here. Trust me. You don't need this. It's going to hurt at first, but you'll move on. You have to."

She cries some more. I hold her. No one knows me like this woman. And she knows me well enough to know the fight has left me. We lay there in my bed, clinging to one another, but both of us know the truth. This is our goodbye.

Maybe a half hour or an hour later, she gets up, cleans her face in the little in-room bathroom and takes a seat in the chair next to my bed. She tries to talk to me. I give her short answers, each one a snip of the invisible cord that has bound us so intricately and tightly together for the past two and a half years.

Finally, the nurse comes in and tells Kalaine she needs to have the room cleared so she can examine me to be discharged. My mom pokes her head in the door.

"We're breaking you out of here, Bodhi!"

Mom has no idea of what I've done—what I had to do because I love Kalaine more than life.

My mom waits in the hall. The nurse gives me and Kalaine a moment. Kalaine kisses me on the forehead, leaving a trail of kisses on my skin. And then she walks away—like I asked her to. And even though my heart screams at me to beg her to turn around, I don't. I'm doing this for her. Anything else would be supremely selfish.

I'm a drowning man. If she stays, she'll drown right along with me.

KALAINE
(ONE MONTH AFTER OUR BREAKUP)

He will be sorry for the way he treated you,
don't you worry about that.
~ Nikki Rowe

It's been a month since Bodhi broke things off—the most excruciating month of my life. I went to the competition and I won first in women's heats just like I promised him I would. He went home to California, and I think he changed his cell number, or he blocked me, because he's stopped answering any of my calls or texts. Then I stopped calling and texting because a woman can only take so much rejection before she starts to implode into a very dark place.

To top that off, Kai officially announced his voluntary retirement from the pro circuit. It had been a long time coming, I sensed it for probably the past six months to a year. But I think Bodhi's accident flipped the switch for my brother. Kai's not even casually surfing these days. And this week he got a call from a guy who owns a resort on an island off the coast of California, inviting him to come run their water sports rentals and lessons. He said he's considering it.

"What's with the men I love? They're all leaving me for California," I moan to Leilani.

We're manning the counter inside my uncle's food truck, taking orders for plate lunches from tourists and locals. I don't need the work, but I have to stay busy or I'll spin out into a grief-stricken mess.

"Sweet kaikua'ana, I don't pretend to understand men." Leilani takes money from the guy at the window and hands him his change.

The guy decides to insert himself into our conversation. "We're pretty easy. Feed us. Tell us we did a good job at whatever we're doing at the moment. Satisfy us with physical affection. Bam. You nailed it."

"Thanks, bruh. If only." Leilani rolls her eyes.

"Women are the complex creatures," the guy continues. "Full of nuance and mystery."

"Nuance and mystery, huh?" Leilani leans closer to the window to size the guy up.

From where I'm sitting, he looks attractive. Typical caucasian surfer, here to soak up the North Shore vibes.

I prop my hip on the counter behind us while my uncle continues to cook Spam on the cooktop and then cut the chicken he just grilled for the teriyaki.

"Yeah." This guy runs a hand through his shoulder-length hair. "Women are like flowers. Delicate, but also strong enough to withstand a storm. Each one unique in its beauty. Men are like coconuts."

I almost laugh. This guy is trying hard with the poetic lines, that's for sure. His eyes look sincere, though.

"I don't know what the heck you're talking about," Leilani says with a chuckle. "But I like you."

All it takes is that little bit of encouragement and this guy's all, "Wanna grab a bite sometime?"

"While you're here for what? A week? No thanks, cute

tourist boy. I'm not one of the souvenirs you get to collect like a stamp on your passport. Thanks, anyway."

"Nah. It's not like that, beautiful wahine. I'm actually moving here. I just got a place with some friends here in Haleiwa."

Touché. As cheesy as this guy's lines are, he somehow carries them off because of the sincerity in his eyes when he says them.

"Hmmm. So you're a haole. I'll think about it."

The guy beams.

"My name is Stephen. But my friends call me Scoop. Where will I find you ... ?"

He trails off, leaving room for Lei to fill in her name. She doesn't.

Then he adds, "Can I get your number?"

"Nah. You'll find me."

With that, she hands the Styrofoam box my uncle passes to her out the window.

"Take care, cute haole."

"Cute, huh?" He beams up at her like a little puppy begging for a treat.

"Cute enough that if you track me down, I might let you take me to coffee or a smoothie. Dinner's next level. You have to work your way up to that."

"See?" he says, winking at her. "Complex. Mysterious. Evasive. Women are far more challenging to figure out than men."

"Well, I hope you're up to the challenge, then." Leilani gives him a smile and turns to me, indicating she's finished with her little flirt session.

The guy takes the hint and leaves.

"I'm not going to make nearly enough money today with you chatting up every tourist that comes to the window." My uncle sounds serious, but he smiles at Leilani.

"You'll do fine. Besides, I'm ensuring they come back."

"Looking for you, not my fried Spam."

"They'll come looking for me, and they'll buy your Spam. Don't worry, anakala."

She calls him uncle, even though she's not remotely related by blood. But Leilani's ohana is mine, and mine is hers.

My time at the food truck does the job of distracting me, but as soon as I'm alone in my VW Beetle, the same feelings overwhelm me.

Bodhi broke my heart. I've never felt so aimless and empty. Tears flow down my face as I drive down the highway leading to the road that will take me back to my parents'. I think back over those days we spent in the hospital just after his accident. And then anger flows through me. How dare he push me out? Why didn't he give me a say? I would have given everything up for him. I still would. That's probably the most tragic piece of this whole situation. I'm not over Bodhi Merrick. I don't know if I ever will be.

When I came home after those first two days in the hospital on Maui, Leilani threatened to call down curses on Bodhi. She said, *I could call my uncle. He's a kahuna. He could bring Bodhi down.* Then she added, *I don't even need my uncle. I might just book a flight to California and rip that man five new orifices. What does he think he's doing?* I just answered her with the truth, *Bodhi's already down, Lei.* I wasn't mad then, but I'm furious now.

My grandma wasn't much better than Leilani. She asked me questions all rooted in our island superstitions:

Did you leave your chopsticks standing up in a bowl of rice?

No, kuku wahine. I know that's bad luck.

Did you cut your nails at night?

Did I? Maybe.

No, tutu. I didn't.

Ah. You wore shoes in the house?

Probably.

No. I am respectful. I always remove my shoes.

Then she announced her declaration. *I'm sorry, Keiki. This boy is not good for you. You need to be rid of him.*

If only. I wish there were an exorcism for the way a man's very essence entwines itself around your heart. I'd go to that ceremony and have Bodhi severed from me the same way he seems to have so easily cast me aside. Even that thought draws up tears. I don't want to have Bodhi removed from my heart. He is my heart.

I just want him back.

Maybe one day I'll find a way to live without him.

I can't imagine that happening, but he left me no choice.

25

KALAINE

Surf and feel your life be changed forever.
~ Nossa Company

I walk home from my talk with Kai, lighter than air. Most people don't get the kinds of second chances I'm being offered.

Bodhi and I might be building something new together. Only time will tell.

I'm surfing again.

And, even Kai and I might be redefining our dynamic.

The crisp morning breeze blows past me, ruffling my hair. But warm rays of sunshine peek through the misty morning fog, reminding me winter is receding and spring is on the way to Marbella.

My phone rings in my pocket, so I pull it out. Leilani's beautiful face fills the screen.

I answer the call, and her voice brings a smile to my face.

"Aloha, Kah! I was this close to sending out a missing persons report on you."

"Shush. You were not."

"You used to call me every day."

"The phone goes both ways, Lei."

"I know! I know. I'm busy helping your poor uncle run the truck, and I've been riding a lot. But there's no excuse. Sometimes I think of calling, but then I don't know what you need. So, I don't. Today, I had to call. I've got news! I'm going to be at a thing in Huntington Beach. Vans is putting on a surf expo and my agent arranged for me to be there since Vans is one of my sponsors."

"You're coming to California?"

"Looks like it. How far are you from Huntington Beach?"

"If you don't count the one hour ferry ride, we're only about two and a half hours north of there. I'll make it happen! I can't believe I'm going to get to see you."

"I can't believe you want to."

"Stop it. You know I do."

"I'm mostly kidding. That's why I called. I'm so stoked. I miss you like crazy."

"I miss you too."

I know I've pushed Leilani away. I had to. I needed the space to get my head on straight after the accident. Maybe, in his own way, Bodhi needed that too, only his dive was deeper and his darkness more profound.

"I've got news for you too," I say.

"You and Bodhi are getting married?"

"No! No." I shake my head and nearly roll my eyes. "We're still taking things one day at a time. But it's promising."

"Says the Magic Eight Ball." She chuffs. "So, what's your news?"

"Wellll ... I surfed this morning."

"What? You surfed! Kah! That's amazing."

"It was incandescent, transcendent, magnificent ..." I gush.

"Okay, Miss Thesaurus. Tell me everything. What finally pushed you into taking that leap? This is huge. I know it. You know it."

"It is."

I spend the rest of the walk home filling Leilani in on every detail of the morning.

"Bodhi's manning up these days, huh?"

"He's being consistent. And he's still irresistible."

"I'm not convinced yet. But I'm leaving the judgment call up to you. I can tell you're in a way better headspace."

"I am."

I fill Leilani in on Megan showing up when we rode in to shore.

"She wants to do an interview."

"What do you think? Are you game? Do you need to wait?"

"I think I'm going to do it. When Bodhi dropped off the face of the earth, that was news. All those reporters came around for a while. I refused to comment back then."

"I know. I remember it all."

"Yeah. But now, this is my story. It's not about him. It's about me coming back from what happened at Mavericks. I want to be the one to tell my story, and I trust Megan to tell it the way I want."

"Then, do it."

"I'm going to."

"Good. I can't wait to see the clip on YouTube."

"YouTube?"

"Yeah. They film the interviews for *Surfer* now. It reaches more people. So, I'm assuming she'll have someone there filming while she takes notes for the physical article."

"Oh. Okay."

"It'll be great, Kah. I always knew you were a phoenix. Nothing's gonna keep my girl down."

"It feels that way."

"I can't wait to see you. I'll text you all the details."

"I can't wait either."

I wonder if Bodhi will come.

Leilani and I hang up and I walk into the house.

Bodhi's dressed from his shower, and singing a song in the kitchen. As I approach, I realize he's serenading Shaka, who is sitting at his feet looking up at him with hearts in his eyes. He's switching up the lyrics to *Summer of Love* by Shawn Mendes.

"It was the winter of Shaka.

Kisses on your snout. Shaka, yeah you're sloppy, you know.

Tangled in Mavs' sheets, ah you lucky dog, you know."

I giggle and Bodhi looks up, his face turning a shade of soft red.

"Hey. Uh. How long were you standing there?"

"Long enough to hear your new chart-topper."

"Hmm." Bodhi hums and walks over to me. "Everything good with you and Kai?"

"Yeah." I smile up at Bodhi as he wraps his arms around my waist and tugs me close. "Really good. He wanted to talk about me surfing. And he agreed to back off a little."

"Kai did? He said he was backing off?"

"Not backing off, off. But yeah. A little less Mother Gothel. A little more of him allowing me to let my hair down and come out of the gilded tower."

"That's awesome. And for the record you've always struck me as more of a Moana than a Rapunzel, but I'm good with either."

"You are, are you?"

"Mm hmm." Bodhi bends and kisses my nose and then my jaw and then he places a tender kiss on my lips. I loop my hands behind his neck and run my fingers through his hair.

When we pull apart, Bodhi says, "I think I'm going to be

riding the high of your surf sesh for quite a while. It felt so good to be out in the water with you again."

"It did, didn't it?"

"Yeah. It really did."

"So ... Lei called. She's got a thing with Vans in Huntington Beach. She's sending me the details. I think I'm going to meet her there."

Bodhi's face morphs from open and relaxed to a forced neutrality.

"Are you okay?"

"Yeah. Definitely. Of course." He smiles again, but it feels scripted.

"And I'm going to do the interview with Megan."

Might as well dump all my big decisions in one fell swoop.

"You are? Are you sure?"

"Yes. Megan's right. Someone's going to tell my story. It might as well be me."

Bodhi runs a hand down my hair. "You kill me, babe. Bravest woman I know."

He places a kiss on my temple and tucks me into his chest so my head rests under his chin.

I almost blurt out the three words I haven't said to Bodhi since the day of his accident. I'm feeling so much love for him right now I can barely contain it. Love and hope. My life will go forward. I'm going to surf. I don't know how far I'll take it, but I'm going to call Dan and see what he says. I know he'll let me call the shots. If I want to go big again, we'll work up to it. If I want to stay on smaller waves and compete that way, we can make that happen too.

And Bodhi is here, holding me. I know we can make a future together. Maybe not the future we had always dreamed of—but maybe. Today, I believe anything's possible.

Bodhi's phone buzzes on the kitchen counter.

"I made coffee. Grab a mug while I see who's texting me."

He picks the phone up and mutters, "Jammer. That man won't take no for an answer."

"You told him no?"

"About San Diego, yeah."

"Why, Bodhi?"

He looks at me like he's weighing out how much to say.

"Let me check this. You've got to get ready for work."

Really? Something in my chest pulls tight. My head swims a little.

What broke us last time wasn't Bodhi's dip into depression. We could have weathered that together. What broke us was this: him shutting me out.

26

BODHI

Obstacles can't stop you. Problems can't stop you.
Most of all, other people can't stop you. Only you can stop you.
~ Jeffrey Gitomer

I see it in her eyes—the old hunger and drive. And it thrills me. Mavs deserves everything. The idea of her on a big wave again isn't going to be easy for me to work through, but if that's what she wants, I'll support her one hundred percent. I just don't know if I can be the man she needs now. I'm not where she is, itching to get back to our old life, welcoming reporters to spread the private details of the hardest season of my life out into the world for public consumption.

I've got a cush situation here on Marbella. It works. I teach lessons. I surf. I have her. Why can't that be enough? I thought it could. But I was kidding myself. Mavs needs to stretch her wings. She's always lived with both hands open, fearless and free. I wouldn't want her any other way. And I can't be the man who holds her back—I never would be that man. Not then, and not now.

I turn away from her and grab my phone.

Mavs shuffles around behind me, opening cupboards, setting a cup onto the counter with what might be a little more force than necessary. The coffee flows into the cup, then the refrigerator opens and shuts. Milk, sugar, spoon hitting ceramic in rhythmic pings. Every sound echoes into the silence between us—the silence I created by being stubborn and refusing to let her see what's really going on with me.

I turn my attention to my cell.

Jammer: *Just me again. Bugging you until you relent. Tell me you've reconsidered your answer.*

My lips pinch in and I notice my jaw tightening. I texted Jammer a week ago to say I wasn't ready to surf in any sort of contest, even one for charity. Maybe next time. He's not convinced I meant what I said. I lean back on the counter, texting my response.

Bodhi: *Still a no.*
Jammer: *I wish you'd reconsider. We all miss you, man.*
Bodhi: *I miss you too. Maybe I'll come hang another time.*
Jammer: *What would it take to sway you?*
Bodhi: *Nothing, man. It's a hard pass this time. Really.*
Jammer: *You're breaking my heart over here. Promise me you'll come hang within the next few months and I'll lay off.*
Bodhi: *I promise.*
Jammer: *I'm going to hold you to that.*
Bodhi: *I know you will. Gotta jet. Take care, Jammer.*
Jammer: *You too.*

Mavs has turned toward me, leaning back on the counter adjacent to mine. She lifts her mug to her mouth and takes a sip.

"What did Jammer have to say?"

"He wanted to change my mind. I told him maybe next time."

"Why?" Her eyes implore me to crack open. "Bodhi, you can talk to me. I'm not fragile. I won't break."

"It's just ..." I stride over to her, taking the mug from her hands and setting it on the counter. Then I wrap my arms around her waist. "It's not my thing, I guess."

Mavs looks up at me. "Bo. This is me. Tell me what's going on. Don't shut me out."

Her unspoken *again* hangs in the air.

I close my eyes. She's right.

A war rages inside me. I don't even know why I won't tell her. Maybe she'll push me. She'll definitely call my bluff. She's so courageous. Maybe I'm not made of the same stuff she is.

I look her in the eyes. The honey-golden brown is soft and sweet as ever. The way she's looking at me ... I could conquer the world. For her, I would.

"I'm afraid, Mavs." As soon as those words fall from my lips, it's as if I'm stripped down in front of her, unable to hide anything. "After how things were, I'm finally good. I surf every day. I teach. I take people on the adventures they save all year to go on—and I get paid to do that. You're here. We're ... good. If I don't go down to San Diego, it won't all be up in my face." I trail the back of my hand down from her temple to her chin.

Now that I've started, I'm a parishioner in her confessional. My thoughts flow like private admissions into the safety between us.

"When I fell at Jaws, and came out of that accident in the hospital, I had clinical depression. The day I sent you away, I didn't have a label for it, but the doctors figured it out that week. My whole world went black. I couldn't snap myself out of it. I've never experienced anything so grim and hopeless. I came home to Mom's, and it got worse. She dragged me to a counselor and a psychiatrist. I had no motivation, but I went for my mom.

"After my surgery, Mom called Kai and he showed up. He had just started working here at the resort. He knew how badly I had hurt you, but he still came and checked in on me. Whatever Mom told him made him set aside his anger at how I had hurt you enough to be willing to reach out. After that first visit, he'd show up every few weeks like a leaky faucet with a slow drip, relentlessly wearing me down.

"One day he made the suggestion that I consider moving in with him. The next visit, he said, *Your mom already raised you. Get out of her hair and come stay with me.* I wouldn't have if he didn't put it that way, and he knew it. So, I packed my stuff the following week, took the ferry and moved in with your brother. Before you know it, I was working at the watersports shack, still doing online therapy sessions with my counselor once a week, and tapering my meds. And a while after that, I got back in the water."

"I didn't know all that." Mavs smiles up at me softly.

"How would you? I didn't tell you, and Kai never would. He knows it's not his story to tell. But, now, I'm good. I haven't had to face down that kind of persistently bleak outlook since I got better. Some people fall into that pit and never get out. I was one of the lucky ones. I'm out. But I could fall in again. It scares me to think that could happen. And seeing those guys—so many of my old friends—living their lives, still being sponsored, or even better, being the sponsors for other surfers? That could crack me, Mavs. I just can't take that chance."

I confess my deepest reality to her. "I miss it every day. Not a day goes by that I don't ache for the thrill of the big rides, the way we'd sit up planning our next adventure, the hunger and the bliss of it all. With you here, that longing has dissipated. But it never leaves. Maybe I'll crave those kinds of waves—our old life—every day until I die."

"I know, Bodhi. I can tell. Your life here is so good. But it's like you're one of those birds that flies into a window thinking he can keep going. Then, he backs up and flies at it again. You're hitting an invisible barrier. Maybe it's time to bust through. Or maybe not. But if not now, when?"

"I don't know, Mavs. But I can't go this time. I just can't."

"Okay." She reaches up and cups my jaw with her hand. "I won't push you."

She stands on her tiptoes and loops her hands around my neck and tugs my head down so she can kiss me. I pull her close and kiss her like it's our last one. She melts into me and I hold her, pulling back to tell her what she means to me. I've said everything short of professing my love. I can't do that when we haven't even decided where things are headed between us.

"You did awesome out there today." My hands remain looped behind her while I look down into her eyes.

"I did, right? It was amazing. I'm still riding the high."

"You earned that. Ride the bliss all the way until dawn patrol tomorrow."

"I will. And, Bodhi?"

"Yeah?"

"Consider San Diego."

I nod my head, but I know I probably won't. Not taking that risk probably makes me the world's biggest hypocrite. The thing is, I'm good here. I'm finally good.

I stare into Mavs' eyes. She's lit up from the inside. Ready to take on the ocean and an interview already. I feel her slipping away from me, moving forward in only a few short months in ways I haven't in the two years since my accident.

I just got her back and now she's ready to jump with both feet into a life I can't stomach. And just like last time, I can't ask her to put a brake pedal on her life just because I'm unwilling or unable to move forward.

27

KALAINE

Love is a lot of things, but safe isn't one of them.
~ Mandy Hale

"So, you came here?" Megan asks me.

Megan and I are sitting on one of the patios at the back of Alicante. The resort roped off the area for us.

I nod. "Yes. My brother, Kai Kapule, lives here."

"Kai was a pro surfer at one point."

"Yes. He retired a little over two years ago."

"I remember his career well. Send him our regards from *Surfer* mag."

"I will."

Megan's cameraman joined us for the interview. Just like Leilani predicted, he's filming me while Megan asks questions. She's not writing anything down this time since she'll have the film to watch and draw material from later. Megan and I agreed not to mention the name or location of the island so we don't draw a crowd of people here who would invade my privacy.

"And what happened when you arrived?"

I don't tell her how Bodhi answered the door the day I showed up on Kai's porch. I already decided to leave his name out of this whole interview. This is my story. He'll remain anonymous.

"I ran into an old friend. That person was instrumental in getting me past my fears. I just surfed for the first time again last week."

"So you're physically able to surf again."

"I am." My voice lifts. "I didn't know if I would. But I am."

"That's totally understandable after the kind of accident you endured."

Megan already walked me through a series of questions so I could give a rundown of what happened at Mavericks.

"Will you be getting back into the circuit?"

"I'm considering it. I just talked with Dan two days ago. We're figuring out next steps."

"Dan Hale, your coach and jet ski pilot?"

"Yes. Dan Hale."

"Well, that's exciting news!"

"It is. I don't know what we'll decide, but we're working out options together, and Dan's talking with my previous sponsors."

"I love hearing that. The world of surfing will welcome you back with open arms. I hope you know that."

"I do. I'm fortunate. And I love our ohana—our surfing family."

Megan smiles and then she asks me a question that takes me by surprise.

"So, do you see Bodhi Merrick much these days?"

I school my features. If I even flinch, I'll give everything away on camera. I'd like to shoot Megan a *what the heck* look.

"I hear from him. He's doing well."

"Good. I'm glad to hear it. Our readers and viewers would love to know if you two are ever getting back together."

"We've each been through a lot. We're supportive of one another. He's a special man."

"Okay. So you'd rather not talk about Bodhi."

Ding. Ding. Ding. And the winner is, Megan!

"This interview is about me, my accident at Mavericks, and my recovery. I'd like to focus on that. If Bodhi and I ever officially get back together, we'll call you. Does that work?"

"It works, Kalaine. I hope I didn't overstep. It's sort of my job to ask the hard questions—the ones everyone wants me to ask on their behalf."

"I get it."

We go on to talk about my plans. I mention the Vans event in Huntington, which is the weekend before the charity surf event in San Diego—the one Bodhi still refuses to attend. Then we wrap up and the camera finally turns off.

"I'm sorry, Kalaine." Megan looks contrite. "I didn't mean to go into a subject that was off limits by bringing up Bodhi. I just figured when I saw the two of you together ..."

"We're still figuring things out. It's not at the level where either of us wants details out in the public eye yet."

"I should have asked you off camera first. I'm truly sorry."

"No problem. I trust you to keep things between us until I get a hold of you with any status update. If I ever have one."

I stop talking. No need to yammer on about all my uncertainties with Bodhi. Ever since our talk in the kitchen we've been more affectionate, even in front of Kai.

It took a lot for Bodhi to tell me all his fears and the details of what happened after his fall. He comes across as easy-going, and he is, but admitting his struggles has always been an issue. It's like he thinks his weaknesses will hold me back, so he tries to protect me from them. I'd love to be the woman who teaches him that weakness is strength when it's shared with the ones we love. I'm not sure if he's going to extend me that privilege.

∽

I'M SITTING on the couch with Shaka, reading a book I picked up called, *Life on the Edge: A Story of Ten Big Wave Surfers.* My phone rings with an unknown number. In small print under the area code, it says, San Diego, so I answer.

"Hello?"

"Hey, Kalaine. It's me, Jammer. Do you remember me?"

"Sure, Jammer."

"I just saw the piece on YouTube—your interview with Megan Woodruff from *Surfer*?"

"Yeah? I didn't realize it was live yet. I was out in the water this morning and then I went to work. I'm just curling up with a book right now. Actually, you're mentioned in one of the stories."

"Is that *Life on the Edge*?"

"It is. How'd you guess?"

"I'm not included in too many books—not like you and Bodhi. Anyway, I was calling you about something specific. Not just the interview."

"If it's about getting Bodhi to come down, I don't think I can help you out."

"Nah. He's already shot me down a bunch of times. I'm getting the hint. He wants me to back off. I've left him alone after the last string of texts we sent one another."

I run my hand down Shaka's back.

"What do you need then?"

"Well, I wasn't aware you were back in the water until I saw the vid on YouTube. I thought you might want to come hang. You'll know a lot of people down here. You said you and Dan were considering what's next. There are a lot of shoulders you might want to bump into—people who might be instrumental in helping you get back into contests and even some new sponsors. If not that, you could just see some old friends. Ride some waves if you want. Or not. We'd all love to see you."

"Wow. That's ... thanks. Can you give me a minute to think this over? I'd really love to say yes. I just need to think."

"Sure. Take your time. And if Bodhi wants to come along, his invite is open. No pressure on either of you."

"No pressure?" I tease Jammer.

"Okay. Well, a little pressure. Just enough to get you to say yes."

I smile. "Thanks, Jammer. I'll let you know."

We hang up and I set the book aside. I don't really need to think this over—not for me, I don't. But with Bodhi refusing to go, I think I need to talk to him.

Bodhi comes home from work alone right around dinner time. He's carrying a bag of tacos with him. Kai had to do something, he didn't say what, so it's just me, Bodhi and Shaka in the house this evening.

"Hey, babe," Bodhi sets the bag of tacos on the counter and pulls me into his arms.

There's something lighter about him since we talked the other day. It's like he needed permission to choose this life. I'd never push him into something he doesn't feel ready for. He didn't push me. I don't think he knows what really caused our demise last time. It wasn't his inability to move forward. It was how he shut me out. I don't know what we'll do if I start surfing again professionally, but I know we can make anything work if we're both willing to communicate and be real with one another. For a man who lets everything he's thinking fall right out of his mouth, he has the hardest time being vulnerable when it matters most.

I lean into his arms. He cups my jaw and looks down into my face like he's holding something precious, but also, like he's about to say goodbye. I know he isn't. We just overcame a massive hurdle. Still, the expression on his face sends a shot of apprehension through me. I want to assure him we're good. We can ride this wave too—whatever it brings.

"I love you, Mavs."

The air nearly leaves my lungs. I actually gasp.

"You ... love me?"

"I always loved you. I never stopped. I love you so much it breaks me. And then it puts me back together. You are the only woman I'd ever consider making a life with. I love you."

I feel tears prick the corners of my eyes and fall down my cheeks while a smile stretches my face wide. "Bodhi, I love you so much. I missed you."

I sob a little, the weight of how much we've endured and how much I missed him washing over me in one powerful swell. "I love you, Bodhi Merrick. No matter what."

He leans in and claims me with a kiss so fierce and full, I almost tip backwards. His hands still cup my jaw. I grip the sides of his shirt at his waist and hold him to me. We kiss with forgiveness and hope and hunger and healing. And then our kisses soften, and Bodhi's stroking my hair and pulling away to say things like, "I missed you so much," and, "Never again, Mavs," and, "You're it for me." The things he mutters are nearly incoherent strings of promises and regrets and declarations, all punctuated with soft kisses to my jaw, my mouth, my cheeks.

I pull back and our eyes meet. "Bodhi, you aren't losing me."

I have to say what I sense he's thinking.

"I might go back to competing. That doesn't mean you have to. We can make anything work as long as we do it together."

He's quiet. His eyes soften. There's this unspoken moment between us where I am the private witness to something shifting inside him. We stand there, gripping one another, wordlessly coming home.

"I never wanted to be the one to hold you back." His voice is low and serious.

"You don't hold me back. No one has ever believed in me

like you do. I wouldn't have gotten in the water without you. You push me forward. You need to see that—the power and influence you have. You make a difference. I need you."

He smiles at me. "Back then, after the accident, I was so crushed. I couldn't stand the idea of you giving everything up for me. You had so much momentum. It was your time to shine. I didn't want to put a dimmer on how far you could go."

"I understand that now. But it would have been so much better if you could have given me the choice. It was my decision to stay or move on. You took that from me."

He smooths my hair and then he places a soft kiss on my forehead.

"Forgive me, Mavs. I wasn't in my right mind. My headspace was so messed up. All I could think was that I was going down like a sinking ship, and I couldn't bear to take you with me."

"And it nearly killed me to watch you drown while shoving me onto shore."

"I know, babe. I know. If I could go back and do it over ..."

"We're not going back. We're moving forward."

"Agreed. Moving forward. I'm here. And I'm yours, Mavs. I'm in. I don't want to push you out. Just promise me you won't let me hold you back."

"I can't promise that."

His face contorts a little.

"I won't promise not to bend or sacrifice for you. Life isn't about grabbing up our own joy and achieving our own goals at the expense of the people who matter most to us."

He's not convinced. I see it in his eyes, so I press on. "When you choose life with someone, you choose to include them. This is a partnership, Bo. And if we go forward together, we'll both be giving something up—probably regularly. But I believe what we'll gain in exchange for those concessions will be worth it."

"How'd you get so smart?" He smiles down at me.

I smile back and lean into him so he can hold me.

"I want this, Mavs. Us. I want us. All of it."

"Then let's get it—all of it, together."

~

"Is that everything?" Kai asks me for the third time.

"Yes. I'm not moving out, I'm just going away for four days. Chillax, Kai.'"

"I'm so chill. This is me, your not-intense-bodyguard being super-chill."

He waves a hand up and down in front of his torso and then raises both hands in a gesture of innocence. He is getting better. But old habits die hard. I'm giving him grace.

I went to Huntington to see Leilani last week. She and I rode together. It was the sweetest time, seeing her, riding waves together, hanging out afterward. A few reporters approached me when I came out of the water after a sesh with Lei. I talked with them about my plans. Dan and I decided I'd start preparing to compete again. Bodhi is one hundred percent behind me. Would I rather he be at my side? Yes. But we have an understanding. I won't push him. And he won't withhold his heart. He'll let me in, and we'll navigate the hard choices together.

I pick up my duffel and walk toward the door. Bodhi's teaching a surf lesson this morning, so Kai brought a golf cart around to take me to the ferry. I throw my things into the cart and take the passenger seat next to Kai. As he pulls away from the house, I stare at the porch, remembering the day I showed up here, confused and searching. Bodhi answered the door— the man I didn't want to see, but longed for at a cellular level with a yearning that never diminished despite two years of separation. And now, I'm on my way to surf in a competition for charity—to see my surfing ohana, the family of extended friends who live for that one next ride.

A part of me believes Bodhi should push through his resistance and come along, but I haven't said anything since our conversations weeks ago. If our relationship is going to work, I have to give him the honor of choosing his own pacing and limits.

Kai parks the golf cart at the edge of the sand. We grab my things and walk toward the ferry. I wish Bodhi were here to see me off, but he's got his job. He's teaching someone to surf. That's important in its own way.

As I come to the end of the dock, a man emerges from the interior cabin of the ferry. I expect a crew member to help me with my board.

I blink. "Bodhi?"

"Yeah." His face breaks into a lopsided smile.

"What are you doing here?"

I look back at Kai. "Did you know he was here?"

I can't believe he came here just to see me off.

Kai smiles and tips his chin toward Bodhi.

Bodhi steps off the boat and onto the dock. "I couldn't let you move on without me. Not this time. I called Jammer last night. I'm coming to San Diego. I'm going to surf with you there. And I'm even going to play with the band."

I throw my arms around Bodhi's neck.

"You're coming! Are you sure?"

Bodhi holds me tight and murmurs into my hair. "I'm sure, Mavs."

Then he pulls back and looks me in the eyes. "I got to thinking. And then Kai and I were talking a few nights ago. I can live a half life, playing it safe, or I can go all in. And I want the whole picture. I want you and me together, traveling, surfing, all of it. I don't know when I became the guy who played it safe. But I'm ready to risk again."

I smile up at Bodhi. "You are the bravest man I know."

Bodhi's voice is quiet, obviously trying to keep his words between the two of us. "You make me brave. You make me want to take all the chances."

He smiles down at me, and then he winks before leaning in so his mouth is right next to my ear. In a soft voice, scratchy with emotion he says, "Kiss me, Mavs."

I tilt back so I can see his face. I'm unable to contain my smile. "Oh? Who's demanding kisses now?"

Then I rise up on my tiptoes to give Bodhi a light kiss. He kisses me back and I lose myself in him until my brother clears his throat. Loudly. Twice.

"Okay, you two. My work here is done," Kai says as Bodhi and I separate.

"Your work, huh?" I laugh.

"Definitely. Where would you two be without me? Now get on the ferry before it takes off without you."

I walk over to Kai and give him a hug.

"Take a few waves for me, Kah."

"Okay," I promise him. "And you do me a favor while I'm gone."

"Anything."

"Check in on Mila."

The blush rises up his cheeks faster than fire on dry leaves.

Mmm hmmm. That's what I thought.

EPILOGUE
BODHI - FOUR MONTHS LATER

Love's about finding the one person
who makes your heart complete.
Who makes you a better person
than you ever dreamed you could be.
~Julia Quinn

"How's surfing's *it* couple doing today?" Kai smirks at me and Mavs when he walks out from the hallway into the kitchen.

"That joke just doesn't get old," I deadpan.

"It really doesn't."

"It kind of does." Mavs smiles over at her brother.

Mavs called Megan a few months ago when we got back together, and Megan released a lead story about surfing's "it" couple rising up from the depths. I rolled with it, even though that kind of publicity is not my jam.

I'm rolling with a lot of things these days.

After Megan's story released, other sports magazines got in

on the action. Mavs and I have been featured and interviewed in a bunch of crazy-big publications. Hello, *Sports Illustrated*. Kai teases us all the time asking how the "it" couple is doing, or asking for my autograph in front of customers just to stir the pot and spur them to ask questions and even request my autograph. It's all good. If this is the price of having my girlfriend back in my life, I say, bring it.

"You two about ready?"

"I'm ready." Mavs smiles up at me. "Are you?"

"To watch you teach a bunch of kids to surf? Yes. This is going to be epic."

Shaka wags his tail.

"You stay here, buddy." I point to his dog bed in the living room.

I don't know why we have that fluffy pillow thing for him, he still sleeps in Mavs' bed at night, and then he naps on the floor—right next to the dog bed, but never on it.

"He can come," Kai says.

"Shaka?" I look at Kai. "You're saying he can come? We're doing a lesson."

"I know. He can ... you know ... hang with me. Or around outside the shack. Whatever."

Mavs and I exchange a look. Kai's softening to our dog, but he still doesn't want to admit it.

"Okay. Come on, Shaka. Let's go surf." I smile down at our mutt. He's scrappy and rough around the edges, but he's the best dog on the island as far as I'm concerned.

Shaka wags his tail. Mavs isn't the only one who found a renewed love for the ocean this year. Shaka loves getting out on a board with me.

The four of us walk down the street until the beach comes into view and then we turn and walk across the sand toward the watersports shack. A group of kids has already gathered out front on the benches. A few parents linger, chatting. We get everyone suited up and assigned a rental board and then Mavs and I lead our students down toward the spot on the sand where we will start lessons.

Once everyone has their boards laid out on the beach, Mavs takes over. She's signed on with Alicante to teach lessons whenever she's home on Marbella. Her time is split between training for her competitions, traveling for surf contests, and living here on the island. She still helps Mila part time when she's home. Kai hired on another two part-time employees to fill in so I can have more flexible hours too.

The six junior wannabe surfers are lined on the sand, facing the ocean, each one with a foam trainer board next to them.

Mavs smiles and addresses the group of five boys and one girl, probably all ranging between the ages of eight and eleven.

"Hi, everyone. I'm Kalaine, but you can call me Kay or Kala or Kah. I'm going to be one of your instructors today. And this is my friend, Bodhi. He and I are going to be showing you the basic moves and techniques you'll need to start surfing. We'll practice here on the beach, and then we'll take you out into the waves once everyone has the hang of the basics."

"You're Kalaine Kapule?" the student named Leena asks Mavs.

"I am."

"You're my idol. I want to be a surfer because of you."

Mavs smiles warmly at the girl and thanks her.

We run through the moves, showing the kids how they'll drag their arms to paddle out into the water, and then we practice popping up. Once everyone has a hang of the moves they'll need, we lead our class down into the shorepound and show them how to walk their boards out. Then we take them into waist-deep water and help them mount their boards.

Mavs and I paddle alongside the cluster of students, calling out instructions and watching for their skills and safety. Eventually, a few stand up and catch waves. We ride and float in the water for an hour, and then everyone paddles back to shore.

It never gets old: the excited chatter and beaming smiles of our students after they've caught their first waves, or even when they didn't learn to stand, but spent an hour in the water pushing their own limits. And now I get to share this experience with Mavs.

I watch her come out of the water, her long brown hair falling in wet waves down her back, her smile wide. She looks over at me.

"Fun?" I ask her.

"I loved it. Did you see Leena catch that last wave?"

"I did. She's no grommie—not yet. But she did great for a first day."

The urge to lean in and kiss Mavs tempts me, but we're technically at work with six sets of eyes fixed on us. We lead the group up to the dock where Shaka meets us, his tail wagging wildly.

Parents congregate inside the shop and out front near the benches, retrieving their children one by one. Some set up lessons for later in the week so their child can build on the skills they learned today while they're here on vacation. Others thank us and head back to the resort for the day.

Leena lags behind.

"Um, Miss Kalaine?"

"Yes?" Mavs smiles at her.

Mavs already tugged her wetsuit zipper down so the top hangs loose at her waist, revealing her swimsuit underneath. She's toweled off her hair into a mess of wild curls.

"I ... um ... could you ..." Leena looks around and then back at Mavs. Then she sticks a small notebook out. "Could I get your autograph?"

Mavs beams. After all she's been through, nearly losing her life and then her profession, she's bounced back and even gained a new generation of fans. She takes the notebook and scrawls something in it, then she turns to Leena's mom.

"Should we take a photo together?"

"Would you?" Leena nearly squeals.

"Of course."

Leena's mom lifts her phone and captures a few shots of Mavs and Leena. I walk over and offer to photograph the three of them.

When they leave, I turn and pull my girlfriend into my arms.

"Can I get your autograph too?"

"Hmmm." Mavs taps her chin and pretends to debate my request.

I kiss her chin and then her nose.

"I could be persuaded," she says, leaning back and looking me in the eyes.

"Oh yeah?"

"Yeah."

"Challenge accepted." I tug Mavs toward me with my hands looped behind her back. I lean in and place a kiss on her lips. She returns my kiss with equal tenderness. We've come so far. Not a day passes that I don't think of all we nearly lost, individually and as a couple. Each moment like this is a gift.

Kai walks out the shop's back door.

"You guys are going to run off my customers."

I pull back from Mavs, keeping my arms wrapped around her waist.

She turns her head toward her brother. "We just gave six lessons for you. I'd say we're good for business."

"Maybe in the water, but all bets are off once you two hit the shore."

We laugh.

"I'll be in," I say. "Give me a minute to say goodbye to your sister."

"She's not going overseas. You two will see one another in a few hours."

Kai acts disgruntled, but he's as happy as we are that we've made it through the hardest season of our lives.

I pull Mavs back in for another kiss. "I'll see you at home this afternoon. Maybe we can hit the evening glass off."

"I have to hit it. I promised Dan I'd ride every day."

"Great. It's a date."

"You're getting lax, Bo. Coming home to me does not count as a date."

"I'll make it count. Just you wait."

She smiles, then stands on tiptoes and kisses me, and then she turns and calls Shaka. Once she's changed, she and our dog make their way back to our house. I watch them go before I head into work.

∽

THE FOLLOWING WEEK, we're at the US Open.

No. Not that one.

Mavs and I do not golf. We're surfing.

Most people don't know about the world's largest surf competition unless they live in Huntington Beach, California, aka "Surf City," or they're into surf culture. Mavs and I aren't competing, but we're hoping to compete next year. This week we're hanging with friends, watching the contests, catching waves when the heats aren't underway, and hooking up with our sponsors.

And we're interviewing with Megan later today—Yes. Megan from *Surfer*.

"Did you see that wave Justin caught?" Mavs runs up the sand through the massive crowd of people sitting in a continuous, colorful sprawl of beach chairs, umbrellas and towels—all here for the competition.

"I saw it!" I loop my arm around Mavs' waist when she approaches. "He's definitely advancing."

"That alley-oop was insane!" She's nearly buzzing with excitement.

"It was. He killed it." I tug her into my side.

Leilani walks up behind Mavs. I flew her in for the contest. She and Mavs haven't seen one another in a while. Though, now that we're surfing more, we cross paths with Leilani and a bunch of our old friends in the most unusual places. So far, we've been to Australia and South America over the past four months. We've got a European tour scheduled three months from now.

"This is the life!" Leilani says. "Give me a sunny day on the beach watching hot surfers kill it out on the water any day. I'm in my personal version of heaven." Leilani comes over and gives Mavs a squeeze. "And seeing you! That's icing!"

"And you too, I guess." Leilani gives me a playful shove as Mavs steps back into my side and I wrap an arm around her.

Of all Mavs' family and friends, Leilani held a grudge against me the longest. I don't blame her. I held a grudge against myself. But we've made our peace now that she sees how happy Mavs is being back together with me.

Friends we've known for years cluster around us. It feels like old times, only better. Life tore Mavs and me apart, but we've been stitched back together—stronger and with an invisible extra layer of something we didn't have before. I wouldn't wish our ordeals on anyone, but coming out the other side I can see how they refined us and gave us an immeasurable appreciation for one another, surfing, and life.

"Hey! It's Kalaine and Bodhi!" a kid who can't be over fourteen shouts.

When I glance toward him, he's pointing at us, and his friends are all staring in our direction.

I tip my chin to the kid. A few other heads turn our way.

Whenever we're off Marbella, we're noticed by someone. I'm sure all the attention will level out, but not anytime soon—not after today.

Something else catches Mavs' eye. Her brows draw in, and she looks up at me, then over toward the judges' stands.

"Is that ...?" She squints and steps away from me a little so she can see more clearly.

"Kai?" Mavs shouts her brother's name.

Heads around us turn to see what she's shouting about.

"Huh. Looks like it." I answer her casually.

"That's Kai! I'd know that man anywhere," Leilani says.

When I glance up the beach, Kai's walking across the sand toward us, a big smile on his face.

He reaches us, and Mavs asks, "Kai, what are you doing here?"

He pulls her into a hug. "I thought I'd join you. I never take time off, so I figured it was time for a break. Besides, I wanted to see the Open."

"You wanted to see the Open? Are you feeling well?" Mavs looks even more confused.

"Yeah. Why?" Kai's whole demeanor is casual and calm, as if he just takes the ferry, drives nearly three hours and shows up in Huntington everyday when he's supposed to be manning the watersports shack back on the island.

"It's just that pro surfing hasn't been your thing since you retired." Mavs narrows her eyes at Kai like she's trying to solve a riddle.

"Well, today, it is."

"How are the heats lining up?" Kai asks me, obviously trying to redirect his sister away from her line of questioning.

When Mavs looks at Leilani, Kai glances over at me and winks.

"Hey. I think Jammer's up next." I tell Mavs, hoping she'll look out toward the ocean.

She scans the ocean, surveying the lineup of surfers while she shades her eyes with her hand.

Leilani pulls Kai aside and the two of them start talking.

"I can't tell which one he is from here," Mavs says to me. "Let's go down toward the water."

"Give me a minute," I tell her. "I've gotta grab something."

I hold Mavs' gaze so she doesn't focus on what's going on around us. My smile spreads when she looks up at me. She's oblivious to the crowd parting to let my special guests through. The couple comes and stands a few feet behind her.

Before Mavs has a chance to look around, I drop to one knee in the sand, grabbing the box from a pocket in my swim trunks.

"Bodhi, what are you doing?" Her brows draw in.

Kai has his phone out, recording everything.

Mavs follows my gaze to where I accidentally glanced in Kai and Leilani's direction. They're both smiling, and Kai's holding the phone out to capture this moment.

"Kai, Why are you ...?" Mavs asks. She turns back to me. "Wait! Bo?"

I don't give her time to say the next words. I look up at her, reaching my hand out so I can catch hers in mine. I run my thumb across her knuckles. "Mavs, you're everything. I knew it the first day I met you in that parking lot at Mavericks. It was almost as if a small voice inside me said, 'She's the one.'"

Mavs claps her free hand over her mouth. Her smile pulls her cheeks up and her eyes fill with tears.

"I don't believe in love at first sight. But I do believe in us. I won't ever be able to tell you what it means to me that you gave us another chance. You know you are my forever. I want little Bodhis and little Mavs running on the beach with us. I want to take you on adventures, chasing down waves. I want to watch you soar, and catch you when you fall. I want to be the man at your side now, and long after we take our last waves. Tell me you'll be my wife. Will you marry me?"

Tears are streaming down Mavs' cheeks. She falls to her knees in front of me.

"Yes, Bodhi! Yes!" She throws her arms around my shoulders.

When she pulls back, I slip the ring on her finger while we're both still kneeling on the sand. And then I kiss her. The salty taste of her tears mingles with the sweetness that's always waiting for me whenever our lips connect.

We kneel there, oblivious to the crowd forming around us, losing ourselves in the moment—this moment we've waited a lifetime to experience. I'm vaguely aware of the clicking of cameras, so I pull back, swiping a curl away from Mavs' face and smiling at her. Then I extend her my hand, and we stand up together. She leans into me and I loop my arm behind her back.

Mavs' father approaches us.

"Kalaine?"

Her had snaps around. "Makuakane?" She uses the Hawaiian word for *father*. "You're here?"

Her father smiles, and I can see the moment when Mavs' eyes rove the group of people closest to us, catching on her mom.

"Makuahine?" She says the Hawaiian name for *mother* when she sees her mom.

"Yes, Kalaine," her dad answers. "We are here. Bodhi made arrangements for us to be here to witness him asking you to marry him."

Then Leilani rushes Mavs. "You're engaged!" She throws her arms around her best friend.

They rock together in a hug, saying words I can't understand to one another before releasing each other.

"Bodhi," Kalaine's father addresses me.

His face is serious.

"We are washing the past out with the tide today—keeping what is meant to remain on shore, and letting the debris float away into the water to be shaped like sea glass into something more beautiful. This is a new day. When you called me to ask for my daughter's hand for the second time in my life, I told you that the past was now behind us. I release you and Kalaine from your mistakes and bless you into your future together. You are the man to whom I am entrusting my daughter's heart. Care for her. And now, you will officially be our ohana."

He walks toward me, extending something small.

I reach my hand out. Kalaine's father places a piece of jewelry into my palm.

"This is a Hawaiian necklace. The pendant is engraved with your Hawaiian name. We are naming you Makoa. You are still Bodhi, the awakened or enlightened one. And I believe you have lived up to your name. But Makoa means, the brave one. Any man can hide from life—hide from his past and the pain it caused him—and many do. It takes a brave man to rise up from the waves that threaten to take him under. Now you are Makoa."

I look at the necklace, thumbing the pendant with Hawaiian characters engraved in the metal. I start to put the necklace on. Mavs steps nearer to me and clasps it for me. Her hands linger on my neck and her honey-brown eyes lift to mine.

"You don't take that off."

"I know. I've seen other guys wearing theirs. I just never thought I'd have one."

"I love it." She smiles at me. "And, thank you for asking my father for my hand. It means the world to me that you would do that."

"I needed to know he was good with us now."

"They love you, Bo. We all do."

I wrap my arm around Mavs and turn to Mr. Kapole. "Thank you for this, and most of all for your blessing. I love Kalaine. I will cherish her and keep her heart safe. You can trust me."

The people around us start to gather around to look at Mavs' ring and my necklace. There are lots of hugs and shouts of joy. Reporters who are here for the event come by and take our photo. Kai makes his way through the throng of people until he's standing by my side.

A group of female surfers who are old friends of ours surround Mavs, congratulating and hugging her.

Kai pulls me into a hug and claps me on the back. "I'm honored to call you brother."

"I always thought of you as a brother." I leave my hand on his shoulder when he pulls back, squeezing once to emphasize my words. "I wouldn't be here without you."

"You'd have done the same for me." He smiles warmly.

"I would."

My eyes scan the crowd for Mavs. Always. I'll always seek her out when we are separated. Maybe it took her coming to us, broken and nearly defeated, but in the end, I know we would have found our way back to one another somehow. She's my missing piece, and I'm hers.

She sees me searching for her, and she beams over at me. I pat Kai on the back and walk toward my future wife. When I reach her, I pull her into my arms and kiss her on the forehead, allowing my eyes to drift shut so I can breathe in the smell of tropics and flowers and saltwater. Not a day will pass that I won't treasure the gift of this woman in my life. Nothing makes a man appreciate what he has more than nearly losing it for good. When I look into Mavs' eyes, I see all my own emotions reflected back to me.

"I love you, Mavs."

"I love you too, Bodhi. Always."

Have you read all the Love Trippin' Stories?

You can read Cam & Riley's story in *Are We There Yet,* a road trip romcom.
And find Ben and Summer's story in *A Fish Out of Water,* an enemies to lovers romcom.

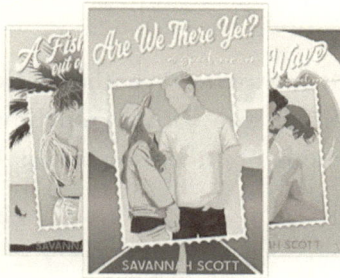

Coming June 2024: Kai and Mila's Story in *Resorting to Romance,* a single mom, fake dating romcom.

If you love laugh-out-loud, small-town, closed-door romcoms, come on over to Bordeaux, Ohio (pronounced Bored-Ox) **The Getting Shipped Series** is Savannah's well-loved stories set in rural Ohio with found family friendships, meddling townspeople, and book boyfriends so hot they could pop a whole row of corn.

Have you heard of **the Sweater Weather series,** set in Harvest Hollow? You can fall in love with a Frenchman in Savannah's story from that famous multi-author series: *A Not So Fictional Fall.*

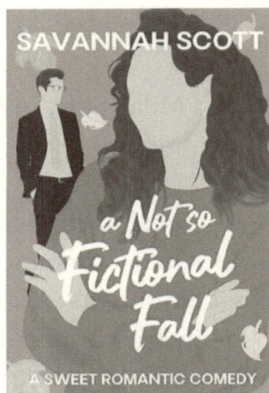

And then, if you still need to hear another man call a woman "Cher," pick up *He's So Not My Valentine,* a single mom romcom with heart.

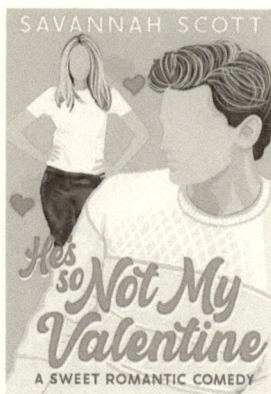

Want to make sure you get updates from Savannah Scott?

Be one of the readers who hears about new releases first, gets to participate in special giveaways, and sees sneak peeks into Savannah's writing ... join her weekly newsletter for all this and more. **https://bit.ly/SavannahScottNewsletter**

Looking for a sweet group of readers who share life and books together? Join Savannah's Sweet Readers Facebook Group at **https://www.facebook.com/groups/pattyhscottssweetreaders**

Or Follow **Savannah on Instagram @SavannahScott_author** And follow Savannah on Amazon for automatic notifications of new releases directly in your inbox. **https://bit.ly/savannah scott**

All the Thanks ...

I want to thank **Gila Santos,** my copy editor. You are a sweet cheerleader and you see my blind spots. Thank you for believing in this story and me.

Tricia Anson. Goodness gracious. You are my friend, my proofreader, my personal assistant, the keeper of my sanity, and a gift in my life. I can't imagine what I'd do without you. Here's hoping I never have to find out.

Jessica Gobble, You are my bestie and my sister from another mister, Thank you for believing in me and praying over me all these years.

To my **Awesome "Shippers" and especially the CORE Team** who love me and my books so thoroughly, and to the **AMAZING Bookstagram Community.** I am so thankful for the way you support each book I write. Your sharing and celebrating of my work helps get these books out into the hands of other readers.

Thank you to **Mary Goad** for this cover. You just keep outdoing yourself!

Thank you **Jazmine Dean** for answering all my pro surfer questions as I was polishing this story. You inspire me as you press against boundaries and reach for opportunities, riding the waves for all women, and leaving your mark in this sport. Watching you is art and beauty.

Thank you **Shauna Douglass** for your insight into Hawaiian culture and specifically her guidance about the significance of Hawaiian jewelry with a person's name on it. Shauna, you inspired my imagination to create that whole extra-special moment in the epilogue between Bodhi and Mr. Kapule. Thank you.

Most of all, I want to thank **God** for calling me to be a story-teller and giving me the ability to make others smile and laugh.

I thought you'd like to read some more of the quotes I gathered while I was writing Mavs and Bodhi's story ...

Kalaine: There's nothing like that feeling of waiting for a guy. It's the loneliest feeling in the world ~ Hilary Winston

Bhodi: Ex-girlfriends are like car wrecks. You shouldn't want to know the details, but you do. ~Allison van Diepen

Either: Life isn't about how you survived the storm. It's about how you danced in the rain. ~ Unknown

Either: Out of the water, I am nothing. ~ Duke Kahanamoku

Either: Man cannot discover new oceans unless he has the courage to lose sight of the shore. ~Andre Gide

Either: You can't stop the waves, but you can learn to surf. ~ John Kabat-Zinn

Kalaine: When life gives you lemons, squeeze one in your hair and go surfing. ~ Unknown

Savannah

Made in United States
Troutdale, OR
05/12/2024

19822896R00202